KABU KABU

BOOKS BY NNEDI OKORAFOR

KABU KABU

PRIME BOOKS

KABU KABU

Prime Books
www.prime-books.com

For more information, contact Prime Books:
prime@prime-books.com

ISBN: 978-1-60701-405-8

"Funny how all things people don't understand seem to be 'cursed.' "

—**Zahrah Tsami from *Zahrah the Windseeker***

CONTENTS

FOREWORD

Whenever I'm grabbed by a book or an author I tend towards overkill. And when I find authors who take on the world while incorporating mythologies that are so fresh and different I begin to hoard their work.

This is what happened when first I read Nnedi Okorafor's work. I love that she writes of young women who are strong and facing the challenges not only from their changing bodies but from family and friends. More often than not, the stories are based in modern or future Africa, which is rarely shown in science fiction and fantasy. And even the magic is indigenous. Nnedi changes our perception that Tarzan is still an accurate portrayal of the continent and surrounds us with ancestors and stories that engage us as one world.

Her short story collection, *Kabu Kabu,* takes us on rides of the heart and mind, her characters could be any of us on the planet, and her stories invite us in rather than keep us at bay. Science fiction used to be a genre that didn't feel inviting to me. I always loved it, but I didn't feel I was part of it . . . that is until I read Octavia Butler and now Nnedi. When you read Nnedi you never feel as if you've lost time you'll never get back. Instead you find yourself wanting to write her pleading that she expand her short stories and make her novels never-ending.

In short, get somewhere you want to be, gather your snacks, turn your music down low, and step on in.

Whoopi Goldberg
NYC 2012

THE MAGICAL NEGRO

Lance the Brave stood on the edge of the cliff panicking, his long blond hair blowing in the breeze. Behind him, they were coming fast through the lush grassy field. All Lance could do was stare, his cheeks flushed. Once upon him, they would suck the life from his soul, like lions sucking meat from the bones of a fresh kill. He held his long sword high. Its silver handle was encrusted with heavy blue jewels and it felt so right in his hand.

He loved his sword; so many times it had helped him bring justice to the world. He'd fight to the end. His life for his country. If only he knew how the amulet around his neck worked. The ruby red jewel bounced heavily against his chest as if to taunt him more with its difficult riddle. He was never very good at riddles. He took a deep breath, a tear falling down his rosy cheek.

"My life for my country," he whispered, trying not to look down the cliff. "If it must come to this."

But it could have been better. It could have been more.

Any moment now. It wouldn't be quick, but painful. The shadows were savage beasts. The horrible black things were known to skin a man alive, tear off his fingernails one by one, boil a man's flesh until it fell apart. The shadows would dirty his very soul. The shadows came from the very heart of darkness.

I never should have gone there, he thought.

The shadows were almost upon him, devouring the light that shined on the grassy field. They left only rotten filthy blackness behind. Lance closed his eyes, whispering a silent prayer for the welfare of his beautiful fair wife and lovely daughter, Chastity, back at the castle. When he opened his eyes, he nearly fell over the cliff. *What is that?* he thought.

Standing between him and the approaching shadows was an equally dark figure. The African man floated inches above the grass, his large crown of puffy hair radiating from his head like a black explosion. His skin, a dirty brown, almost blended in with the shaded evil approaching

11

him. He turned to Lance, held up a dark black hand and brought it to his thick lips.

"Shhh, no time," he said in a low smoky voice. He wore no shirt or shoes and carried no weapons. *He'll be killed*, Lance thought sadly. He didn't like the idea of someone else dying on the cliff with him. This moment was about his martyrdom only. Lance shook his head, his long blond hair shaking.

"Please," he said. "You must . . . "

"Look, there's no time, so just listen," the African said. "The amulet responds to your heart."

The shadows were only meters away. *Who is this man?* Lance wondered. *Where did he come from? How can he levitate?*

"Look deep within yourself," the African said. "You have the power, you just haven't tapped into it . . . "

The black man's eyes suddenly bulged and a dark red spot ate its way into the middle of his chest. He'd been pierced with an evil blackness deeper than his own. He fell to his knees, coughing up blood. The shadows paused behind him, as if to savor the death of the black man. Lance watched him with a sad frown. The man only had moments to live.

Then the African man looked up at him. Lance would have jumped back, but even in his fear, he knew to do so would send him prematurely plummeting to his death. The African man looked angry. Angry as hell.

"Yo, what the *fuck* is this bullshit!" The African quickly stood up and looked at the red hole in his chest oozing blood and other fluids. "Aw *hell* no! It ain't goin' down like this. Damn, *how* many *times*?"

He turned to the shadows and held up a black finger.

"Y'all should know better. You know what I can do to you. You ain't that stupid."

The looming shadows retreated a bit. Lance was shocked. Could this man possibly be commanding the shadows? The shadows were pure power. *How can* he *control them?* Lance numbly wondered. The black man turned to Lance and pointed a finger.

"Look . . . *fuck you*." Then he looked up at the blue sky and said, "My ass comes here to save *his* ass and after I tell him what *he* needs to do,

I get sixed? Whatchu' think I am? Some fuckin' shuckin', jivin', happy Negro still dying for the massa 'cause my life ain't worth shit?"

He cocked his head and looked back at Lance.

"I'm the mutherfuckin' Magical Negro, what makes you think I'm gonna tell you how to use that damn amulet you been carrying around for two months because you too stupid to figure how to use it and then fuckin' die afterwards? What world is you livin' in? Some kinda typical fantasy world from some typical fantasy book? Like I ain't got no family of my own to risk my life fo' and shit!"

The Magical Negro reached into the pocket of his black pants and brought out a fat cigar and a lighter. He lit it and took two puffs. He blew several rings and, with a wave of his hand, linked them into a chain that settled around his long neck. Then he laughed as the chain dissolved.

"I . . . I . . . in my heart?" Lance asked. He was terribly confused. He could barely understand the dark man. What a strange dialect he was speaking. *Controlling evil darkness?* Could it be because he had internalized the evil of the shadows? Could that be what turned his skin that horrible color? Blew out his lips? Gave him such a huge deformed nose? Corrupted his hair? Lance frowned. *Why am I thinking of such things in my last moments?* He stepped forward, holding up his sword again, trying to look brave.

The Magical Negro shook his head and said, "Had enough of this." With a wave of his hand, Lance fell from the cliff to his death. The Magical Negro listened for the thump of Lance's body on the rocks below. He smiled. He took a puff from his cigar. He picked up his black jacket that sat in the grass and shrugged it around his narrow shoulders. Then he picked up his black top hat and placed it on his head and laughed a wheezy laugh.

"Sheeeit," he drawled, looking directly at you. "You need to stop reading all this stupidness. The Magical Negro ain't about to get his ass kicked no more. Them days is ovah."

The Magical Negro rested his red cane on his shoulder and leisurely strolled into the forest to see if he could find him some hobbits, castles, dragons, princesses, and all that other shit.

KABU KABU

WRITTEN WITH ALAN DEAN FOSTER

Ngozi hated her outfit. But it was good for traveling.

Her well-worn jeans had no pockets on the back, thereby accentuating the ass she didn't have. She'd accidentally stained her white t-shirt with chocolate after stuffing too much chocolate doughnut too fast into her mouth while rushing. And she had grabbed the wrong Chuck Taylor's: her black ones would have matched better than the red. She'd overslept. Somehow, she hadn't heard her fucking alarm clock. Now she was going to be late for her plane to New York, which would make her late for her plane to London, which would cause her to miss her connection to Port Harcourt.

"Shit." She fought desperately to hail a cab. "*Shit!*" As a stress reliever, the angry repeating of the word helped to lower her blood pressure about as effectively as it did to draw something yellow with wheels closer to the curb—which was to say, not at all.

The day's disaster didn't end here. The long fingernail of her right index finger had broken and she kept scratching herself with it. Her skin was sandpaper-dry from taking a hot shower and not having time to put on lotion afterward. She had forgotten her antiperspirant. Not only did she feel that she *looked* like a pig, despite the cold outside she was sweating like one. *Wonderful*, she thought. Bronchial pneumonia would give her something to look forward to, as well.

The only saving grace was that she'd had the good sense to pack her things the night before. Her backpack, carry-on, and large suitcase were in far better shape than their owner. She stumbled out of her townhouse and dragged her things down the steps. Outside, the full moon was still visible in the early morning sky. The sun wouldn't be up for a while. Nothing like leaving for another continent after a restful night's sleep.

She saw it then. An unprepossessing vehicular miracle heading up the street in her direction. *Too much to hope for,* she thought wildly. She started jumping up and down, waving wildly and shouting. "Taxi! Oh please God, let it be a taxi!"

As it drew nearer, Ngozi first sensed and then saw that it was traveling too fast, buoyed along by a cushion of heavy-based music. She frowned. Her frantically waving hand dropped to her side and she took a step back. The cab had the sleek but stunned look of a hybrid vehicle. Might be a Toyota or Honda. In the darkness she couldn't see the logo. The car was weirdly striped green and white and lizard-like. Even from a distance she could see that the exterior was pocked with way too many dents and scuffs, like an old boxer past his prime. As it came closer, she hunted in vain for a taxi number or business logo on the passenger-side door. Neither presented itself. Instead, there was a short inscription:

Two footsteps do not make a path.

Standing in front of a fire hydrant, the only open space on the stretch of street, she gawked at the oncoming vehicle. Despite the seriousness of her situation, she made a choice that was as easy as it was quick.

"I am not," she muttered to herself, "going *near* that thing." She glanced down at her watch and bit her lip. She was out of options.

The taxi screeched to a halt, and backed up impossibly fast. Then it zig-zagged crazily into the undersized and very illegal parking space before her. It was the most adept bit of parallel parking she had ever witnessed. Not to mention quasi-suicidal. Barely an inch of clearance remained in front of or behind the cab. She shook her head and chuckled. "This guy *must* be Nigerian. Just my luck." In the back of her mind she felt a twinge of caution. But she didn't have time to waste.

The driver turned his music down and jumped out, shrugging a leather jacket over his short-sleeve blue shirt to ward off the chill. He was short, squat, medium brown-skinned, and possibly in his early forties. *Definitely Igbo,* she decided.

"I take you wherever you need to go, madam," he announced grandiosely. His accent immediately confirmed Ngozi's suspicion. It was quite similar to that of her own parents.

"O'Hare," she said.

"No problem."

She hefted her backpack up and stepped to the cab's passenger door as he loaded the rest of her luggage into the trunk. "I'm running late. *Really* late."

"I see," he responded with unexpected solemnity. "Where you headed?"

She was too busy wrestling with the back passenger door to reply. She grew even sweatier. The door wasn't budging at all. Loading a traveler's baggage and taking off before he or she could get in was a widespread taxi scam everywhere in the world. The cab driver shut the trunk and smiled at her. "Let me get that for you," he said. "It doesn't open for just anyone." He was chuckling to himself as he came around and grabbed the handle.

Wrapping his fingers around the worn, smudged metal he gave it a simultaneous twist and tug. The door swung wide with a curious non-metallic *pop*. Her nose was assailed by the unexpected aromatic scent of cedar wood and oil, both in much stronger concentration than was typical for the usual generic, commercial car deodorant. She slid inside. And promptly froze.

Nestled snugly between the front seats was a large leafy potted plant. On the ceiling of the car but presently shut was a slightly askew sliding skylight. A wealth of skillfully hand-wrought rosaries and glistening cowry shell necklaces drooped from the rearview mirror. Most startlingly, the entire interior of the cab was intricately hand-inlaid with thousands upon thousands of tiny, multicolored glass beads.

"Wow," she whispered, running an open palm carefully over the car's interior. The feel was smooth but bumpy, like a golf ball turned inside-out. *This must have cost a fortune*, she thought. It was as if she had stepped inside the world's most elaborate handicraft necklace. Gazing at her unexpectedly ornate surroundings she tried to imagine someone, or even several someones, taking the time and patience to complete the intricate work of art.

Further up front was something that looked decidedly out of place in the bead-encrusted, shell-strung interior. Set into the dash beside the battered heating and air-conditioning controls was what looked like a computer installation. Rotating lazily on the screen was a three-dimensional image of a bushy ceremonial Igbo masquerade mask. At least, that's what Ngozi guessed it to be. As a choice of screensaver, it was a distinctly unsettling one. She shivered. She'd never liked masquerades. Especially the ones at certain parties back home that turned so violent people had to hold back the performers with thick ropes. The damn things were supposed to be manifestations of spirits of dead people and they looked and danced like insane monsters. Serious nightmare material.

The driver got in and slammed his door shut. If he noticed the anxiety in her expression, he chose not to remark on it.

"You never answered my question," he said. Throwing his right arm over the top of the front passenger seat, he twisted to look back at her as he started the cab. Another surprise: despite the vehicle's scruffy appearance, the engine's purr was barely audible. Definitely a hybrid, Ngozi concluded. "How do I know where to take you if you don't tell me where you're going?"

"I did." Ngozi frowned. "Didn't I say O'Hare? United Airlines. I'm, ah, going to New York."

"Got relatives there?" the man inquired. "You visiting your folks?"

"No." She wavered and finally confessed, "I . . . I'm going to Nigeria. Port Harcourt. My sister's getting married."

He grinned. "Thought so. You can't hide where you're from, O. Not even with those dada dreadlock on your head. You still an Igbo girl."

"Woman," she corrected him, growing annoyed. "Woman in a *big hurry*. I'm a lawyer, you know." *Fuck*, she thought. *Shut up, Ngozi. How much does he need to know to get me to the airport, man? Next thing he'll try to scam me out of all my money in some fiercely tricky specifically Nigerian way.*

"Ah, a big Igbo woman, then," he murmured thoughtfully.

"And I was born and raised here," she added, unable to resist. "So I'm Igbo, Nigerian, and American."

The driver laughed again. "Igbo first," he said as he shifted into drive. Jamming the accelerator, he roared out of the illegal parking space with the same lunatic adeptness with which he had darted into it. Flinching, she grabbed the back of the seat in front to steady herself and held her breath. *Oh my God, I feel like I'm in Nigeria already.*

As they accelerated out onto the street, he turned the music back up. Listening, Ngozi smiled. It was Fela Kuti, Nigeria's greatest rebel musician. She loved the song that was playing . . . "Schuffering and Schmiling." Crooning his unique command of mystery, mastery, and music, Fela spoke to her through the speakers:

"You Africans please listen as Africans
And you non-Africans please listen to me with open mind.
Ahhhh . . . "

Ngozi found herself, as always, lulled into reminiscence by his honeyed words. She thought of her father's village. Where the dirt roads became impassable every rainy season. Where any effort to improve them was thwarted by friendly thievery, lies, and jealousy. Last time she had visited her father's village with her parents and sister and their departure had been marked by a small riot. It was caused by cousins, aunts, uncles, and strangers battling into the rooms the four of them had just left. They hoped to grab whatever the "visitors from America" might have left behind.

Among the desperate, hopeful scavengers had been Ngozi's cousin who was so smart, but unable to afford medical school. And her uncle with the Hausa tribal marks on his cheeks from when he was a little boy. Those three vertical lines on each cheek had served for more than decoration. They were all that had allowed her uncle to survive the civil war of the sixties.

Ngozi let herself slump back against the surprisingly soft seat. She had not been home in three years. Chicago, America was great. But she missed Nigeria.

"I want you all to please take your minds out of this musical contraption and put your minds into any goddamn church, any goddamn mosque, any goddamn celestical, including sera-phoom and cheraboom! Now—we're all there now. Our minds are in those places. Here we go . . . "

She smiled to herself. That was Fela—West Africa's greatest anti-colonialist. Angry, obnoxious, wonderful, and thought-provoking all at the same time.

They turned onto Halsted and headed south, weaving through traffic at a high speed with an intensity and determination that earned the cab several furious honks and not a few Chicago-style curses from the startled drivers they shot past. Ngozi hung on for dear life. What ought to have been an opportunity for her to cool down was instead one for more sweating as the driver skirted airport-bound limos and huge semis by scant inches. She considered telling him to drop her off at the next stoplight. Up front he was swearing and laughing and at times it was impossible to tell one from the other. His hands worked the horn as if it were a second mouth.

Eventually he glanced up at the rearview mirror. She struggled to look back with an expression other than that of sheer terror.

"Why you wear your hair like that?"

Instantly Ngozi's fear turned to exasperation. She wasn't even in Nigeria yet and already she was getting this typical antediluvian macho shit. "Because I like it this way," she snapped. "Why do you wear *your* hair like *that*?"

"Is that any way to speak to your elder?" the cab driver commented, sounding hurt. "Miss big fancy lawyer with no ass."

Ngozi's eyes widened. Her blood pressure, already high, went up another twenty points. "What?"

The man laughed afresh. "Do you even *speak* Igbo?"

"No. Not a damn word. You got a problem with that?"

"*Ewoooo!*" he exclaimed disapprovingly. "Of course I do! You are incomplete, *sha*."

"Oh, give me a break." She rolled her eyes. "You don't know me."

Dodging around a slow bus, he took a wild turn to the left, which threw her sharply to the side. Straightening, she searched the back seat. "How come you don't have any seat belts back here?"

"What you need those for?" he asked, eying her in the mirror. "You in the back."

"Maybe because you drive like a maniac?"

"Don't worry, I get you there alive."

They had turned onto a side road flanked by uniform rows of houses marching in brownstone lockstep. None of the intersections they crossed appeared to have street signs, including the one they were rocketing along.

"Have you ever been to Nigeria, Miss?"

"Many times. A lot of my family is still there. I try to visit as often as I can."

That shut him up. She smiled. *Nigerian men and their bullshit assumptions*, she thought. Her smile vanished when the cab's speakers went *DOOM!* The entire vehicle shook. She clapped her hands over her ears. *"What the fuck?"* she screamed.

"Watch your language, Miss big lawyer."

"First you criticize my hair, now you criticize my language. Do I look ten years old to you?"

"Got a stop to make," he said. He fiddled with the dashboard computer, where the masquerade mask had given way to an image of a young man. "Don't worry, we won't be late."

Within a minute, they pulled up in front of one of the brownstone buildings. The man whose visage smiled from the screen was standing out front cradling a briefcase. The image on the monitor didn't convey his height and build. The man stepped up to the front window.

"Festus," the driver said. He reached out and slapped hands with the man. "What's up?"

"Can you take me over to Vee-Vee's really quick?" Festus' accent was an intriguing mélange of Nigerian and British English—and something else. Perfectly-styled jeans enveloped his long legs. A finely-cut long-sleeved navy shirt could not conceal his muscled chest.

"Vee-Vee's?" Ngozi frowned as she leaned forward. "I know that place. That's too out of the way. I can't miss this flight, man!"

"Relax," the driver urged her. "I said I get you where you need to go."

Bending low, Festus peeked inside the cab. Ngozi had every intention of persuading him to find another taxi. Initially. The soft glow of street lights revealed smooth brown skin, perfect perfect lips, prominent cheekbones. Festus was utterly and unabashedly gorgeous. Her urgency dissolved like a pat of butter in hot broth.

The driver got out and opened the door for his second passenger. Ngozi felt her ears pop. She knew she should slide as far away as possible from this man, but what she wanted to do was slide as closer. She swallowed hard, not moving either way.

"Hi," was all she could say.

"Hey." He held her eyes with a gaze that was more than forward. A shiver ran through her from her periwinkle-colored toenails to her "dadalocks." He pulled the door shut as the driver started the car, then turned toward her. "I'm Festus McDaniel."

Despite feeling more than a little overwhelmed, she had to laugh. "Is that your real name?"

"When I need it to be."

"Then my name is Ororo Munroe."

"Ah, an X-Men fan."

She could not have been more surprised if he had announced he was the pilot for her forthcoming flight. "You, too?"

"When I need to be," he repeated, this time punctuating it with an undisguised leer. He scooted closer. Ngozi was annoyed to find that she did not mind, especially after her edgy go-round with the cab driver. What was happening? This was not like her. Her temples were pounding. She felt her eyes closing, her lips parting.

"Hey!" the driver yelled. Her eyes snapped open. "Festus! This is my passenger. *Back off!*"

Ngozi blinked again. Her mind cleared and the throbbing in her blood faded. Festus' face was close enough to hers that she could smell his breath. It was, unexpectedly, slightly fragrant of mint. And a saltiness she could not immediately place. Not only was he the most gorgeous man she had ever seen (and she'd seen plenty), he smelled really really good.

She pressed her temples harder. *What the* hell *was I just doing?* That leer . . . Or had it been a sneer?

Whatever it was, it was still there, plastered across his face as he leaned away and stared at her. Adrift in confusion, Ngozi could have sworn she saw fangs retreating under his upper lip. What the *fuck*? She pressed herself as close to the door and as far away from him as possible.

"What goes on in your head right now?" he asked softly.

"Huh?"

"Don't mind him," the driver advised her. He was scowling at Festus as he tossed something over his right shoulder. Ngozi felt it land in her lap. "Suck on that," the driver said, watching her through his mirror. "It'll make you feel . . . more like yourself."

She looked down, found herself staring at a cherry Jolly Rancher. Her fingers worked mechanically as she unwrapped the candy and popped it in her mouth. Flushed from embarrassment, she turned to the window to avoid the other passenger's unwavering gaze. All sweetness and tartness and fake cherry-ness, the candy dissolved slowly in her mouth. She did feel better.

Having lost her attention, Festus chatted with the driver in rapid Igbo all the rest of the way to Vee-Vee's. Ngozi tried to translate what they were saying but all she caught were bits and pieces like "419," "the money," and "oyibo," which meant either "white person" or "foreigner."

It took much less time to get to Vee-Vee's than she had anticipated and she was more than a little shocked when she checked her watch. Only fifteen minutes. She attributed the accomplishment to the driver's unsurpassed, if wholly maniacal driving skills.

They pulled up to the Nigerian restaurant and the passenger eased out, his movements as supple as a dancer's. As he stepped over the curb he looked back at the cab and blew a kiss in Ngozi's direction. She winced and tried to look away, and instead found herself following him as he strode inside. As he entered, he thrust first one arm and then another into a neatly-pressed suit jacket. He slipped it easily over his shoulders. He looked sharp. *Is that Armani*? she wondered. A frown creased her face. *Wait a minute. He wasn't carrying that when he got in the cab.*

"Sorry about that." The driver apologized. "But he tips well."

"Of course, he does," Ngozi mumbled, still confused. "Someone like that . . . " Her voice trailed away.

Once again the driver cranked up the music and, wonder of wonders, both passenger and driver remained silent for the duration of the drive to O'Hare. As the cab pulled up to the United Airlines terminal a check of her watch showed that she had barely a half hour before take-off. The instant the car stopped she jumped out, yanking her pack and purse after her. While the driver was unloading her large suitcase from the trunk, she fumbled in a pocket for her cell phone. It wasn't there. Her heart started pounding. She checked her purse, then her carry-on.

Passport, purse again, backpack. Underwear. Deodorant. All present and more or less accounted for. Only one thing still missing. Only one thing . . .

Obligingly, the driver helped her drag her suitcase into the cab. Then he got in the driver's seat. Soon the security people would shoo them off.

"I'll drive around," he said, when a security guard began yelling at them to move on. "You search."

She quickly unlocked her suitcase and began rummaging frantically within. Futile. She knew damn well that her cell had been in her jacket pocket. She glanced again at her watch. The numbers continued to tick away relentlessly. She had fifteen minutes left—and that is if they didn't lock the boarding gate on her.

"Where the hell?" she asked, rising hysteria in her voice. "Where the hell *is* it? No time to get another boarding pass! I can't miss this flight! I can't miss the wedding! I have to be there for her."

She had a horrible sinking feeling. She grabbed her wallet. "Credit card, credit card, come on," she whispered. She'd need that for her new boarding pass. It wasn't *there*! Her license, library card, office building i.d., insurance cards, Sam's Club card, World Wildlife Foundation card, they all sat in their usual slots. Except her credit card. Inside, she screamed and frothed at the mouth. On the outside, she stayed calm.

They arrived back at the terminal and she threw open the rear door of the taxi and began searching. Seat creases, floor, under the front seat. Ten minutes left. Getting back into the car and slamming the door, she tilted her neck forward and rested her forehead against the cold metal of the hood, defeated.

"They do all this stupid crazy traditional shit," she mumbled, talking as much to herself as to the silently staring driver. "My sister was born here like me. I can't let her go through this alone."

He closed his door and looked in the rear-view mirror. "I'm sorry," he murmured. "I truly am." He paused. "The security guy is coming. We go around again?"

"Whatever," she muttered.

They drove away from the terminal. At that moment revelation dawned on her—and it was not pretty. She looked up sharply and when she met his eyes in the mirror, she knew. "You've got to be kidding!"

The driver let out a short sigh and nodded sadly, knowingly. "He isn't common, but he can be a thief."

"Festus." Stupid, she told herself. Big lawyer, she was. Uh-huh, right.

"Yep," the driver confirmed.

"*Dammit*." She screamed. "My own fault, too. I should have left earlier, given myself more time. Skipped the damn make-up."

"I've heard about the hours lawyers have to deal with," he said. "The pressures."

Ngozi couldn't bear it anymore. The tears came. She wasn't thinking about herself. Her mind was full of visions of her sister being toted around like some parcel, being forced to say things she had not been raised to believe. Her sister was marrying an Igbo man she had met in college. Fine. That was her sister's choice. It didn't mean Ngozi had to like him, and she never had. He was always making snide comments about how Ngozi was thirty-five, childless, and unmarried. Once he had even, quite deliberately, called her "Mr. Ngozi." Then he had insisted on a traditional wedding in the village for all his relatives to attend. She didn't really want to go, but she had no choice. She *needed* to be there, for her sister.

The driver continued to stare at her in the mirror, but by now she was too miserable for his steady gaze to make her any more uncomfortable than she already was. He pulled onto the side of the highway and turned around. "Look," he said, "my job is to get you where you need to go. I promised you I would do that. I—know other ways to get you where you need to be."

She wiped her nose on her sleeve, not giving a damn about the hygienic or visual consequences. "What? Like a flight from another airport? Midway?"

He shrugged. "It's sort of a . . . a private transport set-up."

She stared back at him. Heroin drop-offs, 419 scams, and all sorts of other Nigerian-oriented shady business flashed through her mind. Hadn't she already been victimized once this morning? "I'm a lawyer," she reminded him. "It's my duty to uphold the . . . "

"You want to be there for your sister, right?"

Her insides clenched. She was past desperate. "I have to be."

Her answer appeared to resolve something within him. "So we go."

She started to say something. Finally, motivated more by resignation than any real hope, she got in. "Can I use your phone to cancel my credit card and pause my cell service?"

★

They drove down South Wabash Avenue for ten minutes, exited onto Congress, and turned onto a small commercial road. The increasingly industrial surroundings were unnerving her anew.

"Now then: I only have one request," he told her.

She frowned. "Request? What are you talking about? What kind of 'request'?"

"Stay in my cab."

"Why would I want to . . . ?"

Doom! For the second time that morning Ngozi felt her head rattle. When her vision cleared she found herself looking toward the dashboard computer installation. The picture had reverted back to the image of the disquieting masquerade mask. She felt a fresh jolt of anxiety.

Get a hold of yourself, she thought uneasily. "You aren't picking anyone else up are you?" she asked.

"A man must make his bread," the driver said. "Don't worry. I get you there." Turning down still another side street, he slowed to a halt in front of a carwash. It was operational, but not especially busy.

"Have another passenger to pick up," he declared.

"Oh, whatever." Thoroughly beaten, Ngozi leaned back. She took a deep, deliberate, calming breath. It didn't help. With nothing to do and nothing to look forward to, she peered indifferently at the carwash. A glistening silver Mercedes emerged, paused briefly at the exit, turned left and drove off. Behind it, oversized tan and brown brushes continued to spin. She'd heard of twenty-four hour car washes, but had never had occasion to make use of one.

"So who are we . . . "

"Shhh," the driver hissed. He was staring intently at the car wash. Bemused and exhausted, Ngozi followed his eyes.

She let out a startled gasp. "Oh, great. What now?"

Then she saw. The largest spinning brushes detached itself from the interior of the car wash. Still rapidly spinning, it came toward them, as if it had officially checked out and was leaving work for the day. Ngozi trembled, unable to look away. It whipped water from itself as it approached.

"What's—what is—you see that?" Ngozi babbled. "Are you seeing . . . "

"You better move over," the driver advised her. "It's going to be a tight fit."

She gaped at him. "Say *what*?"

The apparition continued advancing toward the idling cab. Ngozi guessed it to be about seven feet tall, four feet wide. It hadn't looked that huge when it first came out. A giant spinning carwash brush. Oh sure, right, why not? Then she heard it.

"Oh shit, this isn't happening," she heard herself whisper.

Tock, tock, tock—the thumping of a small drum. Frantically she grabbed at her nearest door handle. She no longer cared where she was or where she needed to be. She was going to get the fuck out of that insane cab and away from its crazy driver and make a run for it.

The door would not open. The handle wouldn't even budge.

"Let me out!" She kept her voice as calm as she could. Looking back she saw that the giant brush was almost to the cab. Her eyes blurred with tears of terror and distress. She blinked them away. "Please, sir," she stammered. "Lemme out. *Right now.*"

"Now you just take it easy, big lawyer," the driver admonished her. "She won't hurt you. She just needs a ride."

A thousand clashing, conflicting impossibilities were flying through Ngozi's mind. That that thing approaching the cab was a masquerade. But masquerades were mythical beings. They were the spirits and ancestors. They didn't exist, except in legend.

A remnant of full moon still lingered in the sky, its baleful light now illuminating entirely too many of her surroundings. She was in a part of the city she had never seen before. No street signs. First a strange man steals her emotions and then her cell phone and credit card. And now this *thing* was going to get in the cab. With her.

It stopped outside the passenger window. Up close, so close, too close, she could see its body was a thick column of shredded raffia, pieces of cloth, and strings of red beads. She tried to open the door again. The handle wouldn't move.

"Open!" she heard herself screaming, "Plea . . . !"

A sudden breeze from nowhere filled the interior of the cab with the heady aroma of palm wine. Ngozi pressed herself against the car door, raising a leg and arm up as a shield. The creature standing outside the taxi dissolved into a rose-hued mist and came wafting slowly in through the window. Pressing against the door now, Ngozi started to laugh uncontrollably. Once fully within the cab the being rematerialized, its fragrant bulk completely filling the seat beside her and threatening to spill over onto her cringing lap.

Rough raffia scratched at Ngozi's face. At least it was dry now. The wooden head perched atop the raffia mass had a stern female face. Now it turned, slow and silent, and stared down at her. She felt every hair on her body stand on end.

"Just stay calm," the driver suggested, unperturbed. "It'll be a short ride. She's just another passenger." As he pulled away from the carwash he turned up the music again. Fela sang:

"Ever day na de same thing
Shuffering and Shmiling!"

As they drove, the masquerade shook to the beat of the music, the raffia that composed its body quivering and shaking.

When it got out of the cab ten minutes later in the parking lot of a bookstore that wasn't open for business yet, Ngozi was left half paralyzed and with nothing more to say. Her arms and right cheek sported fine scratches from the brush of the creature's leaves. And the blast of rose-colored mist the masquerade became when it exited the car had left her clothes and hair damp. Fragrant and sweet-scented, but damp.

"Chicago's a big place," the driver declared amiably. "You work graveyard, you pick up *all* kinds of immigrants who work all kinds of jobs."

Clearing her throat, Ngozi managed to find a voice. Though reduced to something like a whimper, it did resemble hers. "I want to go *home*."

The driver smiled, the driver laughed, just as he had before. "You worry too much, girl. Woman," he corrected himself. "I suppose it part of being a big lawyer. I said I'd get you there."

"Home," she croaked weakly, repeating herself. Slouching low in the seat, she grasped her short dreadlocks. *I am seriously screwed*, she thought. They were barely clear of the parking lot when the car shook yet again.

DOOM!

The image on the monitor changed to that of a rotating ax. Immediately, the driver slammed on the brakes and turned around.

"Where are we—who are you picking up now?" Her voice had turned shrill. "When am I going to get priority here? *When are you going to start listening to me?*"

"Sorry," he murmured regretfully. "Gotta pick this one up."

"Why? Why one more? Will there always be 'just one more'?" She was staring fixedly at the rotating ax on the monitor, trying to square the image with everything else that had happened this morning. Thoughts of her sister's missed wedding were receding rapidly into memory. They had been replaced by: *Will I ever be allowed to get out of this cab? And will I get out alive?*

The man stood under a street lamp on the side of Lake Shore Drive. Encouragingly, dawn was not far away, but the city lights were still on. Staring at this latest phantom, Ngozi couldn't understand why people who passed him on the highway did not use their cell phones to call the police. If she saw someone like him, she certainly would have. She started to reach into her pocket. Then she remembered that Festus guy—who was probably some sort of Nigerian vampire—had stolen her cell phone.

Of course, the driver slowed to a stop right in front of the guy on the side of the highway. The door swung open opposite her. After her ears popped, she could hear the big man breathing, even over the increasing roar of early commuters zooming by on the road. Raspy and heavy his respiration was. He was large, African, and clad in jeans and t-shirt. She couldn't tell what color the shirt was because its owner was spattered from head to toe in what could have only been blood. Once more she found herself scrambling to the far side of the seat. Digging into a pocket, she pulled out the only hard object she had in there. A pen.

Bending forward, he peered into the cab. His eyes met Ngozi's. He smirked.

"Hello there and good morning." His voice was exceptionally deep, somewhere down near the lowest register of which a human being was capable. His accent was Nigerian but very slight. His face glistened as he slid in. Ngozi shut her eyes and squeezed her hands into tight fists. The handle on her door still refused to work. She heard the worn leather beneath the beads creak as the passenger dropped his weight onto the seat. The cab filled with the coppery smell of fresh blood. He said something in Igbo to the driver.

"Sure thing," the driver responded in English, maddeningly accommodating as ever.

The man's breathing remained loud and grinding, as if he was trying to digest something in his lungs instead of his stomach. Every so often he grunted to himself. Trapped, weary, frightened, Ngozi wished the driver would turn his music up loud enough to drown out the sound of the new passenger's merciless respiration.

Not long after but far too much later, the cab finally slowed and stopped. She heard the door open and shut. Her ears popped. Cautiously, she opened her eyes. The sun was just starting to lighten the sky. Had she made her plane, she would now have been an hour closer to where she needed to be, instead of stuck and terrified in the confines of a cab not far from her townhouse. No, this wasn't even a cab. The driver didn't have a license displayed anywhere; it was probably illegal. She'd somehow wound up in a *kabu kabu* right here on the streets of greater Chicago.

"Why didn't you call the police?" She didn't have any energy left to shout.

She stared at where the passenger had been sitting. The space was stained with blood. Her stomach rolled.

"For what?" the driver asked innocently.

She managed to muster a little more volume, a smidgen more outrage. "He was covered in blood!"

"Oh, that. That's just the Butcher's preference." He was counting money as he deposited bills into the cab's lockbox.

"'Butcher'? Butcher of what?"

"Not my place to ask," the driver replied solemnly. "He tips very very well, also. Hates my music, though. Maybe hates all music." He paused. "I take you where you need to go now. No more pick up. It's daytime anyway." He touched the screen and the image changed to that of a waving Nigerian flag.

She had given up trying to predict whether the driver meant anything he said or if she was interpreting his words correctly. She just rolled with it. When he finally slowed to a stop, she wasn't sure if they were still even in Chicago. In front of them were the remnants of what might have been an open flea market a half a century ago.

"My God. A friend of mine told me there were places like this in Chicago, but I've never seen one of them. She calls them 'dead zones.' "

"Ha!" Accelerating slowly, the driver turned the cab into a narrow alley that ran parallel to the ghost market. "Dead indeed, for sure. Lots of *wahala*, places like this. Trouble, trouble, trouble. But plenty useful to folks like me. And today, folks like you."

They drove along flanked by red brick walls. Very red. If Ngozi had not already seen all that she had seen, she would have been sure that this taxi driver, having had his fun, was taking her to a secluded place where he could dismember her at his leisure.

"Why do we have to take this way to get to this mystery airport of yours?" She struggled to keep the shakiness out of her voice.

He opened the cab's skylight. "You see the sky up there?"

It was the first time she had looked up, instead of just out, since she had first entered the cab. "Oh my," she whispered, forgetting her uncertainties. Even as the dawn sky continued to brighten, she could see millions of twinkling stars, with the plump, white, full moon perfectly framed in the rectangular opening. She inhaled sharply as she spotted a shooting star. And then another. And another. Shooting stars at twilight, she thought. What a treat. A large bird soared by, passing low and slow. It was gray with a very large beak. She thought she could see it looking at her, following her with its eyes. Impossible, of course. She was exhausted, and lapsing into anthropomorphization.

"What kind of bird was that?" she asked herself.

Gazing at the expansive, clear, waking sky filled her with more than a little sense of wonder. The weariness dropped away from her like a cheap rapa. The voice of the driver interrupted her unanticipated reverie.

"You might want to hang on for this." It sounded like a warning.

"Huh?"

The car started shuddering as the ground beneath the tires became rugged. With no seatbelt to hold her down she was thrown from side to side, the wind knocked from her lungs.

"*Biko-nu*, just hold on," he shouted over the rumble of the wheels. "It won't last long!"

The bumping became too violent for her to even speak. At any moment she expected the doors to fall off. They would be followed by the floor, the roof, the engine, and finally her seat. In addition to the deafening noise of vibration, the interior of the cab was filled with a rushing sound, as if the earth was whistling in her ears. Above it all she could still hear the rhythmic pounding of the cab's stereo, though she could no longer make out the words of the irrepressible Fela.

Almost as soon as it had commenced, the brutal jouncing stopped. When she had recovered enough to look out the window, she saw that the brick walls had been replaced by trees on both sides of the road. A park. They were driving through one of Chicago's notable parks. At any minute she expected to see the Museum of Science and Industry, or one of the colossally expensive new high-rise condos set in carefully landscaped faux natural grounds.

Up ahead the narrow, badly maintained dirt road joined a paved one. *Must be coming out of the park*, she told herself. As they drew closer she was able to make out the details of the cross traffic. She sank as far down into her seat as her shaking spine would permit.

"Good idea." The driver was watching her in the rearview. "I was going to suggest that you do exactly that."

"S-s-stop the car!"

"Don't worry." He did not slow down. "I'm known here."

The cab's tires screeched as he dug out of the dirt path and pulled onto the main road. A minute later they were stuck in the most bizarre traffic jam Ngozi had ever seen.

Monsters. Insane vehicles. Monsters riding insane vehicles. And every and all things in-between. Creatures sporting every color imaginable, and some that were not. Some insubstantial as mists, their selves half there and half elsewhere. Figments of imagination, fragments of unreality. But not of her mind. She could never have envisioned a fraction of what she was seeing.

They were all traveling, on the move, all heading somewhere. To where exactly was another question to which she did not wish to learn the answer. On the left side of the road they trekked in one direction and on the right in the opposite way. As they moved, they made sounds like the wind in the trees, the water in the river, the bees in their hives. Individual yet uniform buzzing and howling and screeching and whispering that ebbed and flowed to a rhythm only they understood.

She saw a milky gray-skinned humanoid giant walking on all fours. It had very large breasts and what Ngozi thought was a purple vagina. An equally enormous male ghost dragging an immense penis followed her closely. As Ngozi looked on, speechless and frozen by the sight, he thrust into the giant female-thing and the two continued on their way without pause, walk-crawling as they copulated.

Turning away, she found herself gazing at a small truck that looked as if it were fashioned entirely from moist eyes. Each eye stared in a single but different direction from the others. As she looked at it, one after another every one of its intense blue eyes swung around to fixate on her.

"Oh God oh God," she hissed. Shaking, holding herself, she dropped back down on the seat.

It was a position neither her spine nor her curious mind allowed her to maintain for very long. Moments later, she was up again and peeking over the lower edge of the window. Thankfully, the eyeball truck had dropped out of sight. Her cab driver had shifted into a slightly faster interior lane. As he drove on they were surrounded and hemmed in by thousands, by millions of spirits and ghosts and specters.

Some had many legs, some bounced, some drove, some sat inside things that drove. Others crawled or tumbled, flew or dragged themselves along. Shrieking madly, a skeleton woman rode by on a skeleton ostrich. A ghostly man with feet facing the wrong way sprinted swiftly backwards past the cab. A phantom woman walked by on her hands, herding before her a pack of pig-like things that were completely covered with wooly black hair.

"We all must travel," the driver said, keeping his eyes on the way ahead. His hands grasped the wheel firmly. "It is the essence of all things, to move and change and keep going forward and backward and around. Even the spirits and the dead."

He had turned the stereo down low. Clearly, this was not a place where one wanted to aggravate one's fellow travelers. Ngozi tried to concentrate on the muted music as she spoke a silent prayer to whatever gods were hopefully watching over her. She had long since turned her back on Christianity, but she was not an atheist, either. In this moment and in this place, atheism was a joke. She closed her eyes. She didn't want to *see* anymore.

Time passed. Long minutes, or maybe it was a short hour. Unable to keep them closed any longer, she finally opened her eyes. They were on a wide road now.

And alone.

"You see," the driver told her confidently. "We were just passing through." He sighed. "Traffic can be a problem anywhere."

Outside the cab, the terrain looked nothing like Chicago, a city park, or even the far south suburbs. It did not look like any place she had been. The road ahead was old and worn out. The soil on the side of the road was red instead of brown. In place of oak and pine she saw palm, iroko, mahogany, and oboche trees.

Something finally came unhinged in her brain. It was all too much, she'd had more than enough of a morning unreal. Twisting around on the seat, she kicked at the car window as hard as she could. Part of her wanted to stop, but a larger part craved the hopeful tinkle of shattering glass. Her foot merely left a print on the window.

"Ah, what are you doing?" The driver screamed and the cab took a sudden swerve.

"Where are you taking me?" she screamed. "I can't stand this anymore! I'm going crazy! Let me out! Let me out!"

"Where do you think I'm taking you? I'm taking you where you need to be! Are you stupid? Big lawyer?"

Staring wide-eyed at the latest manifestation of impossible surroundings, which happened to be a stretch of palm trees, Ngozi fought to get herself under control. "This can't be," she whimpered. "It can't be."

"If it can't be then how we be here? Lighten up," he instructed her. "I said I get you where you have to go—and I will."

Ngozi shut her eyes. She opened them. "Stop the car."

He glanced at her in the rearview mirror but kept going. She took a very deep breath. "*Stop the fucking car!*" she screamed loud enough to strain the lining of her throat.

He pulled over at a crossroads. Tentatively, she tried the door handle. It turned so easily she almost sprained her wrist. She stared at it.

"It's open." He turned around in his seat. "What did you expect?"

She narrowed her eyes at him. Gripping the handle hard, she pushed. It opened effortlessly. Her ears popped and a rush of warm, humid air caressed her face. Before anything else could happen, she jumped out of the car.

She just stood there.

The sun beat down hard, the heat and light heavy and hot on her skin. A different kind of sun. The air smelled different, too. She sniffed a hint of distant burning wood. A subtle, invisible, but nonetheless very real shift ran through her entire being, like ripples from a stone cast in flat water. She knew where she was.

"But—how . . . ?"

Wordlessly, the driver got out of the cab.

She knelt down and touched the ground. She rubbed the red dirt between her fingers. On the road, occasional cars zoomed by. As if this was all normal.

"Are you coming back in?" He was standing behind her now.

She grabbed a rock, rose, turned, and threw it at him. A part of her wanted the stone to hit him square between the eyes. "All I wanted was a goddamn ride to O'Hare!" she screamed.

"You can't always get what you want." He smiled. That same, damnable smile. "But if you try sometimes . . . "

"Don't you dare finish that . . . "

His smile widening, he sang the last part of the annoying Rolling Stones song, " . . . you get what you nee-eed!"

Bending, she found and threw another stone at him, aiming for the knees. This time she had better luck, and he had less. He let out a yelp and grabbed at himself where the rock had hit. The tide of satisfaction that flowed through her was brief.

"So you do feel pain," she snapped. "Well, that's good. At least you're not some fucking demon."

"Spoken like a true American girl—woman—I must say." He winced, rubbing the bruise he was going to have. "Are you going to get back in the cab, so we can finish this trip and you can pay me?"

"No."

They were silent, staring hard at each other. She felt as if she had just finished two triathlons in a row. Without food. Across Death Valley. Or maybe been chased around the world. Unexpectedly, she found that she had to stifle a sudden urge to laugh.

Cautiously, the driver stepped closer. "Do you trust me?"

Let's see now, she thought. *I got in your cab under the pretense that you would have me at O'Hare airport in half an hour. Instead, I shared the passenger seat with a thieving vampire, a shedding masquerade, some kind of bloody-man butcher, was driven through the traffic of Hell or the Highway Styx or whatever. And now here I am.* Alive. Alive, and more or less well.

"Holy shit, I'm in Nigeria," she said wonderingly.

He held the door open for her as she slowly slid into the back seat. Smiling as he did so, of course. She looked at her watch. The hands pointed to the same time it had been when she left, give or take a half hour. "That can't be right," she mumbled.

Somehow she was not surprised to learn that they were only a short distance from her village. Shouts of joy and wide grins of happiness from three of her aunties greeted her when she stepped out. As the driver unloaded her big suitcase she saw that other guests were also disembarking from cabs similar in appearance to the one that had brought her to the site of her sister's wedding.

Seeing the shock and jubilation on her younger sister's face was worth everything Ngozi had gone through to make it home. Almost. Excusing herself, Ngozi paid the driver.

"Just for the equivalent of the trip to the airport," he told her. "A flat fee. I give you ten percent discount for when I carried other passengers. No charge for the . . . time travel." He smiled that enigmatic smile. "I don't have a meter anyway. No point in putting one in a cab like mine, is there?"

Then other relatives noticed her, and she found herself swarmed with questions, concerns, and love. When she looked back, the cab was gone.

Something on the ground caught her eye. Bending, she picked it up, and grinned. It was a tiny bright red bead. One of the thousands that had decorated the interior of the cab. She doubted the driver would miss it. He seemed to have a good business, and would be otherwise occupied.

"We thought you'd call before you travelled. We were worried about you," her cousin Emeka said as he took her suitcase and carry-on and escorted her to the compound's main house.

"Sorry," she told him. "I got up late and forgot to call before leaving. Then, well, I took some weird Nigerian unlicensed cab, it got kind of crazy."

"Ah, a Naijameican-style kabu kabu." He nodded knowingly. "I hear those can be bad business."

They stopped in the shade of the house. "Emeka, this might sound like a stupid question . . . but am I too late? For the wedding? My watch says . . . well, I don't know how long I was *really* in that, ah, kabu kabu."

Emeka looked at her oddly. "Too late? No, no. The wedding isn't until tomorrow. You are a day early, Ngozi."

She stared at him, then looked down at her watch. So it wasn't broken. That driver. That crazy smiling fucking driver. He was busy, all right. He really had lost track of the time.

THE HOUSE OF DEFORMITIES

Ngozi scowled and clapped her hands over her ears. But she couldn't do it for long because she needed to hang on to the van door. She tried to relax as the orange van rattled loudly down the speed-limitless road but the faster the van went, the more it shook. Ngozi didn't know how everyone else could stand it. In the front of the van, her parents and the driver were all laughing and blabbing about just about everything.

"*Chey*, I can't remember the last time I had cassava! It's almost *impossible* to find in the United States," her mother was saying.

"Yes, well, you have six more days to enjoy it," the driver said.

Ngozi scrunched her face. She hated cassava. The smell prevented her from getting it even close to her mouth. Sharp and pungent in taste, cassava was worse than eating celery and she absolutely hated celery. Ngozi's twelve-year-old little sister, Adoabi, loved it and ate it with the fervor that she normally reserved for plums. But at the moment, Adoabi probably wasn't thinking about cassava.

Adoabi sat beside Ngozi, absorbed in another one of her scary books. This one was by Stephen King, *The Talisman*. Ngozi bit her lip as she watched her sister read. *How does she do it?* she wondered. *She should be carsick as hell. But you probably have to be aware of your surroundings to get carsick.* When her sister got into a book, she might as well have physically flown to a different world.

Adoabi had been reading the book since they had boarded the plane back home in Chicago. She read through the entire flight to London and continued reading through the flight from London to Port Harcourt, Nigeria. She kept reading through the ride to the village and for plenty of nights by candlelight in the village.

The Talisman gave Adoabi sweet nightmares every night but still she read on, craving every page. For Adoabi, the book had spiced up the world. She walked around with wide eyes that often annoyed Ngozi.

"Why don't you calm down or something?" Ngozi told her sister once when she saw Adoabi staring at the forest behind the village. "You look stupid and stuff."

Adoabi had grinned.

"You just don't get it," Adoabi said. "It's like everything around us is alive. Look at all the trees!"

Ngozi had only rolled her eyes at her dreamy sister. It was better to just ignore Adoabi's strangeness.

One night, they were sitting on the balcony. The generator had run out of gas and everyone simply decided to turn in early for the night instead of wasting energy trying to stay cool. Ngozi had tried to sleep but it was too hot. Adoabi was sitting cross-legged on the concrete balcony floor reading by candlelight.

Though it was a sweltering night, a strong breeze waved the trees back and forth, making a *shhhhhhhh* sound. Ngozi froze, a shiver running up her spine despite the heat. She glanced at Adoabi, who had stopped reading and was looking out into the moonlit forest that was a sea of rippling leaves.

"There *have* to be monsters in there," Adoabi said. "Yeah, big looming monsters with huge blue bug eyes and white jagged claws that could easily rake up skin."

"Oh, bullcrap," Ngozi said, rolling her eyes. "Those books are like drugs and they are giving you hallucinations."

"I can't help it, though," Adoabi said with a giggle. "I'm addicted."

"Whatever," Ngozi said, going back inside. She sucked her teeth in irritation, the way she heard her cousins do it and quickly went inside. She'd rather sweat indoors than be with whatever was out there.

"Man, whatever yourself," Adoabi said. "You never listen to me."

"Weirdoes aren't meant to be heard," Ngozi said

"You're the weirdo," Adoabi grumbled, going to back to her book. "Your head's, like, all dried up and stuff."

Now in the rickety van on their way back to the airport, Ngozi saw Adoabi's shoulders shiver and she felt more annoyed. Though Adoabi was only two years younger than she was, she could be so babyish. It was always Ngozi's bed that Adoabi crawled into when she got scared at night. And Adoabi snored like a sleeping dragon. *Whatever,* Ngozi thought, *I think she likes being scared or something. There's no other reason why she'd keep reading that stuff.*

The wind whipped a braid into her face. She glanced at it and pushed it back. When she and Adoabi first stepped off the airplane into the heat of Nigeria, their braids were black. But now they had a reddish tint from the dust that swirled around. Ngozi wondered if either of them would be able to wash it out when they got home. Adoabi didn't really care.

"Dust is natural," Adoabi said.

"Man, whatever, dirt lady," Ngozi said.

Ngozi and her sister teamed up with their cousins, Grace and Rose, throughout most of the two-week visit to their father's village. Rose and Adoabi were the same age and Grace and Ngozi were also the same age.

The four girls, looking like four sisters, were inseparable. Adoabi and Rose had a special love for wildlife. They spent hours and hours mucking around in the bushes and red dirt. The day they smuggled in the robust green stick bug under the dinner table still made Ngozi's skin crawl. The vile thing had somehow ended up on the table next to the bowl of jollof rice. Ngozi remembered that insect was cleaning itself. Neither of their mothers had been happy.

In Ngozi's opinion, she and Grace were much more mature than Adoabi and Rose. Adventure was what they were interested in, not creepy insects and slimy lizards. Ngozi giggled at how scared Adoabi got when the four of them snuck out to an old oracle one moonlit night deep in the forest behind the village. It was Ngozi's idea.

Adoabi refused to go unless Ngozi made a grand promise to her. "I hereby promise to buy you the new Clive Barker book, hardcover, the minute it comes out in return for you risking your life visiting a haunted scary place at my request," Ngozi had to recite before Adoabi and her cousins. It turned out to be a worthwhile exchange, for a haunted scary place was exactly what it was, at least in Adoabi's opinion.

With flashlights, they'd trudged into the tall palm trees and thorny bushes, following what their cousin Grace called a path but was really no more than gaps between the trees. Adoabi clung to Ngozi the entire time, jumping at every hoot and screech. Adoabi said she was sure there were lumbering monsters and hungry headhunters watching them, waiting for the right moment to strike.

"Maybe if you didn't constantly scare yourself with those stupid books," Ngozi snapped. "It's just an old place, that's all." The temple, made of thick slabs of grey stone, was covered with flowering vines, dark green lizards scampering up the sides. Rose said it hadn't been used in decades.

"Yeah, since the missionaries invaded and made people believe that a blue-eyed blonde Jesus was their savior," Rose spat. She grumbled something in Igbo and then said, "You should see my mother! She is truly brainwashed, *o*!"

Rose had stood behind the stone altar and recited spells she'd heard a year ago when she had snooped around the local medicine man's hut. Her older sister, Grace, superstitiously crossed herself.

"Stop playing around!" she snapped. "You are so stupid!"

Rose only laughed.

"Do you think all that Christian stuff is going to help against the old religion? You are confused, girl," Rose giggled.

At that moment, Adoabi stumbled across a pile of old chicken bones and gasped, leaping over to her sister and burying her head on Ngozi's shoulder.

"Those are only the bones of chickens, silly," said Rose, picking one up. "Their necks were rung as sacrifice to the gods."

"You know," Grace said, "in the paper the other day, there was a story about how these men are practicing black magic. They had been kidnapping children and cutting off their heads and using their brains and grinding up their skulls for powerful potions."

Adoabi gasped, glancing around into the shadows.

"What?" Ngozi said, holding her sister's hand.

"No, you're making that up!" Rose said. "I can read, too, you know. There was nothing about 'black magic,' that's just a word these white people like to use to make us afraid of our own power! Don't make me tell you off!"

"You are such a little barbarian, Rose," Grace said. "You are too childish to tell me off!"

Rose sucked her teeth, scowling at her sister. Then she turned to her American cousins.

"It just said that there have been children disappearing lately," she said. "Rumor has it that before the child disappears there's a man wearing a black hat hanging around."

"He probably hangs around places like this for stupid girls like you who believe this nonsense," Grace spat.

"I don't *believe* it," Rose said. "I just don't . . . "

That was when the breeze picked up. It was a cool night but the breeze was warm. Later on, Adoabi said, "It was the breath of whatever ruled the forest." Ngozi didn't know what it was. All she wanted to do was forget that burst of hot air and that smelled like wet soil and mulch after it rained.

All four of the girls had frozen, staring at each other with huge eyes barely lit by the half moon above. Then they all took off, swallowing their screams. They were out at an hour that would get them beaten by their mothers, and even in their horror, they knew to remain quiet. Adoabi didn't stop shaking until they had climbed back into their room through the window and she was under her covers.

Now here she is subjecting herself to more of that, Ngozi thought.

"Whatever," she grumbled, staring out one of the open windows, letting the air blow her face. They passed markets where women sold cocoa yam, dried fish, oranges, tomatoes, and egusi. Goats were tied to the trunks of trees and chickens lay on the ground unable to walk because their legs were tied. She tried to take in as much of southeastern Nigeria as she could. There was only a week before it was time to go. *Back to the United States.* The thought made her heart drop. *Man, who knows when we'll be back.*

The trip from their father's village to the Sheridan Hotel in Lagos would be about six hours long, the driver said. Of course this didn't include the traffic and potholes and haughty military men who liked to make travelers unpack everything in their vehicle until the travelers decided to just pay them off.

"If they actually caught anyone carrying drugs or anything else that was supposedly 'illegal,' I'll bet they'd let the people go if they gave them some of the stuff," Ngozi had angrily said as they pulled away from some military men an hour ago.

Ngozi had eyed her sister as the man with dark smooth skin wearing the green beret and carrying the very big gun walked around the van.

"I swear, man," she said right after, "when he came to my side, I swear, I saw his fingers on the trigger, and his nails were long like the nails of . . . a sloth. And did you see his eyes? They were wild, man. Like he was just waiting for a reason to shoot."

"Adoabi, one of these days you're gonna have a heart attack," Ngozi said. She actually thought the military man was quite good-looking. And she certainly didn't find men with nails long as a sloth very attractive.

They were stopping again and Ngozi looked out the window. Adoabi looked up from her book.

"What are we stopping here for?"

Outside was what Ngozi thought was a restaurant. People sat at wobbly tables drinking Fanta and Star and Heineken beer and dishing up Fu Fu with their hands and dipping it in spicy okra or egusi soup. The front of the "restaurant" was open. Adoabi wondered what they did when it rained. She could see two women cooking in a kitchen-like area at the back. She couldn't see but she imagined that they were sweating and probably very tired.

"We're stopping here for some drinks, so if you have to go to the bathroom, Ike says it's around the back," their father said, stretching his long arms. Their parents had become a lot more relaxed over the last three weeks. They were thousands of miles away from their busy lawyer lives. Ngozi was glad to see them without their beepers and having such a great time. They hadn't been back to Nigeria since before she was born, which Ngozi thought was way too long.

Ngozi looked at the decrepit building with a rusting red tin gate. The air smelled of burnt marshmallows and Highlife was playing from a radio somewhere inside. There was smoke billowing from the back and behind the whole building was lush forest.

"Come on, Adoabi," Ngozi said, grabbing her arm, "I have to go to the bathroom and I'm not going behind there by myself,"

"Ngozi, I really do *not* like this place," Adoabi said, trying not to sound as scared as she was. "I don't know if I even want to drink anything from here. Something's not right."

"Ah man, come on," Ngozi said rolling her eyes.

"It's like stumbling across a circle of mushrooms, knowing not to step into it but not knowing why," Adoabi desperately said.

"Whatever," her sister said dismissively, pulling off the elastic band that held her foot long braids in a ponytail. She let them cascade into her face. "The driver said he stops here all the time and if the place wasn't safe, we wouldn't *be* here."

The driver seemed to have been everywhere. He knew every twist and turn, every pothole, how to get around almost all traffic jams (or at least how to lose the least amount of time in one). And he was the most skilled driver Ngozi and Adoabi had ever seen. They had watched him maneuver the van through amazingly tight squeezes. He wove through a traffic jam with such ease, people around him got irritated when they couldn't follow him. One man had even spit on the van as it passed. The saliva globule had dried on the car door.

"Oh, fine. God!" Adoabi said snatching her arm from Ngozi's long-nailed grasp. As she walked toward the building, Ngozi could hear Adoabi dragging her white sandals in the red dirt. Ngozi frowned but she did not look back at her sister. The closer she got to the building the more she felt a sense of doom but she'd never admit such a silly thing. *I'm not going to let Adoabi's stupidity rub off on me*, she thought. She looked up at the looming shack and quickly looked down at her feet and the dirt. There was a dim red haze that radiated from the building like heat.

"Come on, man!" Ngozi said. "Walk faster. I've gotta go bad!"

"I'm coming! Cool it!" Adoabi said. "It's not my fault you didn't go at the last stop."

"I'm sick of going in the damn bushes!" Ngozi snapped, opening the white gate to the back. "You're lucky you didn't get bitten on the ass by a snake or something."

"Whatever," Adoabi said, following Ngozi through the gate. As soon as she stepped in, she ran into her sister.

"What are . . . "

She heard the yipping before she saw them and when she saw them, her jaw dropped. It was a bizarre procession that looked as if it had come right out of Adoabi's head. Coming toward Ngozi and her sister was a herd of puppies, yipping and tumbling over one another. Their fur was a soft sandy brown, their tiny paws white. Bulldogs.

"What the . . . "

Then she noticed something else, some of the puppies were . . . limping. And they were limping because they had no choice. They each only had three legs! In place of where the fourth leg should have been were smooth furry stumps. Ngozi stared until her eyes got dry. She'd seen a story on the news once about a three-legged dog but she'd never seen one in real life. How the heck were they able to move so fast?

In between tumbles, they got quite a few steps in. And she wasn't merely hearing the "yip yips" of the puppies. There were also "tweet tweets." Running amongst the puppies were . . . pink baby ducks? As if this wasn't strange enough, the baby ducks kept falling, too, as they tried to keep up with the puppies. They were bow legged.

"Pink baby ducks and puppies?" Adoabi whispered. "What's wrong with them?"

Ngozi barely heard her sister. She couldn't seem to drag her eyes from the strange sight that was circling around her sandals. The puppies and ducks ran around the girls' feet, quacking and yapping and falling. A few of the dogs mewled at Adoabi's ankle, smearing saliva on her skin.

"Ewwwww!" Adoabi screeched, rubbing her leg against her ankle.

Then the strange ducks and crippled pups ran through the open gate. Ngozi and Adoabi watched as they scuttled into the dusty parking lot like a school of fish, the slightest movement sending them all in another random direction. But not so random, for they moved in circles, never beyond the parking lot. Ngozi shrugged and began to make her way farther into the back, her urge to urinate reminding her of why they had opened the gate in the first place.

Adoabi reluctantly followed her sister and said, "Man, the bushes are way better than this . . . this . . . house of deformities," she grumbled. "What the hell did we just see, anyway? Pink baby ducks and messed up puppies running around together as if they were of the same freaking genus and species and stuff! What kind of . . . "

"Will you shut up?" Ngozi said, with a look of urgency on her face. She had no idea what kind of weird shit they had just seen. What she knew was that she was through using nature as her toilet. God, what *was* it about Nigeria and the simple toilet, anyway? Or should she say lack of?

That was one thing she had not been able to get used to. She hadn't minded washing with cold buckets of water, not having electricity after eight o'clock, eating one big meal a day or the lack of television. She and her sister had adapted easily to Nigeria, indeed. They loved the food, they'd picked up a little of the language, Adoabi had even carried well water on her head with Rose and Grace every day of their last week at the village.

Ngozi had refused, saying it made her neck hurt. But the issue of having no toilet had not been easy for Ngozi to deal with. When there was an actual toilet with actual plumbing that worked, there was always some plump venomous-looking spider hanging out in the bathroom or a nasty wall gecko scampering in its prickly manner on the ceiling or enormous cockroaches swimming up from the bowels of the toilet like water beetles. All wildlife seemed to migrate to the bathroom. And when there was no bathroom and she had to find a place outside, Ngozi was in constant fear of snakes, mosquitoes or some other sickening organism or some pervert seeing her.

"I'll make it real fast, okay?" Ngozi said.

Thock!

They rounded the side of the shack and came to what looked like a backyard. Or more like a clearing, for there was no fence to hold the forest behind at bay.

Thock!

An old woman of less than five feet with skin as black as the pelt of a panther stood behind a thick wooden table with a machete in her left hand. Sweat glistened on her thin-looking wrinkled skin. She brought the machete down again.

Thock!

Behind the woman was a metal barrel with smoke billowing from it. The forest crept in close behind. The outhouses were just past the woman to the left. Sitting on the ground against the restaurants' back-door was a man. He had his legs pulled close to him.

"You think he's asleep?" Adoabi whispered. She gasped and roughly grabbed her sister's arm. It was midday and the sun felt especially hot. Ngozi could feel the sweat dripping from the sides of her arms.

"What?" Ngozi hissed.

"That man over there," Adoabi whispered. "Oh, I hope he can't hear us."

"What about him?" Ngozi said, moving forward. Adoabi moved with her, her eyes still on the man.

"He's wearing a black hat!" she whispered loudly.

"So what?"

"Don't you remember what Grace said about the kidnapping man?"

Ngozi thought for a minute and then she remembered. She glanced at the man. The hat was covering his eyes.

"Well, he's asleep," she whispered. "Let me go to the bathroom and then we'll get out of here. We don't want to make it obvious that we know who he is and stuff."

Ngozi had no idea whether or not he was that bad man Grace had mentioned. She didn't really believe Grace's story. But better safe than sorry.

The two girls walked past the sleeping man and the woman, trying to mind their own business. There were three outhouses with tin roofs. Adoabi walked with her eyes cast to the red dirt ground.

Ngozi couldn't help but stare at what was on the table that the woman

47

was chopping and what was swarming around and on it. It looked like the entrails of some animal and there was a lot of it. Enough to cover the entire table. Maybe they were the legs of the puppies, she thought. Or maybe they were chopped up whole puppies *and* ducks! And it was the meat that they put in the okra soup that they were serving with the Fu Fu out in front! Her lip curled in disgust.

The woman took no notice of the flies, which rose up in a buzzing swarm around her head whenever she brought the machete down. The woman watched Ngozi with smirking eyes. She gazed blankly back. *How is she not cutting her finger?* Ngozi wondered. *She's not even looking.*

She took a deep breath, trying to calm herself and then looked straight ahead at the outhouses. She stopped. Once again, Adoabi bumped into her sister's back.

"What?" Adoabi hissed.

"Look up!" her sister whispered, sounding as if she were about to cry.

Adoabi looked up. Perched on top of the outhouses were four large black vultures.

"Wow," she whispered, fascinated.

The birds were almost as big as the girls, sitting hunched forward, their tiny heads dwarfed by their meaty bodies. *It never fails*, Ngozi thought. *What is up with creatures and bathrooms? Is it some kind of sick perverse attraction or are they just comfortable around poo and pee?*

Ngozi suddenly understood why the birds were there. The better to watch the meat. She could hear their long talons clacking on the tin roof. There were five more vultures standing behind the woman in front of the smoking barrel, their heads pointing towards what was on the table. Waiting for a scrap to accidentally fall on the ground so they could snatch it up. They didn't dare get too close to the woman. *She could probably do some damage to them with that big knife*, Ngozi thought.

"Go on," the woman suddenly said in a deep heavily accented voice. "Dey no interest in you."

"Go!" Adoabi whispered, shoving Ngozi toward the big birds.

One of the vultures softly squawked and pecked at the vulture next to it, who raised its enormous wings and hopped away sideways. The sound of their talons clacking on the tin grated at Ngozi's nerves. The hot air had grown completely still, as if to amplify the sound.

"Fine, fine, I'm going!" Ngozi said, slapping her sister's hand away and looking at the woman. The woman waved an encouraging hand to her.

"Come with me a little closer, then I'll go," Ngozi said to her sister, no longer caring how her fear showed. "Please? It's scary, okay?"

Adoabi took her sister's hand and the two slowly crept toward the outhouse. Behind them they could hear the old woman chuckling to herself in between chops. *Yeah, I know she finds this just hilarious as hell*, Ngozi thought. *Two Americanized Nigerian girls too afraid of a few birds to relieve themselves. Wouldn't be the first time people have laughed at us for that kind of reason.* But these thoughts didn't make her any less afraid.

The closer they got to the outhouses, the closer they got to the nasty vultures with the nasty long talons. Adoabi stared at the creature above the outhouse on the far left, the one that Ngozi was leading them to. It locked its eyes on Adoabi. Ngozi could see its haggard-looking orangish yellow beak, which had probably torn apart many a dead animal. And maybe some alive. It tapped its claws on the tin and ruffled its greasy-looking black feathers. A tiny squeak came from Adoabi as she tried her best to stay brave. Ngozi didn't want to know what Stephen King induced monsters and demons were going through her sister's head.

Ngozi reached for the outhouse door, pulled it open and they both jumped back. They felt a gust of hot foul-smelling air waft past them. A smell of disease, waste, and rot and . . . something else? Inside was nothing but a big hole in the ground. Ngozi couldn't see the bottom, maybe that was for the better. But she did hear the buzzing of millions of flies. She slapped the back of her neck and then her leg.

Ngozi turned around and looked at Adoabi. When she made eye contact, she knew that she and her sister were hearing the same thing. The same two things. The first was coming from the pit, through the noise of the flies. Howls and sobs. All high-pitched in voice. Like children. Thousands of them. And the sound was coming from far away. Far beneath.

The second new sound was coming from behind them. A wheezy laugh. If either of the teenage girls knew the disease, they'd have described it as an emphysema tinted guffaw.

"Hhhhhheh, hhhheh, hhhheh!"

"It's that man!" Adoabi whispered, tears welling in her eyes. "It's that man! He wasn't asleep, he was only pretending . . . "

"Come on!" Ngozi shouted, pulling her sister knowing if her sister resisted she'd still sprint away. "Let's go! Let's get out of here, man!"

Ngozi took one last look, as her legs began to move. She saw tendrils of smoke snaking from the lip of the pit over the red dirt around it. Then she snapped her head around and took off. She didn't care if she sounded like Adoabi. She was positive that the hole in the ground led to another world, a terrible one. The buzzing had sounded as if it were coming from far away. As if the hole was the entrance to a world filled with rot and decay and millions of blow flies. And soon they would congregate and rush out of the hole in a putrid swarm. It was the place where all those children had been taken.

Ngozi had forgotten her urge to pee. They ran past the herd of ducks and dogs, who had found their way back into the yard, and out the white gate. They didn't stop until they were in the van. Ngozi slammed the car door hard.

The two girls sat huddled together on the hard wooden seat, their hearts beating faster than ever. For once, Ngozi didn't mind Adoabi's tears. Though she didn't cry, herself, Ngozi felt like she would. She peered out the window at the looming forest and shivered. A slight breeze waved the treetops. Never had the forest looked so alive to Ngozi's eyes. She could feel her own body humming like a tuning fork after it's been hit against a surface.

She could hear their parents and the driver coming back to the van talking. She sat up and looked out the window at the field across the empty street. Then she turned to her sister.

"Come with me out to that field," she said, stepping out of the car.

Adoabi sniffed, her tears already dry on her cheeks. She rubbed her eyes, her nostrils flared.

"Great, now we can get bitten by snakes, too? You never believe me when I tell you things aren't right. Why should I do you any favors?" Adoabi snapped, her hands still shaking.

Ngozi could still feel the woman's eyes on her and she scratched at the fly stings on her arms, neck, and legs. *Will that woman send a vulture to follow us?* she wondered. *I'll bet that bad bad man is still snickering to himself.*

"I'll believe you from now on," Ngozi finally said. "At . . . at least when you sound rational."

Adoabi only humphed but she followed her sister into the bushes anyway.

THE BLACK STAIN

There were once two Nuru brothers named Uche and Ifeanyi. Both lived in the booming desert-town of Durfa and both were the sons of a wealthy merchant named Qasim. At the ages of twenty and twenty-one, Uche and Ifeanyi were two of the most sought-after bachelors in Durfa. Both were tall, muscular, and attractive. Both were as hardworking as their father and as polite yet talkative as their mother. And both had the strongest blood of the Nuru's running through their veins. On their mother's side they were said to be direct descendants of the first Nuru tribesmen the goddess Ani brought to earth from the sun after she awoke.

Ifeanyi was good in math and he spent most of his time as an accountant in the large stone building with the mysterious etchings on the front. This building was his father's store. At the age of nineteen his father had bought the building from a woman who wore a thick black burka. She'd sold it to him for a pathetically cheap price. Being a man of opportunity and knowing that women should never involve themselves in deals as complex as the buying and selling of property, his father quickly took the building off her hands and made it his store. Months later, he married and from then on, the store proved to be a place of fortune. Ifeanyi had even been born in the backroom when his mother had stayed at the store too late. She'd been trying to get some last minute paperwork done before retiring home to give birth.

From boyhood, Ifeanyi had loved his father's large store. Now as an adult, he maintained the store's books and helped his father sell and catalog scrap metal, old computers, capture stations, and many other bits of tech, those very items the priestesses of Ani deemed evil. Ifeanyi justified this by telling himself that the more he sold these items and thus got people to use them, the sooner these things would wear down and crumble back into the dust they came from. He was merely helping along the process.

Each day, on his way into the store and when he left, Ifeanyi ran his hand over the building's etchings. They felt nice on the pads of his fingers. Ifeanyi helped run his father's store with a steady hand. He was firm with his father's Okeke slaves, working them hard and beating them when it was necessary. His father's Nuru workers respected him and found him charming, though like his father, he never gave them bonuses or days off. Ifeanyi wanted to please his father by closely following the doctrines of his tribe and surpassing his father in successes. He believed in the Nuru way that was his birthright, privilege, and obligation. He looked to the sky every night and smiled knowing the sun was out there and he was a fine example of a Nuru man.

His younger brother Uche was the same, except where Ifeanyi worked in the shop, Uche worked on the road collecting and purchasing materials and items to stock the shop. Being out so much exposed him to all the different kinds of Nurus of the Seven Kingdoms. The wealthy, the poor, the educated, the uneducated.

Uche often found himself in Okeke villages shouting at Okekes to decide who would go with him for his next large haul. Be they old computer parts in Ronsi or computer chips in Suntown, the black-skinned Okeke *always* had to argue, bargain, and waste time over who would go. To Uche, the Okeke were a foul dimwitted people and he hated dealing with them even more than his brother did.

Where his brother would have them beaten, Uche liked to have them whipped when they got things wrong. Praise Ani. No punishment was too great for one of the Okeke tribe; they were the people who had angered the goddess Ani when she awoke from her peaceful sleep. They were the descendants of the ones who'd created the evil technology in the darkness before the light.

Uche spent very little time in the store. The walls were too constricting and the clean dust-free robes his father expected him to wear while in the store were uncomfortable. Uche liked to sleep under the stars so he could gaze at them and try his best to remember the home of his ancestors on the sun, a star in itself. *What must it have been like to live in an Okeke-free world where everything was green?* he'd wonder. He was sure that on the sun, beneath its powerful aura, all things were lush and greener than the plants that grew around the rivers. The fertile fragrant land of the sun was nothing like the desert wasteland beyond the Seven Rivers Kingdom.

Nevertheless, Uche travelled into the desert often. This fateful day, it was for scrap metal. He had been to the dead city several times in the past three years. It was a long journey but always fruitful.

He had heard of the dead city months ago when he came across an Okeke madman. The man was a nomad out in the desert. He was in Durfa for reasons Uche didn't know. With his foul breath, blank eyes, and black thin arms flinging about as he spoke, he told Uche of an ancient "ghost metropolis" heavy with rust and valuable metals. Supposedly, it had been one of the Okeke's wicked dwellings from before Ani pulled in the sun. The arid desert had preserved it like a tomb. Intrigued, Uche quickly gathered a team of slaves and Nurus. He took the Okeke nomad as a guide and off they went.

Ten days later, Uche saw it. One of the Okeke's great and terrible empires. Glass, metal, concrete towers slowly crumbling back into sand, as they should. The ancient edifices were enormous, tilted this way and that, like a forest of dying palm trees. The place was silent but it had the same odd feeling, Uche noted, as when he touched the etchings on his father's building. He never mentioned how much he disliked those etchings, but it was a large part of why he preferred to stay away from the shop. He had the same feeling now. He wanted to leave. But the wealth! So much metal they could simply pull off, load, and bring back. This first trip to the ghost city assured the survival of his father's shop for at least another five years. And his subsequent trips increased the family empire tenfold.

Now, for this next trip, his plans were a little different. His caravan would be three times bigger. He planned to collect as much metal as possible. Word had gotten out about the whereabouts of his secret treasure trove. When he found out who had told, if it was an Okeke, he'd have him killed. If it was one of his Nuru workers, he'd discreetly have him whipped bloody.

It was rainy season, a time where life was happiest in Durfa. And it was the week of the rainy season festivals. Uche hated to leave at this time but he had no choice. Time was of the essence. There was plenty of metal in the ghost city but he wanted his choice of the best of the best. He was *entitled* to it. He was the one who'd found the ghost city, wasn't he?

He gathered together a large group. Ten of his strongest Nuru men and thirty Okeke, including a family of seven of his most hardworking. Two of the Okekes were women. It would be a long trip, so the women were necessary. He and his group set out for the ghost town at dawn with fifty camels and eleven scooters.

★

The first two days they made excellent time. Travelling during the night and camping in weather treated tents during the day. The Okeke women cooked and serviced. Everyone else, including the Okeke men, relaxed and settled into that half-alert, half-dream-like state one must adopt when moving through the desert.

On the third day, Uche's world became a most horrible nightmare. The ungwa storms came. His portable had predicted not a drop of rain. Their three capture stations could barely pull enough condensation from the sky to produce enough water to drink. It didn't make sense. His cursed portable must have malfunctioned. Or maybe it was one of those rare cases where the goddess Ani wanted to show her might over the ancient human technology she so hated. He wanted to dash his portable to the dry sandy ground and grind the tiny device with the heel of his sandal. But he had no time for that. He had to run. They all had to run.

Before the rain came, the killer lightning struck. Out in the open desert, within a few hours, with nowhere to run, all of Uche's men and nearly all the Okeke were struck dead by the wild lightning. Only Uche and two of the Okeke family members survived and it was completely by chance. Uche, an Okeke woman named Efem, and her older brother named Bakele, found themselves running across the packed hard ground, lightning blasting the sand into glass all around them.

When the deluge of rain came, they tried to run through a valley. Uche and Efem managed to grab onto the neck of a palm tree and pull themselves onto a stone cliff, but Bankele was not so lucky.

Efem screamed and screamed as she watched her brother swept away in the churning brown flood waters. She tore off her tattered red rapa and bent her legs, preparing to jump. Her eyes were wide with shock and defeat. Uche grabbed her arm. He pulled her to him and held tightly as she tried to tear away from him. She'd slapped and punched at his face, tried to bite his hand, glared at him with wild eyes. Uche held on. He quickly grabbed her rain-soaked rapa from the ground with his free hand. Then he slapped her with it. Then slapped her again. And again. *Smack! Smack! Smack!* Until she stopped fighting. She let him drag her up onto the high point of the slab of stone.

The skies were black. From where they cowered, it looked as if the desert had become a great river, a mythical ocean. Uche stared and stared, his arm locked around the woman who'd started fighting again. She still wanted to throw herself in the water. As he stared, he had a vision. He saw water as far as the eye could see, the shining sun high in the sky. He called Ani's name with his mouth wide and the woman screamed louder, now calling Ani, too. And that was when he saw it. A cave of stone not fifty feet away.

★

Dragging Efem with him, he made it to the cave where he threw her down. He threw her soaked rapa at her. Then he fell to the hard dry ground beside her and passed out.

The lightning-filled ungwa storms lasted for seven days. It took another three for the waters to drain into the always-thirsty desert. Uche had his backpack of supplies, so they had food. Nevertheless, once Efem recovered her wits by the second day, she proved to be more resourceful.

Within the first two days, out there in the middle of nowhere, so far from the Seven Rivers Kingdom, Uche quickly forgot Ani's teachings. Efem did, too. And by the third day, they began to talk about their lives. Uche told Efem about how much he hated the etchings on his father's building. He'd never told this to anyone. Efem told Uche how most Okeke stayed away from his father's building because supposedly something strange had happened there decades ago. They laughed at all this. At first, Uche was troubled by how smoothly they eased into each other's presence. Regardless, soon, a night came where they carefully talked honestly about what it was to be Nuru and what it was to be Okeke. Uche wanted to resist but instead his mind was blown. That night, Efem slept soundly. But Uche cried quietly for hours, wondering how he'd face the sun knowing that he no longer sought to return to its most blessed lands.

Over the next few days, having nothing else of interest to look at, Uche found himself gazing at the black-skinned woman. No, not black, dark brown. Like the coffee his father liked to drink.

"Your skin reminds me of groundnuts," Efem told him. They'd both laughed. He thought she was right.

He also noticed how smooth her skin was and how dimples appeared in her cheeks when she smiled. He liked to see her smile. The night before they left the cave, they made love and Uche had never been so happy. When he returned to the Seven Rivers, he had so much to tell the people. Both Nuru and Okeke. People. No one would listen but he would speak regardless. Then he and Efem would disappear into the night to live in the desert, which they had come to know better after nearly dying in it.

On the way back, it was as if Ani blessed them despite their moral indiscretion. They found and made a meal of a large tortoise and three water-filled coconuts. In some places, due to the storm's passing, there were fields of delicate pink sweet smelling flowers. Efem found them tasty, Uche found them too bitter. They took their time. When they entered Uche's father's store over a month after they'd left, Uche's brother came running to embrace him.

"Where have you been, brother?" Ifeanyi asked, wiping tears from his eyes. He didn't notice Efem at all. "We saw the big storm on the weather maps. We thought you died out there."

"I nearly did, brother," Uche said. He turned to Efem and brought her forward and Ifeanyi frowned. "We are the only two survivors."

As Uche explained what happened, his brother's frown grew deeper and deeper. The Okeke woman was standing beside his brother and his brother still had his arm on her shoulder. Had he gone mad in the desert? Something was very wrong here.

"What is this woman to you?" he finally asked, interrupting his brother's story.

"I love her," Uche said.

Ifeanyi slapped his brother hard enough to bloody his nose. Efem gasped and stepped back as Ifeanyi turned to her and raised his hand to beat her. Uche jumped in front of her. "Don't you *dare!*"

"Or what?"

There are different accounts of what happened next. Some say that an epic fight ensued between the brothers that left the store and both brothers a shambles. In this version, Efem ran off without a word and Uche never saw her again. In another version, Ifeanyi cursed his brother and his Okeke animal whore and vowed never to speak to him again. In this version, Ifeanyi knew what was to come and so did Uche. Ifeanyi ran out into the street not long after Uche, shocked and confused at his brother's reaction, told Efem to run for her life.

The rest of the story is the same wherever it is told. "Abomination!" Ifeanyi announced. "Mark my words, things are about to go wrong! My brother has created abomination! Ani brought us from the sun. She forbade us to copulate with the filth known as Okeke! That rule has been broken! Darkness will follow!" And then that night, with the help of some of his friends, he dragged his brother to a cornfield where he showed Uche how one is to treat an Okeke woman.

The Okeke woman had already been beaten and was nearly unconscious as Ifeanyi forced his brother to watch him rape her. His friends, who had beaten the Okeke woman senseless, looked the other way, for Ifeanyi's wild actions were an abomination, too. However, they forced Uche's head and held his eyes open, so *he* had to watch. By the next month, there was more abomination, for not only was Efem pregnant but this woman became pregnant, too.

The two women, Efem and the Okeke woman whose name was Hidayah, both the color of coffee, hid amongst their own. They hid their secrets, for fear that their fellow Okeke would take their lives if they knew what they carried in their bellies. Eight months later, in two different places, at the same time, one on time and one premature, monstrosities were born. Half-breed. *Ewu.* Up to this moment, to birth an *Ewu* child had only been a threat from the goddess Ani. Both women described how just as the child emerged, a cold feeling stole over them. They spoke of the sensation of something evil sinking into their bellies.

The children that emerged were horrors. Hair the color of sand, skin the color of sand, eyes light as if they had been staring at sand. One was born with teeth and it bit off the finger of one of the assistant midwives as soon as it took its second breath. The other had long nails and scratched deep grooves in the face of the midwife before she could tie its hands together.

It was clear that a demon had entered the two newborn children. Both midwives bundled up and took the newborns, cursed the sleeping exhausted women, and ran to the elders. The two midwives met at the door of the elders at the same time as the sun was going down on a moonless night. The elders quickly called a meeting and made a decision. They would throw the children into the desert.

They did it that very night, when the sky was black and the air was cold. One child died quickly. However, the other did not. The demon inside this one had a powerful will to live. A pack of desert foxes came along and ate the dead child but gave the living one their warmth. Come morning, the strange child could walk. The foxes were satisfied, and they took and raised it.

The child lived amongst them, feral and wild. Soon the child gave into its violent nature and killed and ate its desert fox family. For years, it existed in the desert. Okeke farmers and caravans would claim they saw a ghost or demon lurking outside the cities on the trails. One day this living legend came into Durfa and it showed up at a large wedding.

The wedding of Ifeanyi. It is not known whether this creature was his or his brother's child. No one knows which survived.

Regardless, this creature stealthily killed everyone in sight except for Ifeanyi, leaving him to tell the gruesome tale. This was the first time anyone had glimpsed an *Ewu* creature. Ifeanyi said it only spoke in grunts and drank blood like water. The people of Durfa ostracized Ifeanyi when in his grief, he admitted to his role in possibly creating this *Ewu* child.

His ostracism did not last long, for within a week the thirty-year-old Ifeanyi had a heart attack and died. His brother Uche followed him soon after when he ate a bad plate of egusi soup and died from the disease that dissolves the bowels. The woman Efem was never seen again and her Okeke relatives were relieved. Many reported that Efem was wiped off the earth by the Goddess Ani. And the other woman Hidayah never bore a child again and soon became a lonely spinster.

Understand that the *Ewu* creature was a lesson from Ani. "When the roots of a tree begin to decay, it spreads death to the branches." Uche and Ifeanyi, the descendents of the True Nuru, had lain and procreated with the very beasts Ani deemed only fit for slavery. The *Ewu* creature was Ani's wrath smote upon the Nuru as punishment for the misdeeds of Uche and Ifeanyi and the greater Nuru people, for no fool is owned or disowned by his family.

One must stop to consider the etchings on the walls of Uche and Ifeanyi's father's store. Were they a black magic? A curse created by a rebellious Okeke that destined these boys to force the creation of the *Ewu* born? Evil is Okeke and Okeke is evil. It is written.

When an *Ewu* child was kindled, Ani made it true that the *Ewu* child, a child born of violence and ignorance and profanity, was a monster. A black stain. A creature of the desert that looked and behaved like neither slave nor master. To create one is to curse one's bloodline— Nuru or Okeke. It is to usher in the demon. It is not to happen. And if it does, stamp it out immediately. It is a useless otherworldly creature deserving of no respect, dignity, or life.

HOW INYANG GOT HER WINGS

She circled high above her village, looking down. It would be the last time she ever saw it as it was. Okokon-Ndem, Calabar, Nigeria, 1929. The rectangular adobe sleeping quarters with cooking fires burning in front of them. Built in a circle. A courtyard in the center. The spaces between the huts filled in by forest. Yam and manioc farms close by. Her forest village, her mother, her father, her sister, her sister. She had only one friend and he was over one hundred years old. The others she resented, but they were her people, so she loved them too. Except Koofrey. She would always hate *him*.

She shed no tears. Instead, she looked ahead. To the east. The sun was rising. It would soon be time to go. She sighed. It had all really started with that dream.

★

Levitation

She sat in a round clearing surrounded by ekki, iroko, idigbo, obeche, camwood, and palm trees that fondly bent their leafy heads toward her. Before her was bliss. Ripe bright orange mango slices. A palm leaf heavy with thick disks of boiled yam, soft but firm, dripping with palm oil and red pepper. A pile of buttery biscuits. Split coconuts, the insides lined with thick white coconut meat. Sweet sweet fibery oranges, peeled and separated into juicy sections.

Beside her, a boy wearing blue beads around his neck handed her a green bottle of palm wine. She grinned at him. Whoever he was.

She'd tasted palm wine once when her father had left a gourd of it beside the cooking fire. She'd drunk from the gourd and ended up stumbling around with a grin on her face. Later, she'd received a terrible beating but not even her mother's strong hands could beat out the memory of how delicious palm wine tasted.

Now, she took a deep gulp. It was warm and sweet, just the way she liked her fruits. The wind blew the treetops and the sound of the shushing leaves distracted her momentarily from the bounty before her. She and the boy looked up into the sky, the grins on their faces widening. Their teeth were white, their skin dark brown and they didn't need a moon to know where they were.

★

Inyang woke with gummy eyes, nostrils flaring, mouth agape, gasping for air. She inhaled loudly. All was black and her heart fluttered. *But tonight's a full moon*, she thought, frowning. *So why can't I see?* She tried to raise her head. It hit something solid and stars burst before her eyes.

"Ah!" she hissed. "I've been buried alive!" Her grogginess quickly dissipated as her mind started working on a plan to dig herself out.

She turned her head and saw a wall gecko, pink blue in the moonlight. *Moonlight*, she thought. The wall gecko scampered to a corner, disappearing into the shadows. She tried to rest her neck. There was nothing to rest it on. She shuddered and fought for something to hold on to. Then she dropped from several feet, coming down hard on her straw stuffed bed with a painful thump. She rolled sideways to the floor.

"Oh no, not again," her oldest sister, Nko, groaned from her bed across the room. "You're too *old* for this."

Her middle sister, Usöñ—whose bed was closest to Inyang's—continued snoozing away.

Inyang got up slowly, her legs shaky. She rewrapped her blue and white rapa around herself. Her head ached but this time she remembered. This time she'd been awake when it happened. She rubbed her temples. She hadn't just rolled out of her bed.

"You okay?" Nko asked, rubbing her short hair, her collarette of beads and cowry shells clicking and clacking as she turned to look at Inyang. The straw in her bed crackled as she sat up.

Inyang nodded, pushing her long coarse hair from her face. She picked up her dark blue head wrap and rewrapped her locks. She looked down at herself and her eyes widened. "Nko! I've been wounded!" she screeched, pulling up her rapa and looking at her legs. But there was no sharp pain, only a dull ache.

There was more clicking and clacking as her sister Usöñ, abruptly sat up. "Wha . . . shut up, Inyang," she mumbled, still half-asleep.

"Open the curtains, Usöñ," Nko ordered. "She rolled out of bed again." Usöñ mumbled as she dragged herself up and pulled open the curtains to let in the moonlight. Nko's many folds of fat jiggled as she hurried to Inyang. "Let me see," Nko said, breathing heavily. Even after several hours of sleep, Inyang's sister smelled like baby powder and the scented oil. Usöñ ambled over, also slightly breathless. The three girls stood in the middle of the room like two healthy baobab trees around a palm tree. Nko pulled at Inyang's blue loincloth and Usöñ started laughing. The blood soaked through the cloth just below Inyang's belly.

"You're fine, Inyang," Nko said, a smirk on her face.

"I'll go tell mama and grandmother," Usöñ excitedly said, running out of the room as fast as she could, which wasn't very fast at all.

Inyang stood there, afraid to move. Her two sisters, who were two and three years her senior, had never spoken to her about how they'd gotten their menses. Thus far she felt no pain other than a dull throb in her abdomen but she wasn't sure. Her mind was reeling. *Blood on clothes. Had nose to ceiling. Blood on clothes. Had nose to ceiling.* She felt dizzy and she wanted to sit down. But she had blood on her rapa. And so she was standing there frowning as she sucked a strand of mango from between her teeth.

★

The next day, Inyang floated in the deeper part of the river, staring at the sky. She was glad no one was around. Mildly nauseous, she could feel the blood seep from between her legs with every movement. Earlier that day, her family had celebrated the coming of her menses with a small afternoon feast. She was *n-kaiferi* now. However, even she knew this didn't matter. She would not be circumcised and secluded for weeks in the *m-bobi*, the fattening hut that made girls beautiful. Nor would she be betrothed to a man. Ever.

In all her fourteen years, she'd never been so aware of her dada hair, the long thick locks of tightly twisted hair she'd been born bearing. They marked her as bizarre, potential bad luck, and unmarriageable. Still, because her family loved her, her father bought her a red loin-roll and her sisters decorated it with beads and cowry shells. Her father didn't bother buying the embroidered multi-colored cap that went with the *n-kaiferi* outfit. It wouldn't have fit over Inyang's long ropes of dada hair.

Inyang had reluctantly danced with her sisters and the other girls. Normally, she would have reveled in the food and laughter and especially the dancing. Inyang loved to dance. Sometimes when she was outside preparing dinner and night was approaching, she'd dance to the rhythm of the forest. Inyang wasn't a small girl, nor was she thin. She was tall for her age and strong and she ate healthily, though she was nowhere as large as her gorgeous sisters. But this afternoon, she wasn't hungry. Her grandmother had smiled at her, handing her a slice of sweet mango, her favorite. This Inyang was able to eat.

"It'll pass," grandmother whispered.

But she knew her grandmother was wrong. Inyang was born the way she was and something strange was happening to her. In her dreams, she had always flown. High, past the trees. Into the clouds or blue clear sky, depending on the weather she experienced during the day. In these dreams, she always felt a current of wind spiraling around her, clockwise, moving her with ease. These dreams always ended with a jarring crash to the ground, and her waking up rolled out of bed. But this time, she'd been eating a feast and when she woke . . . she'd been above her bed. She'd told none of this to her parents when they came to examine her.

Inyang hugged her secret close to her chest and waded back to the riverbank. She pulled herself out of the water, not bothering to look around. Though tradition told her to, she wasn't ready to become so conscious of her nakedness. She arched her back and stretched her arms, letting the sun bathe her body. When she was dry, she wiped away the dribbling blood, tied the rag between her legs and around her hips and wrapped her blue green cloth around herself. She tilted her head back and looked at the sky again. A slight breeze tickled her cheeks. Then she knelt down and got to work. She had a large basket of clothes to wash and it would be dark in a few hours.

★

She spent the next several days pretending as if everything was normal. Ten days later, she was outside standing over the flames preparing dinner. It was the plight of being the third daughter of a third wife. Still, she enjoyed cooking, though her lungs hitched and heaved from the fire's smoke on days when the wind wasn't moving enough. Today, however, the wind whipped and whirled slapping her locks around. She wore them down when she was cooking, when she allowed her mind to wander.

She closed her eyes, inhaling the wind as she stirred the soup. She was making her father's favorite, pounded yam and Edi Ka Kong soup, using plenty of greens, goat meat, chicken, and stockfish for the soup.

As she pounded the yam in the wooden pestle, she noticed herself levitating an inch off the ground. It had been like this for several days. As if her body didn't want to stay on the earth. Resisting the urge made her belly tickle in an uncomfortable way. When she dropped down a second later, she looked around, her heart beating fast. Thankfully, no one had noticed. She finished the rest of her cooking; her feet spread wide, as if such a stance would anchor her more.

After she served her father and several of the elders, uncles, her mothers, brothers, aunts and sisters, she sat down outside to eat. She scooped up the thick soup with small balls of pounded yam and savored every bite, letting herself think only about her food. When she finished, she collected the dishes and set them down in the small storage area attached to her quarters.

Outside, her sisters stood talking shyly to some men in the courtyard. Inyang envied the way their huge squashy behinds and legs jiggled under their colorful rapas and how their lumpy arms couldn't even wrap around their melon breasts. They were beautiful and normal. Her father wouldn't approve of the men being so close to her sisters. *If papa wasn't so busy, he'd chase those men away*, she thought, smiling.

Inyang loved her father. He didn't spend much time with her, since he had twelve children and a yam farm to maintain. But he gave her what little he could. Sometimes he'd stop in her room to tell her how delicious her cooking was. Or he'd come by to say good night to her and her sisters. Once in a while he'd tell her little stories. It was her father who told her about her dada hair and why she was allowed to keep it.

When she was seven years old, her father had found her curled on his bed, crying. Some of the girls she'd been playing with had made fun of her hair again. They'd said that Mami Wata would steal her away in the night and the thought terrified her. "Normally, your hair would be worn the shortest because you're the youngest girl. But you're . . . a little different," he said, sitting her on his lap.

"No one else wears their hair tangled like mine," she said, still sniffling.

"Inyang, your hair is dada," he said with a sad sigh. "You have no choice. This is the way the gods meant for you to be." From the look on her father's face and the look many women gave her, it also meant she was ugly. As she grew older, she was further separated from her age mates and her sisters when they went through marriage preparation ceremonies and she didn't.

She envied the beauty of these girls who were fattened and circumcised. Once she had even snuck to the fattening huts situated on the outskirts of the village. Both of her sisters had been betrothed to men from nearby villages. Because her mother made so much money in the market, her father could afford to send both of her sisters to the fattening house. Few wellborn men of the Efik people would marry a girl who hadn't been secluded for some period of time, the longer the better.

After two weeks of sleeping in her quarters alone, Inyang decided to go see her sisters. She was also curious just how the fattening huts were able to take any girl and turn her into a beautifully fat woman. When she got to the hut, she crouched low along the side. She slowly peered into the window. The smell of sweat, blood, palm oil, and pounded yam hit her face in a hot waft. The room was dark but she heard voices. She wrinkled her nose and dropped back down.

She slowly peeked in again. There were several beds in which girls were lying, not moving, their faces covered in something that looked like clay. White clothes were tied around their necks, wrists, and ankles. Inyang squinted, trying to see her sisters. On the far side of the hut were a group of women and one of the girls. Her legs were spread wide and two women held each one. When the girl started screaming, Inyang took off running. And she did not stop until she was in her special place in the forest. The owl living in the hollow of one of the trees opened one eye and then closed it when it saw it was only her.

She'd sat down amongst the leaves, closed her eyes, and cried and cried. She returned home feeling better. She knew that the girls in the fattening hut were stuffed with rice, beans, plantains, pounded yam, and palm oil. There were special fattening peppers used to make pepper soup. When drunk, this cured bloating and allowed girls to keep eating. Sometimes the girls had to eat chameleons soaked in water, too.

She knew that whatever happened to her sisters in there made them perfect creatures that appealed to the best of men. Something she'd never get the chance to be. Nonetheless, though she envied these privileged girls, when she was alone and sat really quietly, she realized that a part of her was always smiling, happy to be left alone.

Inyang poured water over the scrubbed dishes and sighed. She had so much to figure out about herself and no one she could discuss it with. That night, she lay awake, her sisters sleeping in their beds next to her. Usöñ directly to her right and Nko next to Usöñ. By age and worth. Nko was seventeen and already engaged to be married. Usöñ was sixteen and had several suitors competing for her hand.

Of course, the fact that no one would marry Inyang didn't mean Inyang didn't like boys. This was a secret not even her sisters knew. Inyang had happily lost her virginity last year. Essien had followed her into the shade where she retreated to dry herself from bathing. They were both thirteen years old. He had touched her between her legs and the sensation made her ravenous. He'd smiled when she asked him to touch her again and again. And it resulted in a smooth transition to an act far more mature. The first time felt odd, a mixture of pleasure and pain. The second time had been more pleasure than pain. Since then Inyang'd had five lovers, all who'd been so intrigued by her that they agreed to never tell a soul.

She thought about it, as she lay awake. She blinked, her mind jumping to a new subject. *Can I really fly?* She'd never heard of anyone who could do such a thing. She would ask grandmother. She would go to her small house next to her father's and fry her some plantain and make egg stew to eat with it. She'd use palm oil, onion, lots of red pepper and no salt, the way grandmother liked it. Then she would ask.

If I can fly . . . she thought . . . *But can I?* The thought caressed her cheek. Inyang looked at her snoozing sisters. She pushed the thin cover from her body with a soft kick and looked at her legs. They were long and strong with muscle. Nothing like both of her sisters', whose were heavy with pounds and pounds of dimply fat. But Inyang wasn't saddened by her slimmer legs. They were good for getting her through the forest, at least.

She closed her eyes and tried to capture the sensation. The ability that migrated around her body like a second skin of mist. How it mingled with the air, like taking the strong hand of a good friend. She shivered, her eyes still closed as she felt the tug as she lifted. There was a bump and a whisper from her mother's room next door and she softly dropped back onto her bed, opening her eyes and listening. She heard her mother's soft voice and then a quieter giggle. It was her mother's night with her father. She closed her eyes again.

This time she lifted much more easily and faster. She opened her eyes. Suddenly she wasn't controlling her movement at all. Still she lifted, the ceiling coming closer and closer. She crossed her arms over her face. At the last second, her nose, a millimeter from the ceiling, she stopped, dropped downward and shot through the thin white curtains and out the window. She slowly ascended above her village, her heart pounding in her chest as she looked down. Whatever had pulled into the sky could, any minute, choose to let her fall.

"Please," she whispered. "What is it you want?"

Nothing but the cool breeze responded. She looked at her village below, trying to resign herself to her fate. From above, even as she shook with fear, she noticed how logical the design of her village was; it was so well incorporated into the forest that if white explorers came through the area, they wouldn't see a village. It was the way of her people, an inclusion, not an intrusion. Still, she could tell which building belonged to her and her sisters. She'd climbed up on the roof one night and placed an owl she'd carved there. From where she was, the owl looked so real. She'd carved the owl's face stern, its eyes piercing. Just like the owl she always saw in the tree near her favorite spot in the forest.

A gust of wind flew past her, slapping into her body like a cool burst of water. She deeply inhaled it and, despite her fear, found herself laughing. She looked ahead over the treetops in the pale moonlight and smirked.

She yelped when she started to descend. When she stopped just above her grandmother's room, she almost laughed with relief. Her grandmother was behind this. She floated down, past the adobe roof, to the window to grandmother's favorite wicker chair. Her grandmother was a tiny woman, and so her chair was a tight fit for Inyang. Her grandmother sat across from Inyang in a wooden chair. The old woman's brown skin was crumpled by the sun and hard work. Her tiny feet were tough, she never wore shoes or sandals, and her arms were still strong. Her eyesight was quickly going. But tonight, she seemed to see Inyang just fine.

"Hello, Inyang," she said with a smile, looking right at her.

"Hello, grandmother," she said. "How did you . . . "

"Did you enjoy it?"

Inyang frowned. Her hands still shook from the shock and the fear of being in the sky with nothing to hold her. However, underneath that fear, her heart beat fast for a different reason. "Yes," Inyang said.

Grandmother nodded. She looked both sad and happy.

"I knew you would try tonight," she said. "The weather is right for it and you've always been an adventurous girl. It's in your blood. You can never wait for long." She paused and leaned forward. "You're like my mother's mother's sister, Asuquo," she said. "I never met her. She . . . I never met her. But my mother used to tell me about her, in case I had a child like her. She was wild, took to the forest often."

She paused again. Inyang felt her stomach flip. Her grandmother had no trouble saying what she thought. Inyang's father was highly respected in the village. But still, grandmother was the first person to tell him off when she thought he behaved stupidly. People even came to grandmother for advice instead of going to the village chief, and the chief did not mind because he often visited her, too.

"Her stupid husband ran down the street shouting *Amuosu! Amuosu!*" grandmother said. "They made her eat the chop nut when her husband accused her of witchcraft. The chop nut killed her . . . they wouldn't even give her a proper burial."

Inyang gasped. In the forest, the doomsday plant thrived during rainy season. Its purplish bean-like flowers were pleasing to her eyes. Eventually dark brown kidney-shaped pods would grow from them. The seed inside the pod was the chop nut which was used to reveal *Amuosu* women, practitioners of witchcraft. Inyang knew it was a flawless judge.

"That man was not the husband Asuquo was meant to have," grandmother said. "They never let her go out and find *him*."

"But her husband was right, then," Inyang said. "She *was* a witch. If the chop nut killed her then . . . "

Grandmother loudly sucked her teeth in annoyance. "No, no, she was not *Amuosu*." She leaned back in her chair. "My mother said the day Asuquo died, the wind stopped blowing for an entire year."

"But the chop nut killed her," Inyang said.

"And it will kill you, too," grandmother snapped. "As it kills *everybody*."

"What?"

"You weren't just born with dada hair, you're windseeker, Inyang. Do you know what that is?"

She shook her head.

"It's the real reason why you were never circumcised or taken to the fattening houses like your sisters. As time goes by, we forget more," she said. "It runs small small amongst the women in my bloodline. I thought my grandaunt was the last. You have a true name, Inyang, a windseeker name, but only your mirror can pronounce it."

"I don't understand all this."

"Just listen," grandmother said, her hands grasping the arms of her chair. "And lower your voice. If anyone hears this, they won't ever leave you be."

"But . . . "

"Eventually you'll have to leave here anyway," she said. "Not now but soon, in some years. Windseekers are rarely welcome in one place for long. You'll see. And you must find your other, have a family with him. That's the only way you'll find happiness."

She didn't like the sound of this. She'd resigned herself to her fate of being alone long ago and learned to feel good about it. Still, though the idea of leaving home scared her, it also excited her. If she could fly, she could go anywhere. Anywhere in the world. She blinked. But not if she found her other . . . no, she didn't want to find him.

"Don't give me that look, girl," grandmother said, disgusted. "This is deep tradition. Follow it . . . or suffer the consequences. You ask for too much. Selfish."

Grandmother spat on the floor and looked away. Inyang frowned. She'd never really asked for much of anything, now she was asking too much. *What I want is simple*, she thought. *Not much.*

"I'm through with you," grandmother said, with a wave of her small callused hand. Inyang started to rise again.

"Wait," she said, reaching for grandmother.

"No, time for you to go," she said. "You're just like your stupid great great grandaunt's daughter. See where that will get you."

Inyang rose and floated out the window, to the sky. Her control was restored and she turned to the forest. She flew low over the treetops, letting her hand touch the top leaves and branches of the palm and mahogany trees. She dropped through the forest canopy and wove between the trees. She flew over her favorite spot in the forest. Even from the unfamiliar perspective of above, she was able to find it. She'd always had a superb sense of direction, never getting lost even when she wandered deep into the forest. As if the world was her home. When she had seen enough she flew. Up.

She burst though the rainforest canopy into the sky. She could glimpse her village, and then other villages. The Cross River. She flew higher and higher and faster and faster. The clouds were cool and felt wet. She burst through another canopy, this time a canopy of clouds. Silence. As if something was holding its breath, waiting. She slowed down, in awe of the moon. It was as if she could reach out and touch its rough surface, cut herself on its crevices. She hovered. A cold air current wound around her in a slow spiral. Then it stopped.

"Yes," she whispered, her voice a plume of white vapor that was absorbed before her. It echoed back to her, slightly lower, more sure. She looked around. The air current was back, spiraly around her hot and cold, faster. She nodded and dropped from the sky, slowing down when she reached the surface of the earth. Then she walked home, quietly went to her room and didn't wake till morning.

Koofrey.

"Inyang! Look what you've done to your sheets! Don't you know how to wash?"

Inyang quickly opened her eyes and jumped up, lest be beaten.

"Look at this girl," her mother said. "Go to the river!"

"Inyang, explain this!" her father said.

She looked around. Her sisters were dragging themselves out of bed. She looked at her feet; they were encased in dried mud. Her bed was filthy with it. She'd forgotten to wash her feet when she'd gotten in last night. Her first instinct was to laugh but that would certainly have assured her a beating.

"I'm sorry, papa, mama," she said.

"Is that why you wear a smile on your face?" her mother asked.

Inyang looked away. She'd always been a terribly liar. *Out of all nights why did papa have to spend the night with mama tonight?* she thought.

"Go to the river," her mother said, again.

★

Inyang walked through the forest, a frown on her face. It had been a year since she'd become a woman. A year since she'd learned who she was. A year since everything around her had shifted like dirt during a rainstorm. Nevertheless, learning how to control it came slowly.

She carried the large container of water on her head easily. She was strong and had grown another two inches, her figure continuing to fill out. Everything was changing.

"Inyang."

She didn't turn around, but she put up her guard. She dissected the voice and then let her mind tell her exactly where she was and how far she was from the village.

"Inyang," he said again in his freshly low voice.

She sighed, annoyed. As she did with all the boys after a while, she had grown tired of him. "What do you want, Koofrey?"

"Please, Inyang, just talk to me," Koofrey said, scrambling up to her. He was slightly taller than she was but his legs were shorter and he labored to keep up with her long fast strides. "I miss you."

Inyang didn't reply with words. She merely walked faster.

"Please, Inyang," he said. He was young, only seventeen, but he was also the son of the chief. "How are you going to treat me like this? Like the shit of a goat? Look at me. Look at me, woman!"

He grabbed her arm and she snatched it away, still refusing to look at him. He grabbed it again, roughly holding on. Then he grabbed two of her locks with his other hand, pulling her head back. A shockwave of anger shot up Inyang's spine, but it was diluted by terror. She knew this Koofrey. She had seen him once crush a boy's nose for looking at Inyang.

"Look at me!" he shouted, his voice cracking. He yanked her to him causing her to drop her container of water. It crash-splashed to the ground. He turned her to face him.

"*Who* are *you* to walk away? I will *beat* you," he hissed into her ear. He pulled her into the bushes by her hair, yanking at her blue-green rapa. There was a rip before it fell. Inyang began to shudder but she didn't fight him. He would surely kill her if she did. Her face was hot, as if it were being squeezed.

"You are nothing but bush meat to me," he said, his voice shaking. "You forget who I am. You forget who *you* aren't."

Her mind felt light as all reasoning and thought fell away like the leaves on a tree in high winds. Only helpless outrage was left. It was when he pushed her long locks aside, roughly turned her around and bent her forward, her forehead smacking the trunk of the tree that she blew up.

"I don't need you to look at me, now," he grumbled. But his voice sounded very far away. Her mind was full of hot blood and she saw everything through a red tint. All the important things about her life were decided upon her birth, when she emerged from her mother's womb with a head full of wet dadalocks. No circumcision, no fattening, no husband, no children, no family. And all this she'd accepted as her plight. Now Koofrey felt that she didn't even have the choice in the men in which she found pleasure. *I don't ask for much*, she thought, the anger she'd quietly bottled up for so long coming to a boil. *I am not selfish!*

She grabbed the tree's trunk and kicked her strong leg back, catching him squarely in his belly. She heard him exhale and fall into the leaves behind him. And then she was lifting, her body horizontal as if every part of her was trying to get away from him as fast as it could. She only blinked when blood from the cut on her forehead oozed into her left eye.

She still couldn't control her flying. Sometimes she floated a few inches above her bed in her sleep. Or she'd be walking down the road and find herself floating off the ground. For this reason, she walked close to the trees, which she could grab if worse came to worst. As far as she knew, her flying never manifested when she was around people.

74

Until today.

Naked from the waist down, she rose slowly at first. Weaving around the branches and leaves. Then she picked up speed. Faster and faster. Tears flew from her eyes and the wind thundered in her ears. She knew clearly that her behavior had gotten her into the situation. Koofrey was known for his violent tendencies. This was part of what attracted her to him in the first place. Still her rage burned. *How dare him*, she thought. *How dare him.* She was too high up now to see Koofrey but she wanted to tear him apart.

She flew higher. Higher. She didn't care that she was shivering with cold. Or that she found it harder and harder to breath. *Let me die if the gods will it*, she angrily thought. Higher still. The air current rotated rapidly around her, cooling her more. She could no longer see her forest. Below her the land looked like the drawing her father had once shown of the world. She had to get a hold of herself before she suffocated or froze.

Though she made no sound, she was wailing. Her entire body was numb. Much of her was still down there, with him. That that young man she had controlled for so long had turned into a beast when he realized he couldn't control her. *I am a free woman*, she thought angrily. *It's my only birthright. I go as I please. I go where I please.* She coughed, her body still shaking with cold.

"As I please," she whispered. She was slowing down. She closed her eyes and took in a deep breath, though the cold burned her lungs. She stopped, hovering. She took another breath and then another. Then she opened her eyes and she felt calm. She descended. There was ice on her skin and eyelashes but it melted as she approached the forest. Her mind was too numb to notice that she was controlling the descent. That she flew shaky but easily through the forest. That when she came back to the very spot Koofrey had pulled her to fifteen minutes ago, she landed hard but not too hard.

He was gone. Her blue rapa was still there. She picked it up and wrapped it around her legs and waist. She flew to the river and dropped into it, then she flew high into the sky to dry herself. She flew half of the way home but when she got close to the village, she landed and walked.

In the back of her mind, something had begun to fester.

Amuosu

"This goat woman is *Amuosu*," the chief spat.

Inyang stood at her door, her arms around her chest, smirking as if she'd heard this before. It had only been a few months since Koofrey had tried to attack her. That very day, she had gone to her grandmother and told her all that had happened.

Her grandmother, knowing that the village elders would do nothing for the honor of someone like Inyang, sent Inyang to Odinakachukwu, the oldest man in the village. He was one of the few people there who was not Efik. An Igbo man, he lived slightly off from the village. People liked to say it was because he was slightly "off" in the head. At night, Odinakachukwu liked to sit quietly in front of his home, his midsection wrapped in a dingy cloth, and smoke his special leaves while he gazed at the dark sky, chuckling to himself as if he and the stars shared some inside joke with him.

He was more a hermit than a member of the community. He was tolerated because of the quality goods he sold and his many skills in the mystical. These same skills had gotten him banished from his own village. He was a tiny man with the voice of a lion. But he used words sparingly and he never repeated himself.

Odinakachukwu took an immediate liking to Inyang and also quickly noted Inyang's desires for revenge. With Inyang's mother and grandmother's consent, Inyang began to spend afternoons with Odinakachukwu, who tried to preoccupy her mind by teaching her to read, write, and make plants grow. Nevertheless, Inyang was a good multitasker. So, as she plowed her way through crumbly books and learned the ways of the forest, she was able to do a few other things, too.

What a poor excuse for a man, Inyang now thought, eyeing the approaching chief. She'd purposely played with him, vengefully so. She'd locked him with her eyes one day as she danced the *Abang* dance with several other girls during a wedding celebration. Inyang wasn't fat but she used her voluptuous figure with flexibility and grace. She'd balanced her weight on her toes as she danced. Side to side. Spontaneously turning while wiggling her back muscles down to her waist to the rhythm of the drums. The earth goddess, *Abasi Isong*, must have been pleased that day, for the dance was dedicated to Her. That evening, Inyang had bedded the chief in so many ways that he was ruined for any other woman.

He was old and she had made him feel young. It was her revenge against his son Koofrey, who continued to follow her around at a distance, practically foaming at the mouth with jealousy. There was nothing he could do. The chief would have severely punished him if he touched Inyang. Playing with the chief was also fun. He had four wives but he was drawn to Inyang like a greedy fly to palm sap. *Idiot*, she thought. *Now he can't bear refusal. Like son, like father.*

"Look at how she smiles at my accusations," the chief said, standing before her. "She's a danger to the village and herself."

He was joined by several of the elders. She'd known they were all coming, the entire village knew. The bush radio had broadcast her name loud. Wherever she turned, women slightly turned their heads to each other and whispered. People stepped back from her when she walked by, as if she could change their fate for the worse. The chief would stop whatever he was doing when he saw her, even if it was an important meeting. He was a disgrace. And through it all, she'd smiled and gone about her business.

Her mother often hissed at her, "Behave like a young lady, Inyang. Watch yourself, now, or this village will leap on your back." Her father didn't say a word. He barely looked Inyang in the eye these days. The thought of her own father being afraid of her made Inyang want to laugh.

"If you don't stand for something, you will fall for something," grandmother said whenever she saw Inyang coming in late. "I don't care why you do this to that man but make sure you understand what you are doing. Make sure you have good reason. And make sure you're ready for the consequences."

As more people approached Inyang's hut, they grumbled and kicked up dust with their sandals. All of the chief's wives followed him, as did several other angry women and curious men.

"How dare you accuse my daughter!" her mother shouted, her arm creeping protectively around Inyang. The look the chief gave her mother turned Inyang's smile into a sneer. Her mother was brilliant and brought in a large percentage of the money to the family and it trickled nicely into the village. People in the market looked for her specifically because she never cheated anyone and the vegetables she sold were always fresh. *But the chief looks at her as if she's . . . bush meat,* Inyang thought. Her place as third wife with only one child who happened to be female was never forgotten. Inyang's father had traveled to Onitsha to visit a sick friend, though Inyang suspected otherwise. The chief must have been waiting for him to leave.

"Inyang is nothing but gold to us," senior wife Mary snapped. Inyang bristled more at how the chief raised his chin to her and let her speak. "You need to reevaluate your reasons for making such an accusation!"

"I don't practice witchcraft," Inyang said through clenched teeth. "This is . . . "

"Why should we believe you?" one of the old men asked. His waist and legs were wrapped in red and orange cloth with intricate black designs. He pointed at her with his walking stick and cocked his head. "You move about strangely. One minute you're going to the forest, and the next moment, one of my wives sees you at the river."

Several of the people behind him grunted in agreement. Inyang shook her head. *I hope you are never reborn into this world,* she thought.

The chief stepped closer. He was a strong man of medium height. When she had first gone to him, she had been slightly shorter. Now she was taller. She was the tallest woman in the village.

"There's only one way to make sure," the chief said. "She must be fed the chop nut."

A hush flew across the crowd; even her mothers were shocked into silence. Inyang's nostrils flared, her fist balled, her nails digging into her palms. She squeezed all the muscles in her legs and her abdominals, fighting to keep her feet on the ground. Slowly, the entire village had come out to listen to the commotion. Now the mention of the plant sent many of them back inside shaking their heads. They wanted no part of this.

"You mean to murder my daughter, my only child," her mother asked, quietly.

"Are you admitting she's a witch, then?" the chief snapped.

Inyang's mother quickly shook her head.

"I mean to make sure my village is free of *Amuosu*, as my forefathers did," the chief said, looking Inyang straight in the eye. Inyang looked back unflinchingly. *I hope you are never reborn*, she thought again. *I am so tired of this place. Tired.*

Inyang looked away when her mother glanced at her. Then her mother looked at Inyang's second mother. "As you wish," she said.

"Tomorrow, evening, when the sun sets, the chop nut will decide," the chief declared. Inyang sucked her teeth in disgust.

When the elders and chief were gone, her mother and senior mother Mary escorted Inyang inside. "Now you see what your mischievousness has gotten you into?" her mother snapped.

Inyang only scowled at her feet.

"What's done is done," Mary said. "This child has never belonged here. She was practically born exiled."

Inyang could hear her mother's silence. She brought her head up, her eyes heavy.

"She's right, mama," Inyang said.

All her things were the color of the sky. She'd dipped her many woodcarvings in indigo dye. All her rapas and shirts were a shade of blue. She owned two necklaces made of wooden blue beads and one pair of blue earrings. Even her skin was so black that it was blue. It was a color she had always been attracted to.

"You have to leave by morning," her mother said quietly.

★

79

Inyang circled her village one last time. Half way around, she saw a speck separate itself from the treetops. She hovered for a moment, then she smiled. The owl pumped its powerful wings. Its yellow eyes glowing wide. It flew around her and hooted three times. She laughed and began her flight east.

The owl flew next to her for an hour, then it hooted three times again and turned back. It was heading home, where it belonged. Inyang didn't turn to watch it leave. Instead, she looked ahead. She would never see her people again, even when she returned so many years later. But she had a memory old as a strong tall healthy tree and she never forgot her family, her people, her place.

Nevertheless, Inyang still had to come to terms with tradition. Even a bird can't fly away from what's expected of it. Inyang would see war, death, love, and life. But always it would come back to the fundamental problem of tradition. And above tradition, her fixed inevitable fate.

ON THE ROAD

A tiger does not proclaim its tigritude. It pounces.
—Wole Soyinka, Sub-Saharan Africa's first Nobel Laureate

I slammed the door in the child's face, a horrific scream trapped in my throat. I swallowed it back down.

I didn't want to wake my grandmother or auntie. They'd jump out of bed, come running down the stairs and in a string of Igbo and English demand to know what the fuck was wrong with me. Then I'd point at the door and they'd open it and see the swaying little boy with the evil grin and a huge, open, dribbling red-white gash running down the middle of his head. Split open like a dropped watermelon.

My stomach lurched and I shut my eyes and rubbed my temples, my hand still tightly grasping the doorknob. *Get it together*, I thought. But I knew what I'd seen—a jagged, fractured, yellow-white skull, flaps of hanging skin, startlingly red blood, and some whitish-grey jelly . . . brain? I shuddered. "Shit," I whispered to myself.

The boy had been standing in the rain. Soaked from head to toe, as everything outside was from the strange unseasonable three-day deluge. He'd been smiling up at me. He couldn't have been older than nine. I gagged. I couldn't just leave him out there.

Knock! Knock! Knock! In hard strong rapid succession. "Oh God," I whispered. "What the hell?" Every hair on my body stood on end. I took a deep breath. Before really thinking about what I was doing, my hand was turning the knob and pulling the door open. I kept my eyes down. His wet black shoes were clumped with red mud. Gradually I brought my eyes up, past his soaked navy blue school uniform pants, to his worn-out and cracked black fake leather belt, his tucked-in white dress shirt, the brown skin of his throat, his little boy face . . . cleaved open, all the way to his eyebrows. *Fuck!* I thought.

In all my five years as a cop on the south side of Chicago I'd *never* seen anything like this. Never. The boy laughed and spoke to me in

Igbo, water dripping from his lips. "You, too," he said, his voice so much like that of the little boy that he was. "Me and you."

"You need . . . help," I whispered. I was about to reach out, despite my repulsion. I'd seen plenty of dead, mutilated, bleeding bodies. A year ago, I'd had a boy's life blood run over my hands as he stared sadly into my eyes. He'd been stabbed five times. His blood had been so warm on my hands and it remained under my nails for days. And that wasn't even my worst encounter with death. So I wasn't easily shaken. But this boy standing before me shook the hell out of me. He should have been dead or dying; not knocking hard on the door, smiling and saying ominous things.

Before I could reach for him, he reached for me. Lightning fast. He tapped my right hand. Just before it happened, I had a flashback of when I used to play tag in grade school. I loved playing tag.

"You're it," the boy said in Igbo. He laughed again.

The touch of his finger burned like a hot rough metal poker. I yelped. Then it was as if my very *being* was repulsed. I flew back about five feet before landing hard on my ass, the air knocked from my chest, my teeth rattling. Sharp pain shot all the way to my fingertips and toenails. I hit the coffee table and groaned as the clay vase on it fell to the floor and broke in two.

I heard footsteps upstairs. I looked at the door. The boy was gone.

"*O'u gini?*" Grandma shouted from the top of the stairs. She barely had her blue rapa wrapped around her waist and she looked much older than her eighty years. Auntie Ama probably was still sleeping, as she remained upstairs. Grandma looked at the door and then met my eyes. "Were you outside?" she asked.

I shook my head, trying to get up. Both my hands felt numb, though the boy had only touched one.

"But you opened the door," she said, still looking at the door like she expected armed robbers to burst in.

I didn't answer. So much adrenaline was flooding my system that I'd begun to feel faint.

"Who was at the door?" she demanded. When I didn't answer,

she narrowed her eyes at me, sucked her teeth and said, "Stupid, stupid girl."

★

Three days before, it had started raining cats and dogs. Out of nowhere. Thunder rolled in the skies, lightning crashed. The wind shook the trees and turned the red dirt to red mud. Three *days* of steady rain. It had stopped only minutes before the boy showed up at the door. This kind of weather *never* happened in this part of Nigeria during this time of the year. But who was I to question the doings of nature? Who was I?

I'd laughed to myself thinking, *of course, it just* has *to happen right when I arrive.* I was only going to be in the village visiting my grandmother and grand aunt for two weeks and now the entire first week was going to be a guaranteed mud and mosquito fest. Little did I know that this was the least of my worries.

★

I told my grandmother everything. Without a word, she frowned and walked outside into the rain. I followed her. Squishing through the mud, we looked all over the yard for that creepy boy. Grandma even looked in the chicken coop and behind the noisy generator. We didn't find a trace of him. Even his footprints had disappeared in the mud. Above, the sky churned with exiting rain clouds. Already I could see peeks of sunlight but I was too bothered to be happy about it.

We went back inside. I took off my muddy shoes, picked up the two vase pieces and plopped down on a kitchen chair, rubbing my lower back and forehead. I was sore but I actually felt okay. I didn't mysteriously grow sick or break out in blue hives or start speaking in tongues. I was fine.

"Grandma, he should have been *dead*," I said yet again, pressing the pieces of vase together, as if that's all it would take to put it back together. "I saw *brain*. Who would do that to a child? And where the heck would he *go*? This is so weird."

"Why were you stupid enough to open the door the second time?" she suddenly asked, crossing her arms over her chest, irritated. "If you see a monster at your doorstep, the wise thing to do is shut the door." She sucked her teeth and shook her head. "You Americanized Nigerians. No instinct."

"He was *hurt*," I insisted. "You can't just . . . "

"You knew better," she said, waving her hand dismissively at me. "Deep down, you knew not to open that door."

Okay, so she was right. I don't know why I opened the door again. It was like my hand had a mind of its own. Or maybe it was some sort of grim fascination? I put the vase pieces down.

"You feel alright?" Grandma asked.

I nodded, rubbing my hands together. They still felt a little numb.

She sighed. "We'll have to keep an eye on you."

"Have you ever . . . "

She held up a hand. "We speak of it no more," she said. "The mud is still wet."

Whatever that means, I thought. I got up, went to the bathroom and shut the door behind me. A large black wall spider occupied the ceiling corner above the toilet. A tiny pink wall gecko eyed it from the other corner. I chuckled despite myself. In the village, one is rarely ever truly alone. Not even in the bathroom.

I wiped my face with a towel and stared at myself in the mirror. I patted down my short 'fro and used some toilet paper to wipe the sweat from my brow. I laughed and said, "Chioma, you're fine." *Just some weird shit, that's all*, I thought. *Maybe the boy's head wasn't as bad as it looked.*

I froze, the smile dropping from my lips. I smelled something. I sniffed at my clothes and my skin. No, it wasn't coming from those either. Not from me. But close to me. Like something unnatural breathing down my neck. Movement on the ceiling caught my eye. The wall gecko was slowly moving in on the spider. I quickly left the bathroom and sought out Grandma. She was sitting in the living room with my grand Auntie Amaka.

They both wore the same blue rapas but Grandma wore a t-shirt that I'd brought her from America and Auntie Amaka wore a white blouse. Their rough wide feet dangled from the couch; their smallness always gives me pause as I'm over six feet tall. They looked at me with furrowed brows. Two old Igbo women with wrinkles so deep their eyes almost disappeared under the folds of skin whenever they made any facial expression.

"I'm fine." I assured them.

They knew I was lying. Yet they said nothing.

I laugh about it now. Of course they wouldn't have said anything.

★

That boy set something upon me. I was sure of it. Shit like that didn't just happen and that was it. Plus, I could still smell that weirdness in the air. Only I seemed to notice. It was like a bit of foulness. Something unpleasant definitely still lingered. Something unpleasant stayed.

The first few days, it was just that smell and odd shifts in the air. I'd be on my way to the bathroom and the leaves of the faux houseplant behind me would quiver softly. I'd turn around to see if someone was there. No one ever was. But that smell lingered a bit before fading away like an old fart. I started hearing whispers behind me, especially when I was the only one home. These were also accompanied by that smell and the sound of footsteps outside the house, loudly squelching in the drying mud. Not something you want to hear while in a rural village deep in southeast Nigeria. You're basically cut off from the rest of the world here. And then there were the lizards.

Normally, they ran about like squirrels, especially the large pine green and orange ones. They'd run up the cement block walls that surrounded the house, weaving between the protective shards of glass and razor wire at the top. They'd stop and do their lizardly push-ups. They were like little foul-tempered dragons. Corner one and you'd get to see just how wild and dragon-like they could get. I'd once seen one accidentally run into a plastic bag. The thing went temporarily insane when it couldn't figure out how to get out. Normally, the lizards of Nigeria were a source of hilarity for me.

When they started showing up everywhere accompanied by that unpleasant smell, they weren't so funny. I'd sit on the porch and three would show up and just look at me. If I stayed in one place for too long, those three lizards were joined by another seven. They'd scramble close. Watching me. As if they were waiting for something spectacular to happen. They only left me alone when I went in the house.

Being police, I know how to observe and listen. I'm *always* aware of my surroundings. I know when I'm being followed. Even when I'm on vacation in my mother's village visiting my grandmother and grandaunt. *Dammit, I wish I brought my gun*, I thought. How silly I was.

★

Days after the encounter with the boy, I had the shock of my life.

Upon my grandmother's request, we went with Auntie Amaka to the village market. I was glad to get out of the house. Even if the "mud was still wet," whatever that meant. It was your usual affair. Piles of tomatoes here, piles of peppers there, boiled eggs, sacks of groundnut, stacks of hugely overpriced cell phone cards, bunches of plantains, pungent dried fish, flies, women in traditional or European style clothes with their nosy eyes and ears and sharp-tongues, dodging the hot mufflers of overzealous shortcut-seeking *okada* drivers. I'd normally have enjoyed this, but I kept noticing lizards lurking too close to me and the boy was still on my mind.

I closely followed my grandmother and auntie as they bought dried crayfish, plantain, oranges, and so on. I guess we were going to have a feast tonight or something. As we walked, I felt like I was being watched again. When the feeling grew too intense, I whirled around, my hand going to my hip for the gun that wasn't there. I saw nothing but people going about their business. I sucked my teeth, my nerves sparking.

"Shit," I whispered. "This has got to stop, man. It's driving me nuts." Being this jumpy was so unlike me. We were standing at the booth of a fruit seller when I caught a whiff of sugariness, sweet and flammable. I turned my head toward the scent and met the eyes of a scruffy-looking palm wine seller.

"Good afternoon," he said, leaning on his ancient-looking dusty bicycle. His large brown gourds full of palm wine dangled from each handlebar. A basket of filled and empty green glass bottles hung from the front of the bars.

"Good afternoon," I responded, still preoccupied. I turned the other way and there *he* was, standing in the road. The boy who should have been dead. He wore a spotless pair of navy blue pants and a white pressed shirt. It was tucked in. And his head was shaven close. Nothing but a slightly gnarled grey brown scar ran down the middle of his head. He looked like a perfectly normal kid. Except for the knowing way he smiled at me. I stared back. He nodded, laughed, and continued on his way, school books in the crook of his arm. No cars came down or from up the road. A lizard scrambled across the street feet from him.

"What the fuck?" I whispered to myself.

The palm wine seller laughed and elbowed me. He leaned toward me and lowered his voice. "That boy's probably going to be the smartest kid in this village's history."

"W . . . why do you say that?" I asked, glancing at my auntie and grandmother. They were haggling hard with some old man over a large pineapple.

"You saw him, right?" he said. He pointed at me with a well-calloused finger. "It was you. Least that's what people are saying."

I wanted to ask, "What people?" Instead I just asked, "How can he be okay?"

The man nodded. "They took him into the forest."

"Not the hospital?" I asked, frowning.

"The hospital would have been no good for that boy."

"*Who* took him?"

"The women, of course." He kicked at a man inspecting his gourds of wine. "You buying or not?"

As the seller haggled with the customer, I watched the boy walk into the market crowd across the road. I watched until I couldn't see him anymore. I felt something cool against my hand and looked down. The tapper smiled, pressing it into my hand. A green bottle of palm wine. "On the house. You'll need it soon. One for the road."

I smiled uncomfortably, taking the bottle. "Uh . . . thanks." I had no intention of drinking it or anything else offered by a stranger that wasn't properly sealed. I mentally patted myself on the back again for thinking to bring all those packets of ramen noodles, my jar of peanut butter, and canned salmon.

"What . . . what happened in the forest?" I asked him, lowering my voice and grasping the bottle.

He paused then only shook his head as he laughed. "You ask too many questions. Go and drink that while you can."

★

That night, I tried to just go to bed and forget about the whole thing. Of course, I couldn't sleep. Outside, the warm wind blew hard. It should have been soothing but it wasn't. I could hear wet footsteps underneath the sound of the wind, squishing just below my window. Though my room was on the second floor of the house, I didn't dare look out.

I considered closing the window but that would have been like shutting myself inside a furnace. *Squish, squish, squish.* Someone was definitely just below my window. And was the ground that muddy? When I could take it no more, I grabbed a can of beef ravioli from my suitcase and went to the open window. Any weird shit I saw out there was going to get hit with that can.

I saw nothing but deep darkness. The power had been turned off an hour ago. Still, that piercing sensation of being watched increased tenfold. I stepped back and pulled the curtains closed. Of course that didn't help. The wind made the curtains billow out like ghosts. I pulled them back open and spent the rest of the night huddled in my bed, staring at the window, the can in my lap, knowing whatever had smashed that boy's skull in was still out there. And now it was interested in me.

★

"What's wrong with you?" Grandma asked as I dragged myself into the kitchen. I felt sluggish but it was the kind of sluggish you feel after hours and hours of deep sleep. I was so rested. I'd finally fallen asleep near daybreak and now it was late evening. I'd slept the entire day away. It wasn't jetlag; I'd gotten over that by my second day there. Something else had made me sleep for over twelve hours.

My belly grumbled with hunger. My grand Auntie Amaka was just walking in. She looked me up and down with way more scrutiny than I was willing to tolerate when I was so hungry. I resisted the urge to roll my eyes. She loudly sucked her few uneven white teeth.

"What?" I snapped, as I ladled some freshly made stew over the plate of steaming white rice my grandmother handed me. I loved my Auntie Amaka. She talked a lot of shit about everyone. But once in a while her scrutinizing eye turned to me. Like now. The woman hadn't even finished walking in.

"She's looking thin," she told my grandma in Igbo, ignoring me. As if I couldn't understand the language.

I scoffed. Maybe I'd lost a pound or two since getting here but I was still my usual thick-bodied Amazon build. My nicknames in the village were "giant" and "iroko tree."

Grandma nodded. "Like it's hollowing her out."

"So it can fill her up," Auntie Amaka finished.

"I don't think I've lost a pound," I said, sitting down with my huge mound of rice and stew. My mouth watered. *Gosh, I do feel empty, though,* I thought. *But I'm about to solve that problem.* I dug my spoon in, inhaling the smell of the spicy red stew and fragrant rice.

"Not physically," Grandma said.

I shook my head. "Whatever," I said, the spoon halfway to my mouth.

A loud bump came from the back of the house. Then a crash. I put the spoon of uneaten rice down. "What the . . . " Then a great roar that made me nearly jump out of my skin. About ten large brown, black, and orange lizards skittered into the room, from the hallway, their tiny claws whispering on the wooden floor. Some climbed the walls, others scuttled across the floor. Neither grandma nor auntie moved. My eye sought the nearest weapon. There. A large knife in the sink. My grandma had used it to chop meat. I jumped up and grabbed it.

A horrified look on her face, grandma grabbed auntie's shoulder and started speaking in rapid Efik, a language they only spoke when they didn't want me to understand. I frowned at them, but I was more concerned with whatever the hell was in the house.

The deep guttural roar came again, this time closer, from down the hall. The sound touched my very being. I held the knife more tightly, trying to think. I knew this was the thing that had been following me, biding its time. This was the thing that had smashed that boy's head open.

The movement of a black lizard on the wall caught my eye. I held the large knife more tightly, ignoring my grandmother and auntie's now angry and loud argument. I only vaguely wondered what the hell they were shouting about. Slowly, knife held before me, I moved toward the hallway. I could see a large shadow creeping forth. Whatever it was was breathing deep and hard. The air grew warm and took on the smell of tar. I realized that this was what that weird smell reminded me off. Tar and maybe soil or crushed leaves?

I glanced at the front door. Still open. I ran for it. This thing meant to take me. On instinct, I knew this. I ran out of the house. It was after me, not my grandmother and auntie. At least I could save them. I surprised myself. I really *was* one of those people who would happily die to save the ones they loved.

I ran onto the dirt road. At some point, I must have dropped the knife. It was pitch dark out there. People were awake most likely. Deep in their homes. But tonight, no one played cards on the porch. No one stood in the doorway, smoking a cigarette. I think people sensed it was a bad time to be out. So I ran and I ran alone. I wasn't even wearing flip flops.

I could hear it coming. Slobbering. Wheezing. Blowing a strange wind. The smell of broken leaves and tar in the air. The half moon in the sky gave a little light. I could have sworn there were hundreds of lizards running with me, some crisscrossing my path. It felt like I stepped on some as I ran. I only managed to stay on my feet because I knew the shape of the dirt road.

I passed the last home and entered the stretch of palm trees.

My eyes had adjusted to the darkness. *I'm going to die out here*, I knew. *Just as the boy should have.* A burning heat descended on me from behind. I fell to the dirt road, coughing as I inhaled its dust. Lizards scampered over me like ants on a mound of sugar. I felt their rough feet and claws nipping at my skin. Something grabbed my hands as a great shadow fell on me. Yes, a shadow in the darkness. It was blacker than black.

The air was sucked from my lungs.

My eyes stung with dust.

The road beneath me grew hard as stone, as concrete.

My arms were pulled over my head and ground into the concrete beneath me.

First the left hand and then the right. At the wrist. Something bit right through. I felt painful pressure then tendons, bone, blood vessels snapping and cracking and then separating. I heard it; the sound was brittle and sharp. Then the wet spattering and squirting of my blood. I only smelled warm paved road. A pause. Then bright white pain flashed through me, blinding the rest of my senses. *Like Che Guevara*, I thought feebly. *Now no one will know who I am.*

Time passed. I remember none of it clearly.

The sound of grass and twigs bending and snapping roused me, the feeling of hands roughly grasping me. I dared to open my eyes. They carried me. One woman carried my hands, like two dead doves. I almost blacked out again from the sight but I held on.

"Hurry," one of the women said quietly. "She's going to die."

"It takes what it will," another woman said.

"She'll be fine." This was my grandmother's voice. My own grandmother was one of these women!

"It's still best to move faster." Auntie Amaka?

Suddenly we came upon a road. It was paved, black, shiny, new. Something you didn't normally see in Nigeria.

"Listen," one of the women hissed, looking around.

All of them froze. I was too weak to do anything. The edges of my vision were starting to fade. I heard the sound of my own blood hitting the concrete as it spurted to the beat of my heart from the stumps of my wrists. It soaked quickly into the concrete.

"It's coming," one of the women said.

There was a mad scramble. They dumped me on the hard concrete. Two items dropped beside me. *Slap! Slap!* My hands. Then other items. Some cocoa yams that rolled to rest against my leg. Tomatoes that rolled in all directions. A bowl of still steaming rice that shattered, some of the porcelain and hot rice hitting my face. A bunch of cell phones that clattered to the ground, all of them still on. And some other things I couldn't see from where I lay.

"What are you . . . " my voice was weak and I had no energy to finish my question.

After a glance up the road, the women started running off. I couldn't get up, I couldn't speak. Soon, I wouldn't be breathing. Their feet made soft sounds in the grass as they ran into the forest.

I was alone in the middle of a road in Nigeria. I couldn't get up. My hands were cut off. I was going to be run over, bleed to death, or both. All I could think of was how hungry I was. That I'd give anything for sweet fried plantain, egusi soup heavy with goat meat and stock fish, garri, spicy jollof rice, chin chin, red stew with chicken, ogba . . .

I stared at my severed hands. My long fingers were curved slightly. My thumbs were both bent inward. My nails still had their French manicure. The bronze ring my boyfriend gave me two years ago was still on my left middle finger. I could see the palm of my right hand with its small calluses from my regular days at the gym lifting free-weights.

The middle finger of my right hand twitched. I blinked. Then all five fingers wiggled and the hand flipped over, reminding me of a spider flipping back onto its feet. My left hand was rising up, too. Barely a sound escaped my lips as my eyes started to water from sheer terror. I was too afraid to move. If one of them came near me, I knew I'd pass out. Instead they both just "stood" there; again that strange waiting that I'd also witnessed with the lizards.

Suddenly, the concrete grew hot. I tried to get up but fell back. The road shook. And as I stared down the road, I wondered, *what the goddamn fucking hell is that*? I tried to get up again; anything to get away from my hands and the chaos happening up the road.

About a fourth of a mile away, the concrete road undulated as if it were made of warm taffy. It broke apart and crumbled in some places and piled up in others. It rippled and folded and fell back into road as the chaos progressed toward me. I looked at the sky. It was black but starting to burn. I didn't know if this was morning's approach or my own death. I did care. I didn't want to die. But I knew I was dying. Still, not a car came up or down this mystery road. No one would save me. My grandmother and grand auntie had left me.

The noise was deafening. Like a thousand dump trucks dumping hot gravel all at the same time. The air reeked of bitter tar. The closer it got, the clearer its shape. Slabs of road the size of houses arranged themselves into a giant body, tail, legs, short arms, and finally a horrible reptilian head. Vines whipped out of the forests flanking the strange road creature and attached themselves to the slabs. They started snaking up to the items the women had dropped. Snatching up the yam tubers, cell phones, tomatoes. They took every scoop of rice, right down to the grains on my face. Every piece of broken porcelain. They left nothing but me.

It stood several stories high, the vague shape of a monstrous lizard of hot gravel. It snapped and tore connected vines as it moved, only for more vines to reconnect. It slithered toward me, its hot black gravel sizzling.

Vines snatched up my hands, which wriggled about like captured crabs. Then the vines snatched my wrists. They dragged me close to the creature. By this time, I was done. I had nothing left. I don't even know why I was conscious.

The vines connected to my open wrists and I could feel them . . . pumping something into me. It was warm and that warmth ran up my arms, to my shoulders, to my chest, all the way to my toes. I felt like I was going to be sick. How can one who is dying feel sick?

The moment the sensation made it to my toes, I experienced a terrible stab of pain that radiated from all over my body. Like a light switch had been turned on, my mind cleared. Just like that.

I screamed.

My eye landed on the horrific creature again. I screamed again. The vines were doing something to my severed hands and wrists. I could hear a soft wet smacking sound. When I finally chanced a look, I saw that the vines were knitting. They were knitting my veins and arteries.

Lying on my back, I turned my head to the side and vomited. That road monster was hovering over me like an over-attentive doctor. Hot pebbles and stones rained on me. The sky was brightening as the day broke. From where I lay, I could now see that it had several lizards running about its body, mainly those large orange and green ones.

Then the worst happened. Its attention focused on me. Every muscle in my body tightened, every one of my physical senses sharpening. I felt that which is "me" fear for her very existence.

The creature brought its huge stone face up to mine. Within inches. Heat dripped from it like sweat. Its bitter tar odor stung my nostrils. Beneath the stench there was another scent, something distinctively native. That woody, rich perfume that I always noticed as soon as I got off the airplane. There was life and death in that scent. But I was only thinking about death, as the smell filled my nasal passage.

It moved closer, within a half-inch. Its appearance began to shift. Stone became wood, elongating into a giant long-faced mask of black ebony with prominent West African features. I nearly started laughing, despite it all. You saw this face in many markets; it was that generic face of most West African ebony masks. I had many masks with this very face on my wall back home.

But this was the *real* one, the *living* one, the *first* one. This was the face that people were selling. My ears rung and my eyes watched; no species of terror could have been more profound. Its thick lips puckered, the deep deep eyes piercing. Over its shoulders, I could see the hard faces of others. They floated like puffs of powder and undulated like oil. They had large eyes, wide-nostrilled noses, cheekbones like granite. Many of them were familiar to me, also. Even more were not.

Some had what looked like ants skittering about their faces. Others had red eyelids and deep tribal scars on their cheeks and foreheads. Blue horns. The face of a great red bird. A tree frog sitting on its forehead. Eyes like mud. Skin like leaves. Some radiated beautiful liquid light. Others sprouted pink flowers. Spirits, masquerades, ghosts, and ancestors, these were deep deep *mmuo*! I was actually seeing *mmuo*! Me, Chioma, born in the USA. Why *me*?

These ethereal faces crowded far far back, tens, thousands, millions, billions, an infinite number of them peering from infinity. Looking over the creature's shoulders. Watching. Seeing *me*. Like those lizards, they were waiting for something to happen to me. Can you imagine?

My chest felt like a block of ice and my eyes burned. My scalp itched. Then I felt it. It was pleasure and pain, black and white, cacophony and stillness, perfumed and pungent. Something inside me both died and was birthed. I moaned, looking into its eyes. At once, there was clarity. I saw a young woman with a chain of thick red-orange beads woven into her tightly braided hair. She danced slowly, lizards following the movement of her feet. And there was a vertical line scarring each of her ankles. Her feet had been cut off and reattached. Yet . . . look at her dance! *Was she the first*, I wondered? *First what*?

Then just like that, the vines retreated. The lizards scattered. And the road-dragon-monster-ancestor-creature grunted and quickly began to shamble back down the road. It was like they all feared the sunlight. I dunno. What do I know?

When I sat up, I was in the middle of a lumpy dirt road and there was a car coming right at me. I jumped up and ran out of the way. The driver didn't even see me! *Am I invisible*? I wondered. I realized I knew where I was, less than a mile from the house. There was no dense forest near the house, never had been. It was all impossible.

Images of *mmuo* rose and fell in my mind and I swayed. I steadied myself by looking at my hands. Slowly I brought them up. There were dark bruises on my wrists, as if someone had tied them too tightly with heavy ropes. There was dried blood, too. But my hands looked . . . normal. They weren't turning purple or black as they should have been nor were they behaving like independent creatures. And most importantly, they were connected to my wrists. I dared to move a finger. It worked just fine. Except for a weird tingle I felt in the fingertips.

I made a fist and wiggled and flexed all my fingers. Still that weird tingle. But that was it. My hands were still alive and they were my own. I wiped my lips with the back of my hand, the taste of vomit still in my mouth. Even my vomit was gone from the ground.

I walked home.

★

I killed a man once. With my bare hands. This was before I was a cop. It's probably the reason I *became* a cop. It was during my second year in college. I was twenty. He followed me home one night and dragged me between the dorms onto a narrow road that ran between the buildings. He was bigger than me. Stronger, too. I'm tall and a rather strong woman, but just a woman nonetheless. So there we were on the concrete, his hands squeezing the air from my neck. I was seeing stars, galaxies, black outer space. There was a ringing in my ears. My head was full of pressure. Tears were in my eyes. I was fading.

Then something swept over me. I raised my hands and grabbed his neck, too. He looked surprised at first but didn't seem too bothered. Until my hands locked on his neck like a vice. Suddenly I knew I could crush stones with my hands. I crushed his neck like it was one of the stones I was imagining.

My parents are lawyers and somehow they kept it all away from the press. And somehow they kept me out of jail, thank God, though that was the easy part. The guy had apparently done to several women many times within the state what he tried to do to me. Since then, I've always been suspicious of my hands.

Typically when you think of one's identity, you think face, right? The eyes are the windows to the soul. You cut off one's head and the person dies. You see a picture where a woman's face is not shown but her body is and you think misogyny, no? She becomes objectified, nothing but a body. But what of the hands? Fingerprints are more personalized than one's face, more unique.

When we want to really identify a suspect, we go to his or her prints. Again, I think of Che Guevara and the depth of the insult in cutting off his hands. The depth of attempted annihilation. So what happens when your hands kill a man? What happens when those hands are cut off and then start behaving like freed spiders? What happens when those hands are reattached by some fucking dragon monster Nigerian ancestor being made of rolling hot gravel and vines and wood? What just happened to me?

As I slowly walked back to my grandmother's house, my stomach groaned and my temples throbbed. *Grandma and auntie*, I thought. *They just . . . left me there.* I heard the crunch of my bones, the snap of my arteries and veins, the splatter of my blood. I saw my own hands moving about on their own. I saw billions of *mmuo*, all staring at me. I stopped, put my hands on my knees and bent forward. My stomach heaved but thankfully I had nothing in it. Tears dribbled from my eyes. More cars passed me by. I wiped the tears away but more tears came. It took me a half hour to make the ten minute walk to the house. By the time I arrived, I was deeply pissed off.

I threw the front door open. "Grandma! Auntie! Where are you?" I screamed in Igbo. I stood there, breathing heavily, wiping the tears from my eyes, so I could clearly see the looks on their faces. I watched them descend the stairs looking guilty as hell. I shouted and cursed and accused them of everything from black magic and Satanism to witchcraft and juju; anything that would make them feel ashamed, as I knew they both claimed to be good Catholics. Spit flew from my mouth, snot from my nose. My voice quivered as my entire body began to shudder. I started sobbing, images and sounds and scents racing through my mind again. And my grandma and auntie leaving me.

Then I blurted the story of the murderer who tried to murder me and instead got murdered. I laughed wildly through my sobs, feeling lightheaded, frightened, desperate, and confused.

"Oh, we knew about you killing that man," grandma calmly responded.

My mouth hung open. I sat on the couch, my heart slamming in my chest.

Auntie Amaka sat beside me and took my hand in hers. I yanked it away from her. I had a brief thought of leaving my severed hand in her hands. I had to work hard not to screech. "Don't touch me!" I snapped.

"My dear, we could have told you, yes," Auntie Amaka said, delicately. "But once . . . once you opened that door . . . "

"No," Grandma said. "Once it started to rain, I think. And you being here."

"Regardless," Auntie Amaka said. "It was going to happen."

I ran my hand over my face. Who knew what the fuck they were talking about? "What was . . . that thing?" I asked.

"It has many names. We speak none of them," Grandma said.

"Why the boy, then?"

"All we can guess was that it was because he outsmarted a great snake that was meant to kill him," Grandma said. "It was last year. The snake was about to strike as he passed through a field. The boy somehow knew. Before the snake could do the job, the boy smashed its head with his school book."

"Again, not his fault," Grandma said. "It never is."

"So you're saying we were both supposed to die but something . . . "

Grandmother laughed. I felt like slapping her. "You think this is about you?" she asked, ignoring the irate look on my face. "You think it had anything to do with any of us specifically?" She shook her head. "In this village, when it rains for three days during dry season, certain people start . . . getting maimed. Us women know where to take them and what to bring. It's been like that since anyone can remember."

"But we don't know the why or the how of it," Auntie added. "It doesn't happen often. Maybe once every ten years." She shrugged and both women looked at me apologetically.

It was like being the victim of an unsolved hit and run. No one knew the motive. No real answers. No revelation. No "aha" moment. So all I knew was pain, mystification, terror, and the eerie feeling of having my face seductively licked by death. I looked at my hands. The thin green lines on my wrists had faded some. I was heading home in a few days.

★

I sit looking out the airplane window now. We land soon. I never return home from Nigeria the same person I was before. But this time takes the cake.

Minutes after takeoff, I felt a rush of relief like no other. I was glad to be leaving the motherland. After what happened, I needed some serious space. I scratched at a mosquito bite on my arm. It was red and inflamed and I knew I should leave it alone. But, damn, the thing was itchy. Nigerian mosquito bites were always the worst. You never feel them land on you and then you can't stop feeling the itch of their bites.

I was glad to be sitting near the window. The plane was pretty packed, so turning to the window gave me at least a little privacy. I looked closely at my mosquito bite, rubbing it with my thumb as opposed to digging at it with my nail, the way I wanted to. The more I rubbed, the better it felt. The less itchy. The less red.

"Oh shit," I whispered. The guy beside me looked at me with raised eyebrows. I smiled at him and shook my head.

It was as if I'd rubbed off the mosquito bite. My skin was healed back to its usual brown. I quickly got up.

"Excuse me," I whispered as I made my way into the aisle. I went straight to the bathroom. Once inside, I unbuttoned my blouse. I had all types of scratches from the incident. I touched the painful bruise on my side and ran my finger across it. Erased like chalk on a chalkboard. I undid my jeans and rubbed the scratches on my legs. I rubbed my hands all over. Then, naked, I stood up and looked at myself in the mirror. Not a scratch, bruise, pimple, or blemish on my body.

I was thirty-nine years old. Happy with my life. "Why?" I whispered. "Shit, shit shit! No, no, no." I was a cop. And I loved being a cop. *Now what will I become?* I wondered. I considered asking my hands. *But what if they answer?*

I sit here looking out the window at the ocean below. *What will become of me?*

I hear a sharp scream behind me. Then a gasp. "I . . . I didn't . . . he tried to . . . " The sound of commotion. A woman yells, "Get his hands!"

"Oh my God!"

Grunting, screeching, shouting. I jump up along with everyone around me. We're all probably thinking of the same thing. Terrorists, 911. I whirl around to see what's happening. It's a sight to behold.

There are five men piled in the aisle. Two of them are dark-skinned Africans; one wears a white caftan and there is bright red blood smeared on it. One of them is Asian, he wears a black suit with a golden dragon pin on the left breast pocket. Two of them are white men; one in jeans and a t-shirt, another in a navy blue suit. They sit on, hold down, and punch a young white man, mashing his head to the floor. The young man's wide eyes water and he sweats profusely. His face is beet red. He's breathing heavily and babbling, "Get me off this goddamn plane! I want to get off! *Get me off!*"

In the seat before them, a woman lies in a man's arms. She coughs, her hands to her throat. A yellow number two pencil protrudes from the side of her neck. Blood spurts and dribbles down. The man holding her, an old Igbo-looking man in western attire, looks absolutely lost.

I look at my hands. I don't even hesitate.

SPIDER THE ARTIST

Zombie no go go, unless you tell am to go
Zombie!
Zombie!
Zombie no go stop, unless you tell am to stop
Zombie no go turn, unless you tell am to turn
Zombie!
Zombie no go think, unless you tell am to think
—from Zombie by Fela Kuti, Nigerian musician
and self-proclaimed voice of the voiceless

My husband used to beat me. That was how I ended up out there that evening behind our house, just past the bushes, through the tall grass, in front of the pipelines. Our small house was the last in the village, practically in the forest itself. So nobody ever saw or heard him beating me.

Going out there was the best way to put space between me and him without sending him into further rage. When I went behind the house, he knew where I was and he knew I was alone. But he was too full of himself to realize I was thinking about killing myself.

My husband was a drunk, like too many of the members of the Niger Delta People's Movement. It was how they all controlled their anger and feelings of helplessness. The fish, shrimps, and crayfish in the creeks were dying. Drinking the water shriveled women's wombs and eventually made men urinate blood.

There was a stream where I had been fetching water. A flow station was built nearby and now the stream was rank and filthy, with an oily film that reflected rainbows. Cassava and yam farms yielded less and less each year. The air left your skin dirty and smelled like something preparing to die. In some places, it was always daytime because of the noisy gas flares.

My village was shit.

On top of all this, People's Movement members were getting picked off like flies. The "kill-and-go" had grown bold. They shot People's Movement members in the streets, they ran them over, dragged them into the swamps. You never saw them again.

I tried to give my husband some happiness. But after three years, my body continued to refuse him children. It's easy to see the root of his frustration and sadness . . . but pain is pain. And he dealt it to me regularly.

My greatest, my only true possession, was my father's guitar. It was made of fine polished Abura timber and it had a lovely tortoiseshell pick guard. Excellent handwork. My father said that the timber used to create the guitar came from one of the last timber trees in the delta. If you held it to your nose, you could believe this. The guitar was decades old and still smelled like fresh cut wood, like it wanted to tell you its story because only it could.

I wouldn't exist without my father's guitar. When he was a young man, he used to sit in front of the compound in the evening and play for everyone. People danced, clapped, shut their eyes, and listened. Cell phones would ring and people would ignore them. One day, it was my mother who stopped to listen.

I used to stare at my father's fast long-fingered hands when he played. Oh, the harmonies. He could weave anything with his music— rainbows, sunrises, spider webs sparkling with morning dew. My older brothers weren't interested in learning how to play. But I was, so my father taught me everything he knew. And now it was my long-fingers that graced the strings. I'd always been able to hear music and my fingers moved even faster than my father's. I was good. Really good.

But I married that stupid man. Andrew. So I only played behind the house. Away from him. My guitar was my escape.

That fateful evening, I was sitting on the ground in front of the fuel pipeline. It ran right through everyone's backyard. My village was an oil village, as was the village where I grew up. My mother lived in a similar village before she was married, as did her mother. We are Pipeline People.

My mother's grandmother was known for lying on the pipeline running through her village. She'd stay like that for hours, listening and wondering what magical fluids were running through the large never-ending steel tubes. This was before the Zombies, of course. I laughed. If she tried to lie on a pipeline now she'd be brutally killed.

Anyway, when I was feeling especially blue, I'd take my guitar and come out here and sit right in front of the pipeline. I knew I was flirting with death by being so close but when I was like this, I didn't really care. I actually welcomed the possibility of being done with life. It was a wonder that my husband didn't smash my guitar during one of his drunken rages. I'd surely have quickly thrown myself on the pipeline if he did. Maybe that was why he'd rather smash my nose than my guitar.

This day, he'd only slapped me hard across the face. I had no idea why. He'd simply come in, seen me in the kitchen and *smack*! Maybe he'd had a bad day at work—he worked very hard at a local restaurant. Maybe one of his women had scorned him. Maybe I did something wrong. I didn't know. I didn't care. My nose was just starting to stop bleeding and I was not seeing so many stars.

My feet were only inches from the pipeline. I was especially daring this night. It was warmer and more humid than normal. Or maybe it was my stinging burning face. The mosquitoes didn't even bother me much. In the distance, I could see Nneka, a woman who rarely spoke to me, giving her small sons a bath in a large tub. Some men were playing cards at a table several houses down. It was dark, there were small, small trees and bushes here and even our closest neighbor was not very close, so I was hidden.

I sighed and placed my hands on the guitar strings. I plucked out a tune my father used to play. I sighed and closed my eyes. I would always miss my father. The feel of the strings vibrating under my fingers was exquisite.

I fell deep into the zone of my music, weaving it, then floating on a glorious sunset that lit the palm tree tops and . . .

Click!

I froze. My hands still on the strings, the vibration dying. I didn't dare move. I kept my eyes closed. The side of my face throbbed.

Click! This time the sound was closer. *Click!* Closer. *Click!* Closer.

My heart pounded and I felt nauseous with fear. Despite my risk taking, I knew this was *not* the way I wanted to die. Who would want to be torn limb from limb by Zombies? As everyone in my village did multiple times a day, I quietly cursed the Nigerian government.

Twing!

The vibration of the guitar string was stifled by my middle finger still pressing it down. My hands started to shake, but still I kept my eyes shut. Something sharp and cool lifted my finger. I wanted to scream. The string was plucked again.

Twang!

The sound was deeper and fuller, my finger no longer muffling the vibration. Very slowly, I opened my eyes. My heart skipped. The thing stood about three feet tall, which meant I was eye-to eye with it. I'd never seen one up close. Few people have. These things are always running up and down the pipeline like a herd of super fast steer, always with things to do.

I chanced a better look. It really *did* have eight legs. Even in the darkness, those legs shined, catching even the dimmest light. A bit more light and I'd have been able to see my face perfectly reflected back at me. I'd heard that they polished and maintained themselves. This made even more sense now, for who would have time to keep them looking so immaculate?

The government came up with the idea to create the Zombies, and Shell, Chevron, and a few other oil companies (who were just as desperate) supplied the money to pay for it all. The Zombies were made to combat pipeline bunkering and terrorism. It makes me laugh. The government and the oil people destroyed our land and dug up our oil, then they created robots to keep us from taking it back.

They were originally called Anansi Droids 419 but we call them "*oyibo* contraption" and, most often, Zombie, the same name we call those "kill-and-go" soldiers who come in here harassing us every time something bites their brains.

It's said that Zombies can think. Artificial Intelligence, this is called. I have had some schooling, a year or two of university, but my area was not in the sciences. No matter my education, as soon as I got married and brought to this damn place, I became like every other woman here, a simple village woman living in the delta region where Zombies kill anyone who touches the pipelines and whose husband knocks her around every so often. What did I know about Zombie intellect?

It looked like a giant shiny metal spider. It moved like one, too. All smooth-shifting joints and legs. It crept closer and leaned in to inspect my guitar strings some more. As it did so, two of its back legs tapped on the metal of the pipeline. *Click! Click! Click!*

It pushed my thumb back down on the strings and plucked the string twice, making a muted *pluck!* It looked at me with its many blue shining round eyes. Up close I could see that they weren't lights. They were balls of a glowing metallic blue undulating liquid, like charged mercury. I stared into them, fascinated. No one else in my village could possibly know this fact. No one had gotten close enough. *Eyes of glowing bright blue liquid metal*, I thought. *Na wa.*

It pressed my hand harder and I gasped, blinking and looking away from its hypnotic eyes. Then I understood.

"You . . . you want me to play?"

It sat there waiting, placing a leg on the body of my guitar with a soft *tap.* It had been a long time since anyone had wanted me to play for him. I played my favorite highlife song. *Love Dey See Road* by Oliver De Coque. I played like my life depended on it.

The Zombie didn't move, its leg remaining pressed to my guitar. Was it listening? I was sure it was. Twenty minutes later, when I stopped finally playing, sweat running down my face, it touched the tips of my aching hands. Gently.

★

Some of these pipelines carry diesel fuel, others carry crude oil. Millions of liters of it a day. Nigeria supplies twenty-five percent of United States oil. And we get virtually nothing in return. Nothing but death by Zombie attack. We can all tell you stories.

When the Zombies were first released, no one knew about them. All people would hear were rumors about people getting torn apart near pipelines or sightings of giant white spiders in the night. Or you'd hear about huge pipeline explosions, charred bodies everywhere. But the pipeline where the bodies lay would be perfectly intact.

People still bunkered. My husband was one of them. I suspected that he sold the fuel and oil on the black market; he would bring some of the oil home, too. You let it sit in a bucket for two days and it would become something like kerosene. I used it for cooking. So I couldn't really complain. But bunkering was a very, very dangerous practice.

There *were* ways of breaking a pipeline open without immediately bringing the wrath of Zombies. My husband and his comrades used some sort of powerful laser cutter. They stole them from the hospitals. But they had to be very, very quiet when cutting through the metal. All it took was one bang, one vibration, and the Zombies would come running within a minute. Many of my husband's comrades had been killed because of the tap of someone's wedding ring or the tip of the laser cutter on steel.

Two years ago a group of boys had been playing too close to the pipeline. Two of them were wrestling and they fell on it. Within seconds the Zombies came. One boy managed to scramble away. But the other was grabbed by the arm and flung into some bushes. His arm and both of his legs were broken. Government officials *said* that Zombies were programmed to do as little harm as possible but . . . I didn't believe this, *na* lie.

They were terrible creatures. To get close to a pipeline was to risk a terrible death. Yet the goddamn things ran right through our backyards.

But I didn't care. My husband was beating the hell out of me during these months. I don't know why. He had not lost his job. I knew he was seeing other women. We were poor but we were not starving. Maybe it was because I couldn't bear him children. It is my fault I know, but what can I do?

I found myself out in the backyard more and more. And this particular Zombie visited me every time. I loved playing for it. It would listen. Its lovely eyes would glow with joy. Could a robot feel joy? I believed intelligent ones like this could. Many times a day, I would see a crowd of Zombies running up and down the pipeline, off to do repairs or policing, whatever they did. If my Zombie was amongst them, I couldn't tell.

It was about the tenth time it visited me that it did something very, very strange. My husband had come home smelling practically flammable, stinking of several kinds of alcohol—beer, palm wine, perfume. I had been thinking hard all day. About my life. I was stuck. I wanted a baby. I wanted to get out of the house. I wanted a job. I wanted friends. I needed courage. I knew I had courage. I had faced a Zombie, many times.

I was going to ask my husband about teaching at the elementary school. I'd heard that they were looking for teachers. When he walked in, he greeted me with a sloppy hug and kiss and then plopped himself on the couch. He turned on the television. It was late but I brought him his dinner, pepper soup heavy with goat meat, chicken, and large shrimp. He was in a good drunken mood. But as I stood there watching him eat, all my courage fled. All my need for change skittered and cowered to the back of my brain.

"Do you want anything else?" I asked.

He looked up at me and actually smiled. "The soup is good today."

I smiled, but something inside me ducked its head lower. "I'm glad," I said. I picked up my guitar. "I'm going to the back. It's nice outside."

"Don't go too close to the pipeline," he said. But he was looking at the TV and gnawing on a large piece of goat meat.

I crept into the darkness, through the bushes and grasses, to the pipeline. I sat in my usual spot, a foot from it. I strummed softly, a series of chords. A forlorn tune that spoke my heart. Where else was there to go from here? Was this my life? I sighed. I hadn't been to church in a month.

When it came clicking down the pipe, my heart lifted. Its blue liquid eyes glowed strong tonight. There was a woman from whom I once bought a bolt of blue cloth. The cloth was a rich blue that reminded me of the open water on sunny days. The woman said the cloth was "azure." My Zombie's eyes were a deep azure this night.

It stopped, standing before me. Waiting. I knew it was my Zombie because a month ago, it had allowed me to put a blue butterfly sticker on one of its front legs.

"Good evening," I said.

It did not move.

"I'm sad today," I said.

It stepped off the pipeline, its metal legs clicking on the metal and then whispering on the dirt and grass. It sat its body on the ground as it always did. Then it waited.

I strummed a few chords and then played its favorite song, Bob Marley's "No Woman No Cry." As I played, its body slowly began to rotate, something I'd come to understand was its way of expressing pleasure. I smiled. When I stopped playing, it turned its eyes back to me. I sighed, strummed an A minor chord, and sat back. "My life is shit," I said.

Suddenly, it rose up on its eight legs with a soft whir. It stretched and straightened its legs until it was standing a foot taller than normal. From under its body in the center, something whitish and metallic began to descend. I gasped, grabbing my guitar. My mind told me to move away. Move away fast. I'd befriended this artificial creature. I knew it. Or I thought I knew it. But what did I *really* know about why it did what it did? Or why it came to me?

The metallic substance descended faster, pooling in the grass beneath it. I squinted. The stuff was wire. Right before my eyes, I watched the Zombie take this wire and do something with five of its legs while it supported itself on the other three. The legs scrambled around, working and weaving the shiny wire this way and that. They moved too fast for me to see exactly what they were creating. Grass flew and the soft whirring sound grew slightly louder.

Then the legs stopped. For a moment all I could hear was the sounds of crickets and frogs singing, the breeze blowing in the palm and mangrove tree tops. I could smell the sizzling oil of someone frying plantain or yam nearby.

My eyes focused on what the Zombie had done. I grinned. I grinned and grinned. "What is that?" I whispered.

It held it up with two of its front legs and tapped its back leg twice on the ground as it always seemed to when it was trying to make a point. A point that I usually didn't understand.

It brought three legs forward and commenced to pluck out what first was a medley of my favorite songs, from Bob Marley to Sunny Ade to Carlos Santana. Then its music deepened to something so complex and beautiful that I was reduced to tears of joy, awe, ecstasy. People must have heard the music, maybe they looked out their windows or opened their doors. But we were hidden by the darkness, the grass, the trees. I cried and cried. I don't know why, but I cried. I wonder if it was pleased by my reaction. I think it was.

I spent the next hour learning to play its tune.

★

Ten days later, a group of Zombies attacked some oil workers and soldiers deep in the delta. Ten of the men were torn limb from limb, their bloody remains scattered all over the swampy land. Those who escaped told reporters that nothing would stop the Zombies. A soldier had even thrown a grenade at one, but the thing protected itself with the very force field it had been built to use during pipeline explosions. The soldier said the force field looked like a crackling bubble made of lightning.

"*Wahala*! Trouble!" the soldier frantically told television reporters. His face was greasy with sweat and the sides of his eyes were twitching. "Evil, evil things! I've believed this from start! Look at me with grenade! *Ye ye*! I could do nothing!"

The pipeline the men had barely even started was found fully assembled. Zombies are made to make repairs, not fully assemble things. It was bizarre. Newspaper write-ups said that the Zombies were getting too smart for their own good. That they were rebelling. Something had certainly changed.

"Maybe it's only a matter of time before the damn things kill us all," my husband said, a beer in hand, as he read about the incident in the newspaper.

I considered never going near my Zombie again. They were unpredictable and possibly out of control.

★

It was midnight and I was out there again.

My husband hadn't laid a heavy hand on me in weeks. I think he sensed the change in me. I had changed. He now heard me play more. Even in the house. In the mornings. After cooking his dinners. In the bedroom when his friends were over. And he was hearing songs that I knew gave him a most glorious feeling. As if each chord, each sound were examined by scientists and handpicked to provoke the strongest feeling of happiness.

My Zombie had solved my marital problems. At least the worst of them. My husband could not beat me when there was beautiful music sending his senses to lush, sweet places. I began to hope. To hope for a baby. Hope that I would one day leave my house and wifely duties for a job as music teacher at the elementary school. Hope that my village would one day reap from the oil being reaped from it. And I dreamt about being embraced by deep blue liquid metal, webs of wire and music.

I'd woken up that night from one of these strange dreams. I opened my eyes, a smile on my face. Good things were certainly coming. My husband was sleeping soundly beside me. In the dim moonlight, he looked so peaceful. His skin no longer smelled of alcohol. I leaned forward and kissed his lips. He didn't wake. I slipped out of bed and put on some pants and a long sleeve shirt. The mosquitoes would be out tonight. I grabbed my guitar.

I'd named my Zombie Udide Okwanka. In my language, it means

"spider the artist." According to legend, Udide Okwanka is the Supreme Artist. And she lives underground where she takes fragments of things and changes them into something else. She can even weave spirits from straw. It was a good name for my Zombie. I wondered what Udide named me. I was sure it named me something, though I doubted that it told the others about me. I don't think it would have been allowed to keep seeing me.

Udide was waiting for me there, as if it sensed I would come out this night. I grinned, my heart feeling so warm. I sat down as it left the pipeline and crept up to me. It carried its instrument on top of its head. A sort of complex star made of wire. Over the weeks, it had added more wire lines, some thin and some thick. I often wondered where it put this thing when it was running about with the others, for the instrument was too big to hide on its body.

Udide held it before its eyes. With a front leg, it plucked out a sweet simple tune that almost made me weep with joy. It conjured up images of my mother and father, when they were so young and full of hope, when my brothers and I were too young to marry and move away. Before the "kill-and-go" had driven my oldest brother away to America and my middle brother to the north . . . when there was so much potential.

I laughed and wiped away a tear and started strumming some chords to support the tune. From there we took off into something so intricate, enveloping, intertwining . . . *Chei!* I felt as if I was communing with God. *Ah-ah*, this machine and me. You can't imagine.

"Eme!"

Our music instantly fell apart.

"Eme!" my husband called again.

I froze, staring at Udide who was also motionless. "Please," I whispered to it. "Don't hurt him."

"Samuel messaged me!" my husband said, his eyes still on his cell phone, as he stepped up to me through the tall grass. "There's a break in the pipeline near the school! Not a goddamn Zombie in sight yet! Throw down that guitar, woman! Let's go and get . . . " He looked up. A terrified look took hold of his face.

For a very long time it seemed we all were frozen in time. My husband standing just at the last of the tall grass. Udide standing in front of the pipeline, instrument held up like a ceremonial shield. And me between the two of them, too afraid to move. I turned to my husband. "Andrew," I said with the greatest of care. "Let me explain . . . "

He slowly dragged his gaze to me and gave me a look, as if he was seeing me for the first time. "My own wife?" he whispered.

"I . . . "

Udide raised its two front legs. For a moment it looked almost like it was pleading with me. Or maybe offering me a hug. Then it clicked its legs together so hard that it produced a large red spark and an ear splitting *ting!*

My husband and I clapped our hands over our ears. The air instantly smelled like freshly lit matches. Even through the palms of my hands, I could hear the responses from down the pipeline. The clicking was so numerous that it sounded like a rain of tiny pebbles falling on the pipeline. Udide shuddered, scrambled back and stood on it, waiting. They came in a great mob. About twenty of them. The first thing that I noticed was their eyes. They were all a deep angry red.

The others scrambled around Udide, tapping their feet in complex rhythms on the pipe. I couldn't see Udide's eyes. Then they all ran off with amazing speed, to the east.

I turned to my husband. He was gone.

★

Word spread like a disease because almost everyone had a cell phone. Soon everyone was clicking away on them, messaging things like, "Pipeline burst, near school! No Zombies in sight!" and "Hurry to school, bring bucket!" My husband never let me have my own cell phone. We couldn't afford one and he didn't think I needed one. But I knew where the elementary school was.

People now believed that the Zombies had all gone rogue, shrugging off their man-given jobs to live in the delta swamps and do whatever it was they did there. Normally, if bunkerers broke open a pipeline, even for the quietest jobs, the Zombies would become aware of it within an hour and repair the thing within another hour. But two hours later this broken pipe continued to splash fuel. That was when someone had decided to put the word out.

I knew better. The Zombies weren't "zombies" at all. They were thinking creatures. Smart beasts. They had a method to their madness. And most of them did *not* like human beings.

The chaos was lit by the headlights of several cars and trucks. The pipeline here was raised as it traveled south. Someone had taken advantage of this and removed a whole section of piping. Pink diesel fuel poured out of both ends like a giant fountain. People crowded beneath the flow like parched elephants, filling jerri cans, bottles, bowls, buckets. One man even held a garbage bag, until the fuel ate through the bag, splashing fuel all over the man's chest and legs.

The spillage collected into a large dark pink pool that swiftly flowed toward the elementary school, gathering on the playground. The fumes hit me even before I got within sight of the school. My eyes watered and my nose started running. I held my shirt over my nose and mouth. This barely helped.

People came in cars, motorcycles, buses, on foot. Everyone was messaging on their cell phones, further spreading the word. It had been a while since people who did not make a career out of fuel theft had gotten a sip of free fuel.

There were children everywhere. They ran up and down, sent on errands by their parents or just hanging around to be a part of the excitement. They'd probably never seen people able to go near a pipeline without getting killed. Hip-hop and highlife blasted from cars and SUVs with enhanced sound systems. The baseline vibrations were almost as stifling as the fumes. I had not a doubt that the Zombies knew this was going on.

I spotted my husband. He was heading toward the fountain of fuel with a large red bucket. Five men started arguing amongst each other. Two of them started pushing and shoving, almost falling into the fountain.

"Andrew!" I called over all the noise.

He turned. When he saw me, he narrowed his eyes.

"Please!" I said. "I'm . . . I'm sorry."

He spat and started walking away.

"You have to get out of here!" I said. "They will come!"

He whirled around and strode up to me. "How the hell are you so sure? Did you bring them yourself?"

As if in response, people suddenly started screaming and running. I cursed. The Zombies were coming from the street, forcing people to run toward the pool of fuel. I cursed again. My husband was glaring at me. He pointed into my face with a look of disgust. I couldn't hear what he said over all the noise. He turned and ran off.

I tried to spot Udide amongst the Zombies. All of their eyes were still red. Was Udide even amongst them? I stared at their legs, searching for the butterfly sticker. There it was. Closest to me, to the left. "Udide!" I called.

As the name came out of my mouth, I saw two of the Zombies in the center each raise two front legs. My smile went to an "O" of shock. I dropped to the ground and threw my hands over my head. People were still splashing across the pool of fuel, trying to get into the school. Their cars continued blasting hip-hop and highlife, the headlights still on, lighting the madness.

The two Zombies clicked their legs together, producing two large sparks. *Ting!*

WHOOOOOOOOSH!

★

I remember light, heat, the smell of burning hair and flesh and screams that melted to guttural gurgles. The noise was muffled. The stench was awful. My head to my lap, I remained in this hellish limbo for a long, long time.

★

I'll never teach music at the elementary school. It was incinerated along with many of the children who went to it. My husband was killed, too. He died thinking I was some sort of spy fraternizing with the enemy . . . or something like that. Everyone died. Except me. Just before the explosion happened, Udide ran to me. It protected me with its force field.

So I lived.

And so did the baby inside me. The baby that my body allowed to happen because of Udide's lovely soothing music. Udide tells me it is a girl. How can a robot know this? Udide and I play for her every day. I can only imagine how content she is. But what kind of world will I be bringing her into? Where only her mother and Udide stand between a flat out war between the Zombies and the human beings who created them?

Pray that Udide and I can convince man and droid to call a truce, otherwise the delta will keep rolling in blood, metal, and flames. You know what else? You should also pray that these Zombies don't build themselves some fins and travel across the ocean.

THE GHASTLY BIRD

"Do do?" the fat gray bird said, taking a tentative step toward Zev.

It stood on the other side of the yard; the side where Zev's gardeners worked the hardest because they had to not only pull weeds but also to keep the jungle behind the fence from invading Zev's well-kept space. The plump bird had a large, hooked beak, and when it turned to the side, Zev could see a plume of white feathers adorning its tail. Zev dropped the large glass of beer that he held in his hand. He didn't drop his binoculars, which he held in his other hand. He brought them to his eyes.

It was a beautiful sunny day on the Island of Mauritius, the kind of day in which only good things happen. But even on this day, Zev never imagined that his dream would come true.

Zev had a rare day off. Usually, he was lecturing at the university, grading exams, typing up his latest scholarly paper, or in the bush searching for birds to photograph and classify. Today, Zev had huffed and puffed as he dragged his lounge chair to the center of his green short-grassed lawn, away from the shade of his perfectly manicured coconut, guava, mango, and banyan trees.

He'd plopped down with his second glass of beer, the lounge chair creaking loudly under his heavy weight. He was fully prepared to inhale the smells of the roses, lilies, and lilacs in his flower garden and watch the birds visit his cornucopia of bird feeders hanging from his Calvaria tree. Some feeders were filled with seeds, others with dried fruit, and some he'd put fresh mealworms in this morning. The Calvaria tree added its own fruit to the feast, to Zev's delight.

This extremely rare tree had cost Zev thousands to obtain and even more to maintain. Now, not only was it healthy, but it was so healthy that it was dropping its thick-coated fuzzy brown fruits all over the lawn beneath it. Zev had been planning to remind his gardeners to clean up the fruity mess, but now he was glad he'd procrastinated. Look who had come to visit him.

Zev was familiar with many of the birds. One of the regulars was the clumsy white egret that often crash-landed onto Zev's lawn. This bird liked to eat the mealworms. It was there now, happily snapping up worm after worm. Warblers, doves ad pigeons, parakeets, Mynah birds, crows. One parrot that had been visiting his feeders for years would even land on Zev's shoulder and take sunflower seeds from Zev's lips. Watching and interacting with the birds usually relaxed every bone in his body.

Now, however, he was anything but relaxed. He was so excited that his heart palpitated and he had to breathe through his mouth. However, his hands were steady. He'd been preparing for this moment all his life.

He bit his bottom lip hard and snickered to himself. He'd rather have thrown his head back and guffawed loudly enough to shake the skies. But he didn't want to scare this bird away. No. That would break his heart. This was his moment. He felt that now he could die a happy man.

"Ah, look at that beak," he whispered, his eyes starting to feel dry from not blinking, sweat trickling through the hairs of his armpits. "It really *does* feed on the fruit of the Calvaria tree! Round body, plume of white feather on the tail. Oh! I just knew it. It's all correct!"

He was overcome again with shakes from stifling his snickers. After all these years! It was true. As he had always believed. It wasn't a certainty he discussed with his fellow colleagues at the university. Zev wasn't stupid. For an ornithologist to believe that the dodo was not extinct and to be open and adamant about it would first get him ostracized and then quietly fired.

Still, Zev believed what he believed and he was a hardheaded man, so no one could change that. The dodo wasn't the stupid idiot bird that those Europeans liked to portray it as. No. It was simply friendly. There had been no humans on this island! Why would it have a fear of them?

But though they were friendly, dodos were smart, Zev believed. It only made sense. In Zev's books, the dodo was known for being extremely stupid. Some called it an inflated pigeon, others just said it was more like a clumsy turkey.

In their travelogues, explorers boasted about being able to run circles around the bird even when they were extremely drunk. Then they would bop the bird on the head and cook it up for dinner. Then they complained about how no matter what they did to the dodo meat, it remained tough and tasteless as an old shoe. Thus it gained another nickname, the "ghastly bird."

Before men brought their boats, disease, and foreign beasts, the dodo had no predators. Or maybe it was too smart to be prey, Zev thought. They lived in the forests with confidence. They'd lay their one large egg in a nest on the ground in the middle of the forest and be sure that their egg was safe. But when men came with his unfamiliar dogs, pigs, and ship rats, the dodo and their nests had no chance.

But the dodo couldn't possibly be as stupid as it looked. They must have a secret, Zev believed. A hiding place that not even man could find. Or magical powers. Maybe they could disappear and reappear at will or, during certain parts of the night, they could fly without needing to flap their tiny wings. The dodo wasn't some overweight dopey looking creature. That was just a costume.

Once or twice he'd let this fantasy surface in conversations with his girlfriend, Sarafina. When his passion for the subject showed, she laughed in his face and rolled her eyes and said, "I think something is very wrong with you, Zev." She'd broken up with him weeks ago. He'd really liked Sarafina. It tore his heart that a belief he held so close to his soul caused her to leave him. So he pushed it into the back of his mind and got on with his research, his lectures, his life work. He loved birds, so this was not very difficult. So what if he remained a bachelor all his life?

Even if he had married her, he'd have never shown Sarafina the cabinet in the corner of his bedroom where he kept a shrine dedicated to his favorite living bird, the dodo.

In it, there were plaster and wooden carvings of dodos. He had a tiny figurine of the bird made of hummingbird feathers. A large expensive porcelain dodo encrusted with chips of glass. And several stuffed toy dodos. He even had a dodo doll that he slept with at night, when none of his girlfriends slept over, of course. He'd collected dodo trinkets since he was a child growing up in India.

At the age of thirty-five, he had been a highly sought-after professor of ornithology. He could have gone anywhere. But it was Mauritius that he wanted to travel to. The home of the dodo. And now almost twenty years later, he still felt he couldn't have made a better decision. Mauritius was not only beautiful, there was also a healthy Hindi population that reminded him of home when he needed it and an even healthier variety of birds. He wouldn't have been happier anywhere else in the world.

He brought down his binoculars so that he could see the dodo with his own naked eyes. Three dainty mourning doves were battling for seeds under one of the bird feeders but Zev only looked at the dodo. The dodo was looking at him, too, which made his heart beat even faster.

Then it turned around in its lumbery way and ran back into the bushes.

"Wait! Please," Zev said, but only quietly. It had eaten here; it would be back. Zev just sat there, his heartbeat slowing back to normal. Still, there was excited sweat on his brow and his mouth twitched into a giddy grin. He giggled, feeling utterly tickled inside. Then he slapped the side of his face and giggled some more.

He didn't know what to do. He didn't want to move, that he knew. If he moved, the moment would be over. *But there will be other moments,* he thought to himself. He was sure the dodo bird would come back. At least once. And he had to be there to see it; maybe even lure it up close with an especially juicy Calvaria tree fruit. *I should get my camera.*

He waited for a moment and then suddenly jumped up. The longer he waited, the sooner the dodo would return. *Get camera.* And he had to empty his bladder. He ran into the house. There was a bathroom that had a small window facing the backyard. He'd be able to look out the window from there to make sure the dodo didn't return without him. He ran fast, his binoculars bumping against his large belly, tripping over the step into the house but quickly regaining his footing with a gasp for air.

He threw the bathroom door open and unzipped his pants as he looked out the window. As he urinated, he squinted. Then he gasped. "Shit!" He wasn't sure what to do. He wasn't finished, but from where he stood, he could see it. The dodo emerged from the spot in the bushes where it had disappeared, back under the Calvaria tree. Zev directed his stream of urine with one hand and grabbed his binoculars with the other hand. The moment he got the bird into view, the bird stopped eating and looked directly at him.

"Oh," Zev said, his eyebrows rising. He was so excited that he could hear his heartbeat in his ears. He shook himself off and zipped up his pants. He didn't bother flushing the toilet when he left the bathroom. *Forget the camera. No time.* He'd left the backdoor open, so he didn't worry about scaring it away with the sound of the sliding door.

Now all he had to do was walk slowly and quietly toward the bird. He knew he could do that. He was a pro at approaching birds. He believed that he had a special ability to mentally calm the birds with his presence, be it finch, parrot, secretary bird, or grackle. Very few birds ever fled from his presence. Even now, as he slowly walked across the yard, sweat pouring from his brow, breathing heavily with excitement, none of the birds at the feeder paid any attention to him. It was as if he was only partially there. He smiled to himself. No other ornithologist in his department would be able to touch him and all his past girlfriends had been too shallow to see how good he was at what he did.

The dodo hadn't moved as it watched Zev approach. All around him, the world was bright and alive. The air smelled of leaves, flowers, fertile earth soaked by the ocean. He could hear the cars and trucks driving by and people houses away having conversations. He paused for a moment and frowned. One of those voices sounded like his mother.

He would call her today and tell her what he saw, then he'd tell his father, then he'd call that woman Sarafina and tell her if she hung up the phone, he'd call back and tell her again, he'd take pictures and show them to his department colleagues, his research and photos would appear in the top scientific journals, he'd make the cover of international magazines, he would be the expert on dodos, he *was* the expert. All this he thought about as he approached the staring robust bird.

Five yards. Two yards. A yard and a half. Still, it didn't move. It was beautiful. So beautiful that Zev felt weak with joy. Two feet away from the dodo, Zev knelt down on the ground and lay before the bird. He could now see that its eyes were black with flecks of gold and green.

He was wheezing as he watched the bird slowly amble up to him. He could feel his heart laboring in its last throes, as the world around him grew more clear and pungent. Now all he could smell were flowers, oily with sweetness, not his lilacs, lilies, or roses. Some other types of blossoms. He rolled onto his side as the dodo spirit guide stepped up to him.

"Do do?" it cooed again, softly. Zev smiled as the dodo bent its soft head and rested it on his cheek. Then Zev knew no more.

THE WINDS OF HARMATTAN

Asuquo followed her nose and used her bird-like sense of direction. All around her were men selling yams and women selling cocoa yams. She always knew where to find the good ones; they had a starchier smell. Her mother didn't believe her when she said she could smell specific vegetables in the market; but she could.

Asuquo was about to jostle past a slow-moving man carrying a bunch of plantains on his shoulder when an old woman grabbed one of her seven locks. The woman sat on a wooden stool, a pyramid of eggs on a straw mat at her feet. Next to her, a man was selling very dried-up looking yams.

"Yes, mama?" Asuquo said. She did not know the woman but she knew to always show respect to her elders. The woman smiled and let go of Asuquo's hair.

"You like the sky, wind girl?" she asked.

Asuquo froze, feeling tears heat her eyes. *How does she know*? Asuquo thought. *She will tell my mother.* Asuquo's strong sense of smell wasn't the only thing her mother didn't believe in, even when she saw it with her own eyes. Asuquo's face still ached from the slap she'd received from her mother yesterday morning. But Asuquo couldn't help what happened when she slept.

The man selling yams brushed past her to hand a buyer his change of several cowries. He looked at her and then sneezed. Asuquo frowned and the old woman laughed.

"Even your own father is probably allergic to you, wind girl," she said in her phlegmy voice. Asuquo looked away, her hands fidgeting. "All except one. You watch for him. Don't listen to what they all say. He's your *chi*. All of your kind are born with one. You go out and find him."

"How much for ten eggs?" a young woman asked, stepping up to the old woman.

"My *chi*?" Asuquo whispered, the old woman's words bouncing about her mind. Asuquo didn't move. She knew exactly whom the woman spoke of. Sometimes she dreamt about him. He could do what she could do. Maybe he could do it better.

"Give me five cowries," the old woman said to her customer. She gave Asuquo a hard push back into the market crowd without a word and turned her attention to selling her eggs. Asuquo tried to look back, but there were too many people between her and the old woman now.

After she'd bought her yams, she didn't bother going back to find the old woman. But from that day on, she watched the sky.

★

Asuquo was one of the last. It is whispered words, known as the "bush radio," and the bitter grumblings of the trees that bring together her story. She was a Windseeker, one of the people who could fly; and a Windseeker's life is dictated by more than the wind.

Eleven years later, the year of her twentieth birthday, the Harmattan winds never came. Dry, dusty, and cool, these winds had formed over the Sahara and blown their fresh air all the way to the African coast from December to February since humans began walking the earth. Except for that year.

That year, the cycle was disrupted, old ways poisoned. This story will tell you why . . .

★

Asuquo was the fourth daughter of Chief Ibok's third wife. Though she was not fat, she still possessed a sort of voluptuous beauty with her round hips and strong legs. But her hair crept down her back like ropes of black fungus. She was born this way, emerging from her mother's womb with seven glistening locks of dada hair hanging from her head like seaweed. And women with dada hair were undesirable.

They were thought to be the children of Mami Wata, and the water deity always claimed her children eventually, be it through kidnapping or an early death. Such a woman was not a good investment in the future. Asuquo's mother didn't bother taking her to the fattening hut to be secluded for weeks, stuffed with pounded yam and dried chameleons, and circumcised with a sharp sliver of coconut shell.

Nevertheless, Asuquo was content in her village. She didn't want to be bothered with all the preparations for marriage. She spent much of her time in the forest and rumors that she talked to the sky and did strange things with plants were not completely untrue.

Nor were the murmurs of her running about with several young men. When she was twelve, she discovered she had a taste for them. The moment a young man from a nearby village named Okon saw her, however, standing behind her mother's home, peeling bark from a tree and dropping it in her pocket, he fell madly in love. She'd been smiling at the tree, her teeth shiny white, her skin blue black and her callused hands long-fingered. When Okon approached her that day, she stood eye to eye with him; and he was tall himself.

Okon's father almost didn't allow him to marry her.

"How can you marry that kind of woman? She has never been to the fattening hut!" he'd bellowed. "She has dada hair! I'm telling you, she is a child of Mami Wata! She is likely to be barren!"

My father is right, Okon thought, *Asuquo is unclean.* But something about her made him love her. Okon was a stubborn young man. He was also smart. And so he continued nagging his father about Asuquo, while also assuring him that he would marry a second well-born wife soon afterwards. His father eventually gave in.

Asuquo did not want to marry Okon. Since the encounter with the strange old woman years ago, she had been watching the skies for her *chi*, her other half, the one she was supposed to go and find. She had been dreaming about her *chi* since she was six and every year the dreams grew more and more vivid.

She knew his voice, his smile, and his dry leaf scent. Sometimes she'd even think she saw him in her peripheral vision. She could see that he was tall and dark like her and wore purple. But when she turned her head, he wasn't there.

She knew she would someday find him, or he would find her, the way a bird knows which way to migrate. But, at the time, he was not close and he was not thinking about her much. He was somewhere trying to live his life, just as she was. All in due time.

Her parents, on the other hand, were so glad a man—*any man*—wanted to marry Asuquo that they ignored everything else. They ignored how she brought the wind with her wherever she went, her seven locks of thick hair bouncing against her back. And they certainly ignored the fact that, though she was shaky, she could fly a few inches off the ground when she really tried.

One day, Asuquo had floated to the hut's ceiling to crush a large spider. Her mother happened to walk in. She took one look at Asuquo and then quickly grabbed the basket she'd come for and left. She never mentioned it to Asuquo, nor the many other times she'd seen Asuquo levitate. Asuquo's father was the same way.

"Mama, I shouldn't marry him," Asuquo said. "You know I shouldn't."

Her mother waved her hand at her words. And her father greedily held out his hands for the hefty dowry Okon paid to Asuquo's family.

Asuquo had been taught to respect her elders. Somewhere in the back of her mind, she knew her duty as a woman. So, in the end, Asuquo agreed to the marriage, ignoring, denying, and pushing away her thoughts and sightings of her *chi*. And Asuquo could not help but feel pleased at the satisfied look in her father's eyes and the proud swell of her mother's chest. For so long they had been looks of dismissal and shame.

The wedding was most peculiar. Five bulls and several goats were slaughtered. For a village where meat was only eaten on special occasions, this was wonderful. However, birds, large and small, kept stealing hunks of the meat and mouthfuls of spicy rice from the feast. On top of that, high winds swept people's cloths about during the ceremony. Asuquo laughed and laughed, her brightly colored lapa swirling about her ankles and the collarette of beads and cowry shells around her neck clicking. She knew several of the birds personally, especially the owl who took off with an entire goat leg.

After their wedding night, Asuquo knew Okon would not look at another woman. Once in their hut Asuquo had undressed him and taken him in with her eyes for a long time. Then she nodded, satisfied with what she saw. Okon had strong, veined hands, rich brown skin,a nd a long neck. That night Asuquo had her way with him in ways that left his body tingling and sore and helpless, though she'd have preferred to be outside under the sky.

As he lay, exhausted, he told her that the women he'd slept with before had succumbed to him with sad faces and lain like fallen trees. Asuquo laughed and said, "It's because those women felt as if they had lost their honor." She smiled to herself, thinking about all her other lovers and how none of them had behaved as if they were dead or fallen.

That morning Okon learned exactly what kind of woman he had married. Asuquo was not beside him when he awoke. His eyes grew wide when he looked up.

"What is this?" he screeched, trying to scramble out of bed and falling on the floor instead, his big left foot in the air. He quickly rolled to the side and knelt low, staring up at his wife, his mouth agape. Her green lapa and hair hung down, as she hovered horizontally above the bed. Okon noticed that there was something gentle about how she floated. He could feel a soft breeze circulating around her. He sniffed. It smelled like the arid winds during Harmattan. He sneezed three times and had to wipe his nose.

Asuquo slowly opened her eyes, awakened by Okon's noise. She chuckled and softly floated back onto the bed. She felt particularly good because when she'd awoken, she hadn't automatically fallen as she usually did.

That afternoon they had a long talk where Asuquo laughed and smiled and Okon mostly just stared at her and asked "Why" and "How?" Their discussion didn't get beyond the obvious. But by night-time, she had him forgetting that she, the woman he had just married, had the ability to fly.

For a while, it was as if Asuquo lived under a pleasantly overcast sky. Her dreams of her *chi* stopped and she no longer glimpsed him in the corner of her eye. She wondered if the old woman had been wrong, because she was very happy with Okon.

She planted a garden behind their hut. When she was not cooking, washing, or sewing, she was in the garden, cultivating. There were many different types of plants, including sage, kola nut, wild yam root, parsley, garlic, pleurisy root, nettles, cayenne. She grew cassava melons, yam, cocoa yams, beans, and many, many flowers. She sold her produce at the market. She always came home with her money purse full of cowries. She liked to tie it around her waist because she enjoyed the rhythmic clinking it made as she walked.

When she became pregnant, she didn't have to soak a bag of wheat or barley in her urine to know that she would give birth to a boy. But she knew if she did so, the bag of wheat would sprout and the bag of barley would remain dormant, a sure sign of a male child. The same went with her second pregnancy a year later. She loved her two babies, Hogan and Bassey, dearly, and her heart was full. For a while.

Okon was so in love with Asuquo that he quietly accepted the fact that she could fly. *As long as the rest of the village doesn't know, especially father, what is the harm?* he thought. He let her do whatever she wanted; providing that she maintained the house, cooked for him, and warmed his bed at night.

He also enjoyed the company of Asuquo's mother, who sometimes visited. Though she and Asuquo did not talk much, Asuquo's mother and Okon laughed and conversed well into the night. Neither spoke of Asuquo's flying ability.

Asuquo made plenty of money at the market. And when he came back from fishing, there was nothing Okon loved more than to watch his wife in her garden, his sons scrambling about her feet.

Regardless of their contentment, the village's bush radio was alive with chatter, snaking its mischievous roots under their hut, its stems through their window, holding its flower to their lips like microphones, following Asuquo with the stealth of a grapevine. The bush radio thrived from the rain of gossip.

Women said that Asuquo worked juju on her husband to keep him from looking at any other woman. That she carried a purse around her waist hidden in her lapa that her husband could never touch. That she carried all sorts of strange things in it, like nails, her husband's hair, dead lizards, odd stones, sugar, and salt. That there were also items folded, wrapped, tied, sewn into cloth in this purse. *Had she not been born with the locked hair of a witch?* they asked. And look at how wildly her garden grows in the back. And what are those useless plants she grows alongside her yams and cassava?

"When do you plan to do as you promised?" Okon's father asked.

"When I am ready," Okon said. "When, ah . . . when Hogan and Bassey are older."

"Has that woman made you crazy?" his father asked. "What kind of household is this with just one wife? This kind of woman?"

"It is my house, papa," Okon said. He broke eye contact with his father. "And it is happy and productive. In time I will get another woman. But not yet."

The men often talked about Asuquo's frequent disappearances into the forest and the way she was always climbing things.

"I often see her climbing her hut to go on the roof when her chickens fly up there," one man said. "What is a woman doing climbing trees and roofs?"

"She moves about like a bird," they said.

"Or bat," one man said, narrowing his eyes.

For a while men quietly went about slapping at bats with switches when they could, waiting to see if Asuquo came out of her hut limping.

A long time ago, things would have been different for Asuquo. There was a time when Windseekers in the skies were as common as tree frogs in the trees. Then came the centuries of the foreigners with their huge boats, sweet words, weapons, and chains. After that, Windseeker sightings grew scarce. Storytellers forgot much of the myth and magic of the past and turned what they remembered into evil, dark things. It was no surprise that the village was so resistant to Asuquo.

Both the men and women liked to talk about Hogan and Bassey. They couldn't say that the two boys weren't Okon's children. Hogan looked like a miniature version of his father with his arrow-shaped nose and bushy eyebrows. And Bassey had his father's careful mannerisms when he ate and crawled about the floor.

But people were very suspicious about how healthy the two little boys were. The boys consumed as much as any normal child of the village, eating little meat and much fruit. Hogan was more partial to udara fruits, while Bassey liked to slowly suck mangos to the seed. Still, the shiny-skinned boys grew as if they ate goat meat every day. The villagers told each other, "She *must* be doing something to them. Something evil. No child should grow like that."

"I see her coming from the forest some days," one woman said. "She brings back oddly shaped fruits and roots to feed her children." Once again, the word "witch" was whispered, as discreet fingers pointed Asuquo's way.

Regardless of the chatter, women often went to Asuquo when she was stooping over the plants in her garden. Their faces would be pleasant and one would never guess that only an hour ago, they had spoken ill of the very woman from whom they sought help.

They would ask if she could spare a yam or some bitter leaf for egusi soup. But they really wanted to know if Asuquo could do something for a child who was coughing up mucus. Or if she could make something to soothe a husband's toothache. Some wanted sweet-smelling oils to keep their skin soft in the sun. Others sought a reason why their healthy gardens had begun to wither after a fight with a friend.

"I'll see what I can do," Asuquo would answer, putting a hand on the woman's back, escorting her inside. And she could always do something.

Asuquo was too preoccupied with her own issues to tune into the gossip of the bush radio.

She'd begun to feel the tug deep in the back of her throat again. He was close, her *chi*, her other half, the one who liked to wear purple. And as she was, he was all grown up, his thoughts now focused on her. At times she choked and hacked but the hook only dug deeper. When her sons were no longer crawling she began to make trips to the forest more frequently, so that she could assuage her growing impatience. Once the path grew narrow and the sound of voices dwindled, she slowly took to the air.

Branches and leaves would slap her legs because she was too clumsy to maneuver around them. She could stay in the sky only for a few moments, then she would sink. But in those moments, she could feel him.

When her husband was out fishing and the throb of her menses kept her from spending much time in the garden, she filled a bowl with rainwater and sat on the floor, her eyes wide, staring into it as through a window to another world. Once in a while, she'd dip a finger in, creating expanding circles. She saw the blue sky, the trees waving back and forth with the breeze. It didn't take long to find what she was looking for. He was far away, flying just above the tallest trees, his purple pants and caftan fluttering as he flew.

Afterwards, she took the bowl of water with her to the river and poured it over her head with a sigh. The water always tasted sweet and felt like the sun on her skin. Then she dove into the river and swam deep, imagining the water to be the sky and the sky to be the water.

Some nights she was so restless that she went to her garden and picked a blue passionflower. She ate it and when she slept, she dreamt of him. Though she could see him clearly, he was always too far for her to touch. She had started to call him the purple one. Aside from his purple attire, he wore cowry shells dangling from his ears and around his wrists and had a gold hoop in his wide nose. Her urge to go to him was almost unbearable.

As her mind became consumed with the purple one, her body was less and less interested in Okon. Their relationship quickly changed. Okon became a terrible beast fed by his own jealousy. He desperately appealed to Asuquo's mother who, in turn, yelled at Asuquo's distracted face.

Okon would angrily snatch the broom from Asuquo and sweep out the dry leaves that kept blowing into their home, sneezing as he did so. He tore through her garden with stamping feet and clenched fists, scratching himself on thorns and getting leaves stuck in his toenails. And his hands became heavy as bronze to her skin. He forbade her to fly, especially in the forest. Out of fear for her sons, she complied. But it did not stop there.

The rumors, mixed with jealousy, fear, and suspicion spiraled into a raging storm, with Asuquo at the center. Her smile turned to a sad gaze as her mind continued to dwell on her *chi* that flew somewhere in the same skies she could no longer explore. Each night, her husband tied her to the bed where he made what he considered love to her body; for he still loved her. Each time, he fell asleep on top of her, not moving till morning when he sneezed himself awake.

Even her sons seemed to be growing allergic to Asuquo. She had to frequently wipe their noses when they sneezed. Sometimes they cried when she got too close. And they played outside more and more, preferring to help their father dry the fish he brought home, than their mother in the garden. Asuquo often cried about this in the garden when no one was around. Her sons were all she had.

One day, Okon fell sick. His forehead was hot but yet he shivered. He was weak and at times he yelled at phantoms he saw floating about the hut.

"Please, Asuquo, fly up to the ceiling," he begged, grabbing her arm as he lay in bed, sweat beading his brow. "Tell them to leave!"

He pleaded with her to speak with the plants and mix a concoction foul-smelling enough to drive the apparitions away.

Asuquo looked at the sky, then at Okon, then at the sky. He'd die if she left him. She thought of her sons. The sound of their feet as they played outside soothed her soul. She looked at the sky again. She stood very still for several minutes. Then she turned from the door and went to Okon. *When Okon gets well*, she thought. *I will take my sons with me, even if I cannot fly so well.*

When he was too weak to chew his food, she chewed it first and then fed it to him. She plucked particular leaves and pounded bitter-smelling bark. She collected rainwater to wash him with. And she frequently laid her hands on his chest and forehead. She often sent the boys out to prune her plants when she was with Okon in the bedroom. The care they took with the plants during this time made her want to kiss them over and over. But she did not because they would sneeze.

For this short time, she was happy. Okon was not able to tie her up and she was able to soothe his pain. She was also able to slip away once in a while and practice flying. The moment Okon was able to stand up straight with no pain in his chest or dizziness, however, after five years of marriage, he went and brought several of his friends to the hut and pointed his finger at Asuquo.

"This woman tried to kill me," he said, looking at Asuquo with disgust. He grabbed her wrists. "She is a witch! *Ubio!*"

"Ah," one of his friends said, smiling. "You've finally woke up and seen your wife for what she really is."

The others grunted in agreement, looking at Asuquo with a mixture of fear and hatred. Asuquo stared in complete shock at her husband whose life she had saved, her ears following her sons around the yard as they laughed and sculpted shapes from mud.

She wasn't sure if she was seeing Okon for what he really was or what he had become. What she was sure of was that in that moment, something burst deep inside her; something that held the realization of her mistake at bay. She should have listened to the old woman; she should have listened to *herself*. If it weren't for her sons, she'd have shot through the ceiling, into the sky, never to be seen again.

"Why . . . ?" was all she said.

Okon slapped her then, slapped her hard. Then he slapped her again. Only her *chi* could save her now.

Okon brought her before the Ekpo society. He tightly held the thick rope that he'd tied around her left wrist. Her shoulders were slumped and her eyes were cast down. Villagers came out of their huts and gathered around the four old men sitting in chairs and the woman kneeling before them in the dirt.

Her sons, now only three and four years old, were taken to their aunt's hut. Asuquo's hair had grown several feet in length over the years. Now there were a few coils of grey around her forehead from the stress. The people stared at her locks with pinched faces as if they had never seen them before.

The Ekpo society's job was to protect the village from thieves, murderers, cheats, and witchcraft. Nevertheless, even these old men had forgotten that once upon a long time ago, the sky was peopled with women and men just like Asuquo.

Centuries ago, the Ekpo society was close to the deities of the forest, exchanging words of wisdom, ideas, and wishes with these benevolent beings who had a passing interest in the humans of the forest. But these days, the elders of the Ekpo society were in closer contact with the white men, choosing which wrongdoers to sell to them and bartering for the price.

Her husband stood behind her, his angry eyes cast to the ground. All this time he had let her go in and out of the house whenever she liked, he never asked where exactly she was going. He never asked who she was going to see. It couldn't have just been the forest. He had asked many of the women who they thought the man or men she was being unfaithful with was. They all gave different names. Father warned me that she was unclean, he kept thinking.

The four old men sat on chairs, wearing matching blue and red lapas. Their feet close together, scowls on their faces. One of them raised his chin and spoke.

"You are accused of witchcraft," he said, his voice shaky with age. "One woman said you gave her a drink for her husband's sore tooth and all his teeth fell out. One man saw you turn into a bat. Many people in this village can attest to this. What do you have to say for yourself?"

Asuquo looked up at the men and for the first time, her ears ringing, her nostrils flaring, she felt rage, though not because of the accusations. It made her face ugly. The purple one was so close and these people were not listening to her. They were in her way, blocking out the cool dusty wind with their noise.

Her hands clenched. Many of the people gathered looked away out of guilt. They knew their part in all of this. The chief's wives, their arms around their chests, looked on, waiting and hoping to be rid of this woman who many said had bedded their husband numerous times.

"You see whatever you want to see," she said through dry lips. "I've had enough. You can't keep me from him."

She heard her husband gasp behind her. If they had been at home, he'd have beaten her. Nevertheless, his blows no longer bothered her as much. These days her essence sought the sky. It was September. The Harmattan winds would be upon the village soon, spraying dust onto the tree leaves and into their homes. She'd hold out her arms and let the dust devils twirl her around. Soon.

But she still couldn't fly that well yet, especially with her shoulders weighed down by sadness. If only these people would get out of the way. Then she would take her sons where they would be safe, and the caretakers she chose would not tell them lies about her.

"Let the chop nut decide," the fourth elder said, his eyes falling on Asuquo like charred pieces of wood. "In three days."

She almost laughed despite herself. Asuquo knew the plant from which the chop nut grew. In the forest, the doomsday plant thrived during rainy season. Many times she'd stopped to admire it. Its purplish bean-like flower was beautiful. When the flower fell off, a brown kidney-shaped pod replaced it. She could smell the six highly poisonous chop nuts inside the pod from meters away. Even the bush rats with their weak senses of smell and tough stomachs died minutes after eating it.

Asuquo looked up at the elders, one by one. She curled her lip and pointed at the elder who had spoken. She opened her mouth wide as if to curse them but no sound came out. Then her eyes went blank again and her face relaxed. She mentally left her people and let her mind seek out the sky. Still a tear of deep sadness fell down her face.

The four of elders stood up and walked into the forest where they said they would "consort with the old ones."

Those three days were hazy and cold as the inside of a cloud. Okon tied Asuquo to the bed as before. He slept next to her, his arm around her waist. He bathed her, fed her and enjoyed her. In the mornings, he went to the garden and quietly cried for her. Then he cried for himself, for he could not pinpoint who his wife's lover was. Every man in the village looked suspect.

Asuquo's eyes remained distant. She no longer spoke to him, she did not even look at him, and she did not notice that her babies were not with her. Instead, she unfocused her eyes and let her mind float into the sky, coming back occasionally to command her body to inhale and exhale air.

Her *chi* joined her here, several hundred miles away from the village, a thousand feet into the sky. Now he was close enough that for the first time, a part of them could be in the same place. Asuquo leaned against him as he took her locks into his hands and brought them to his face, inhaling her scent. He smelled like dry leaves and when he kissed her ears, Asuquo cried.

She wrapped her arms around him and laid her head on his chest until it was time to go. She knew he would continue making his way to her, though she told him it was too late. She'd underestimated the ugliness that had dug its roots underneath her village.

The elders came to Okon and Asuquo's home, a procession of slapping sandals, much of the village following. People looked through windows and doorways, many milling about outside, talking quietly, sucking their teeth, and shaking their heads. Above, a storm pulled its clouds in to cover the sky. The elders came and her husband brought chairs for them.

"We have spoken with those of the bush," one of them said. Then he turned around and a young man brought in the chop nut. Her husband and three men held her down as she struggled. Her eyes never met her husband's. One man with jagged nails placed the chop nut in her mouth and a man smelling of palm oil roughly held her nose, forcing her to swallow. Then they let go, and stepped back.

She wiped her nose and eyes, her lips pressed together. She got up and went to the window to look at the sky. The three young women and two young men watching through the window wordlessly stepped back with guilty looks, clearing her view of the gathering clouds. She braced her legs, willing her body to leave the ground. If she could get out the window into the clouds, she would be fine. She'd return for her sons once she had vomited up the chop nut.

But no matter how hard she tried, her body would only lift a centimeter off the ground. She was too tired. And she was growing more tired. All around her were quiet, waiting for the verdict.

The rumble of thunder came from close by. She stood for as long as she could, a whole half hour. Until her insides began to burn. The fading light flowing through the window began to hurt her eyes. Then it dimmed. Then it hurt her eyes again. She could not tell if it was due to the chop nut or the approaching storm. The walls wavered and she could hear her heartbeat in her ears. It was slowing. She lay back on the bed, on top of the rope Okon had used to tie her down.

Soon she did not feel her legs and her arms hung at her sides. The room was silent, all eyes on her. Her bare breasts heaved; sweat trickling between them. Her mind passed her garden to her boys and landed on her *chi*. Her mind's eye saw him floating in the sky, immobile, a frown on his face.

As the room dimmed and she left her body, he dropped from the sky only thirty miles south of Asuquo's village of Old Calabar. As he dropped he swore to the clouds that they would not see him for many many years. The wind outside wailed through the trees but within an hour it quickly died. The storm passed, without sending down a single drop of rain to nurture the forest. No Harmattan winds shook the trees that year. They had turned around, returning to the Sahara in disgust.

A year later, on the anniversary of Asuquo's death, the winds returned, though not so strong. Reluctant. They have since resumed their normal pattern. Her husband Okon went on to marry three wives and have many children. Asuquo's young boys were raised calling his first wife "mother" and they didn't remember the strange roots and fruits their real mother had brought from the forest that had made them strong.

As the years passed, when storytellers told of Asuquo's tale, they changed her name to the male name of Ekong. They felt their audience responded better to male characters. And Ekong became a man who roamed the skies searching for men's wives to snatch because he had died a lonely man and his soul was not at rest.

"There he is!" a boy would yell at the river, as the Harmattan winds blew dry leaves about. All the girls would go splashing out of the water, screaming and laughing and hiding behind trees. Nobody wanted to get snatched by the "man who moved with the breeze."

Nevertheless it was well over a century before the winds blew with true fervor again. But that is another story.

LONG JUJU MAN

In my village, everyone knows that there are ghosts.

We treat them like anyone or anything else; nothing new. But that day I walked down the path to my auntie's house to deliver a basketful of eggs was different. I was only nine years old.

My auntie lived a few minutes away, if I took the shortcut through the forest. I always chose to go this way because I liked the feeling of being alone with all the tall trees, chirping and cackling birds, and buzzing insects. Oftentimes if I walked quietly, I'd glimpse a curious monkey high in the trees.

This particular day was warm and there was a breeze in the treetops that went *shhhhhhh* as it passed through the leaves. I was in a wonderful mood. I didn't have a care in the world. I should have known something was off when I heard the owl hoot three times and saw a blue butterfly flutter by. Owls only hoot at night, and if a blue butterfly crosses your path it means something's about to happen—at least that's what my mother always says.

I'm a tiny woman. Back then I was an even tinier girl. However, my legs could move me fast as a terrified gazelle. And where I was short, I was tall in words. But still when I came across the wild mango tree heavy with rotting mangos, I was shocked into silence.

Right there, under the tree, picking the most rotten mangos was a ghost. And not just any ghost, either. It was the infamous Long Juju Man, himself! How frightening he was with long black beard, tall lanky body, and skin so brown it was the color of midnight. I stood there in shock. He hadn't seen me yet. When the wind blew, he would lose his shape, becoming solid again when it stopped.

Everything about him was blue like the ocean on a clear day. He wore a blue caftan that reached his knobby ankles and he was encircled by a soft blue aura. Wherever he stepped, he left a blue footprint that quickly melted away. He was stooping down, gathering the most rotted mangos. Everyone in my village knows that ghosts like to eat rotten fruit, for rotten fruits are beautifully sweet to the deceased.

He smelled strongly of red pepper. Even from where I stood, frozen with fear, I could smell him. My grandfather always said that Long Juju Man was a spicy man when he was alive. On moonlit nights, grandfather used to gather all the children. We would sit outside on the ground at his feet, my grandfather in his favorite chair. He would tell us stories that took us into the past and sometimes into the future. We loved to hear the story of Long Juju Man.

"Fifty years ago," my grandfather said, "Long Juju Man was the most talented sorcerer in the village. He could turn lead to gold, goat feces to blue butterflies; he loved blue butterflies. He could cure even the *nastiest* diseases. And he would do it all free of charge. But he also had a weakness for pranks. He'd make it rain on wedding days. Turn palm wine sour. Once he even used his juju to cast a spell on a chicken he was selling that filled it with air, making it appear plump.

"When he saw you, depending on how you behaved, he would decide to teach you something or play a prank on you. His snickering was most annoying. When you heard it, you knew he'd decided you weren't worthy of being taught and that something embarrassing would soon happen to you. No one knows why he was named after the famous Arochukwu shrine, Long Juju. Maybe because he was powerful as he was deceitful. Some like to say it was because 'his juju went a long long way.'

"But one day, he set up a trap for Joseph Okeke, a fat greedy lawyer known for swindling his clients. Long Juju Man dug a deep pit in front of Joseph's doorstep during the night. He lined the bottom of the pit with feathers he had cast a spell on to make them stick to whoever they touched. Then he cast a spell on the pit to make it invisible. Nevertheless, when he was done, Long Juju Man laughed so hard at the thought of the lawyer falling in that he slipped and fell into the pit himself. The pit was deep and the layer of feathers too thin. The fall killed him.

"But as a spirit, Long Juju Man still had things to do," my grandfather said. "Even after death, Long Juju Man continues playing his terrible jokes. So you all watch out for him. Watch your step at the market. He likes to pretend he is a beggar sitting on the ground. But when you pass him by, he'll stick his foot out and cause you to fall in front of everyone. If you are wearing your best Sunday church clothes, *do not hold babies.* Sometimes he will sneak up next to you and tickle the baby until it vomits with glee. And when you are bringing home a basket of eggs, make sure he doesn't see them because he'll break every single one!"

I remembered this last warning as I looked at the eggs my mother had given me to take to my aunt. My heart was beating fast because I couldn't believe I was actually seeing him, Long Juju Man, the ghostly genius joker. As my mother sent me out, she said, "Make sure you don't break even *one* of those eggs."

I had grumbled about how she never trusted me to do the simplest things. I was a confident nine-year-old. I believed in myself. But now I wasn't so sure. And I was terrified. As I stood there, his strong peppery scent wafted into my nose and I sneezed loudly. He turned around and his first reaction was to grin widely, as if he had a thousand teeth and he wanted to show every single one of them. I looked side to side. *Should I run?* I thought. A ghost could move faster than I could, especially on my short legs. No, I didn't run.

"Well, hello there," he said, snickering. His laugh went "hee hee hee," and if I weren't so afraid, I would have giggled myself. "What'cha got there?"

"Nothing important."

"Don't lie to me, little tiny girl," he said, scowling. "You're barely the size of a mushroom!"

"It doesn't matter, I'm not stupid."

"So you know who I am?" he asked.

"You're Long Juju Man," I said, holding my head up to show that I was not afraid. "And I'm not stupid," I said again. "I'm very very smart."

"No, you're very arrogant," he said, biting into a rotten mango. He closed his eyes, and savored the wonderful sweetness. When he opened them, they glowed bright blue. "Why do you travel alone?"

"Because I am confident in my . . . "

"Arrogance is not like confidence," he snapped, his nostrils flaring. I stepped back, afraid that he would pounce on me. Instead he snickered. "Do you not fear me? Do you not know what I am capable of?"

"Yes, I do," I said. "But I'm not . . . "

"Yes, you are," he said grinning. "Look at you with your puff puff hair and short short legs. I could have been a *jackal* and gnawed at your ankles!"

He melted into a blue haze and became a fox-like jackal with shaggy brown fur and pointy ears. He snarled at me and I shivered, but held strong.

I shook my head. "No, there are no jackals in these forests."

"I could have been a bad bad man come to *steal* you away!" he said, his jackal body loudly exploding into sparkles and blue butterflies and coming back together as a tall, mean-looking man with hunched shoulders, a dome-like protruding forehead and shady shifty eyes.

I shook my head again, "It is broad daylight and that is my uncle's house right over there. He likes to garden and he would hear me shout."

Long Juju Man held up a knobby finger and melted from the bad bad man into a thick fog, so thick that I couldn't see anything but blue smoke.

"I could be *confusion*," he said in a voice that sounded as if it were coming from everywhere. "I could make you lose your way!"

For a third time, I shook my head, this time smiling, "I have a sense of direction like a bird," I said. "I never lose my way."

Then I pointed north. "*That* way is north, toward my home."

Long Juju Man sucked his foggy self in and popped back to his original form. He stroked his beard, squinting at me, a smirk on his face. Then he nodded.

"You are a smart smart girl. That is good. I will be nice and not break your eggs. But I must give you a lesson before I let you go. Are you listening?"

I nodded, excited. I would certainly have a story to tell my friends when I got home. I would brag about how I outsmarted the craftiest ghost in all of history!

"You sure you are listening?" he said, his eyes narrowing.

"Yes, I am listening," I said.

"Good. Here is the lesson: What an old woman sees while lying down, a girl can never see even when she climbs up in a tree," he said. "It is only because I like you that I do not smash every last egg you carry. You should always be humble in your confidence and intelligence."

Then there was a popping sound and he disappeared in a shower of blue flowers that melted before they hit the ground. I quickly ran to my auntie's house, clutching the basket of eggs. When I got there, I was sweating from running and the strain of holding in a great story.

I knocked on the door, still out of breath. I heard the footsteps as my auntie approached the door but I heard something else, too. It was a crunching, cracking sound. I gasped when I looked down at the eggs just as auntie opened the door.

"Ngoli, my child," auntie said, smiling and smooching me on the cheek.

Then she looked at the eggs in the basket and gasped.

All of the eggs had hatched into fuzzy yellow chicks, cheeping and looking about in confusion. Wouldn't you be confused if you hadn't expected to hatch?

From somewhere, I heard Long Juju Man's snickers, "Hee hee heeee!"

THE CARPET

My sister and I didn't go to the market with the intention of buying a carpet for the new house. All we really wanted were some souvenirs to bring back to Chicago. We did buy a few ebony masks, some bead necklaces, a bronze statuette of the mermaid goddess Mami Wata, stuff like that. But those were insignificant in the grand scheme of things. How differently things would have gone at the new house had we not bought that . . . thing.

We were in Nigeria to visit our relatives. Our dad was sick so our mom stayed behind to care for him. I was fifteen and Zuma was sixteen. It was our first time visiting Nigeria without our parents. So, though we'd been there many times, it felt new, different, darker. No, those are the wrong words . . . more mysterious.

We spent the first few days of our trip with relatives in Abuja, which is a city in the central, drier, Muslim-dominated part of the country. On the third day, after we'd recovered from our jetlag, we went with our cousin Chinyere to the market. By the time we got back to the house, someone had picked my pocket of the few naira I carried, a group of Muslim men had shouted obscenities at my sister for wearing shorts, and two men threatened to smash my video camera because I had the nerve to record people at the market. This was a normal day.

On the fifth day, we were getting ready to travel to my father's village. It would be an eight-hour drive south. My parents had a house built in my father's village and my sister and I were to spend three days there before moving on to my mother's village. We went with our cousin Chinyere to the market one last time in search of a few more souvenirs.

"Just *ignore* this man," Chinyere said as we walked through the market and approached a really extravagant-looking booth. The man sitting at it was short and old, his potbelly pushing his long white caftan forward.

"Why?" I asked. My hands were shoved in my pockets to protect my money.

"The Junk Man lost his mind a long time ago," she said. "Everyone knows it."

If he's crazy then why is his booth packed with people checking his stuff out? I wondered. But I kept my mouth shut; I knew it would annoy Chinyere.

My sister, Zuma, was a few steps ahead. She hadn't heard Chinyere. Within moments, she had spotted something interesting and she too was drawn to the Junk Man's stuff. Chinyere groaned and rolled her eyes.

"One man's junk is another man's treasure!" the Junk Man announced, looking Chinyere right in the eye, as if challenging her. He turned to my sister Zuma. "Have a look-see, but none of it's free."

"Look at all his . . . things," I whispered to Zuma.

"I know, man," Zuma said, grinning.

"Just junk," Chinyere snapped, thoroughly annoyed.

The Junk Man's booth was the same size as everyone else's, about twenty feet across, separated from the utensil shop to his right and the basket shop to his left by wooden dividers. But all that was exposed of his twenty feet was a narrow path that led in a semi-circle through his "junk."

Everything was arranged. Some items were on tables, most on the ground, or hanging from nails on the wooden dividers. Knives, ebony statues, bronze statues, rings, necklaces and anklets of various metals, piles of colorful stones and crystals, ancient looking coins, brown, white, and black cowry shells of all sizes, some the size of my pinky fingernail, others larger than my head, scary and smiling ceremonial masks, an eight foot tall ebony statue of a large breasted stern looking goddess, a jar of gold powder, a pile of bejeweled and rusted daggers, baskets and bags of colored feathers.

"What you look for, ladies?" Junk Man asked us in his gruff voice, after helping a customer. The stool he sat on creaked as he shifted. He motioned to all his wares like a proud dragon. "Junk or jewels, I sell it to you at a good price."

"Do you mind if I look at . . . " Zuma pointed to the rolled-up carpet on one of his tables. It had golden tassels on its sides. That must have been what caught her eye. Zuma always loved anything that looked like something Scheherazade would own.

"Go ahead. Don't be shy," Junk Man said. "That's what all this is here for. But *don't touch* the things you don't think you should. And especially, don't touch those parrot feathers over there." He pointed to a bowl full of gorgeous green fluffy feathers. The things were practically begging to be touched. I frowned.

"For some reason, people don't know better," Junk Man said with a smirk. "Then they get home and wonder why all they want to do is chatter about nonsense."

Behind us, Chinyere sucked her teeth loudly and muttered, "See? Told you." Zuma and I looked at each other, uncomfortable. The man was either crazy or, seeing that we were American-born, he was trying to lay the mystery on thick. He thought we were like those stupid tourists who bought stuff because they thought it was "magical," like those people I saw buying fake voodoo dolls in New Orleans. Little did he know we'd been coming to Nigeria since we were five and six years old. The country was more like a second home, than the "dark continent" to us.

"Ooookay," Zuma said. "I'm gonna just look over here." As she moved through all his junk, she kept her hands close to her sides. The Junk Man chuckled and turned back to me.

"American?"

I nodded.

"Sisters?"

"Yeah," Zuma said as she looked at an ebony mask.

"Who's older? You?" he asked, pointing at me.

"No," I said. "She's a year older."

"Nah, that ain't older, you're practically twins," he said. "And you're the older one. Your sister hasn't been around as many times."

"Uh, sure," I said, trying not to look him in his wrinkly nearly black face.

"Parents born here?" he asked.

"Yeah," we both said.

"Then you from here."

I laughed hard. "If you say so."

I heard Chinyere loudly suck her teeth with irritation.

"You interested in that carpet?" he asked my sister.

"Sort of," Zuma said, putting down a large cowry shell and returning to the carpet.

He nodded. "Go ahead and unroll it." He snickered again. "It won't hurt you."

Zuma dragged the rolled carpet to Chinyere and me.

"This will be a good finishing touch to the house," she said. "A good house warming gift."

"I dunno," I said.

From what we'd been told, the house was already fully furnished. I wasn't sure if there would be room for it.

"It'll make the perfect gift, yes," the Junk Man said. Then he laughed again. The three of us ignored him and unrolled the carpet. People passing behind us kept getting annoyed, sucking their teeth and grumbling with impatience because the carpet took up part of the market path.

"Oh," I said, blinking with surprise. "It's really pretty."

"Yeah," Chinyere said quietly, all grins.

The carpet was a bright periwinkle color stitched with intricate symmetric geometrical winding designs of thick black threads. I could stare at it for hours. It was a nice piece of artwork, and the gold tassels were beautiful, too. Zuma quickly rolled it back up and said, "I want to buy this, sir. For . . . two thousand naira." That was about twenty dollars.

The Junk Man paused, looking intently at Zuma. Then he smiled. "Okay, let me wrap it up for you. Come on, bring it here."

Zuma grinned, surprised. But I felt a little annoyed. If a seller agreed quickly, then you'd proposed too high a price. But I know I would have also made the same mistake with such a beautiful carpet. Even Chinyere was surprised.

"It's worth over five thousand naira, I'd think. Even after bargaining down," Chinyere quietly told me. "He really *is* crazy."

★

Uncle Ralph drove us in his blue Mercedes. The eight-hour drive was long, grueling, and hot. We spent the last two hours on red dirt roads pock-marked with deep holes from the rainy season. Dusty and tired, we arrived in my father's village, our relatives running out and hugging, kissing, and inspecting us. The house was enormous and lovely, a white adobe mansion in rural Nigeria. However, when we went inside, we learned that the house was also completely and utterly unfurnished! Empty as hell! Apparently, over the last year, since buying the furniture and placing it in the house, relatives had gone in and taken everything. Piece by piece. Nice.

Beds, couches, dressers, tables, chairs, rugs, a refrigerator, all gone. The house also had no electricity or running water. To make matters worse, it was ridiculously dusty from being locked for months. It seemed massive house spiders dwelled in every corner, proud and fat as Shelob from *Lord of the Rings*. Then there were the pink wall geckos that scurried across the ceilings. These were okay because they were cute and ate the mosquitoes and small spiders; I doubted that they could eat the Shelobs. I also saw a pile of larger droppings upstairs in one of the rooms. Not a good sign.

After getting a tour of the house, we both stood there in what was called the Yoruba Room. Our Aunt Mary and Uncle Daniel stood behind us, quiet. Everyone else who had run out to greet us when we arrived had mysteriously disappeared as we walked into the house. The Yoruba Room was the largest in the house, with high ceilings and a lovely, though dusty, tiled mosaic of frolicking fish on the floor.

"But I thought . . . didn't you say that everything was here?" was all I could ask.

"Auntie, uncle," Zuma said, angry. "What happened?"

Uncle Daniel sighed and shook his head. "No one could stop them," he said. "No shame."

Zuma could barely contain herself. "Why didn't you tell . . . "

"We thought your parents would come with you," their aunt said. "We didn't think they'd come if they knew."

When people travel to Nigeria, they don't usually disclose who is traveling or when. You give as little detail as possible, or risk armed robbers waiting for your arrival or unscrupulous relatives from heaven and earth coming by to ask for this and that. Best to catch people off guard. People knew my father was sick, but they did not know the extent. That he would be having heart surgery soon. I pushed thoughts of my father's illness out of my mind.

"Well . . . " Zuma said. She turned and looked out the window at the sky. Then she said, "We're going to stay here tonight."

I gasped and said, "Zuma, I don't think . . . "

She gave me one of her icy big sister looks. I immediately shut up.

"This is our parent's house and we are their daughters. And we're in dad's village. We stay here," she said, her voice shaky with emotion and her fists clenched. I understood. Our relatives knew our father was sick, yet they took his furniture. This was his house and they robbed it. His home in his homeland. We would honor our father before all of them by staying in the house he and my mother built.

"You don't have to," my aunt said, looking worried. She motioned to the house next door. "Please, you will stay with us . . . "

"No," Zuma firmly said. "We stay here."

And that is how we found ourselves in a dusty, creepy, empty but lovely house in the middle of semi-rural southeastern Nigeria with no running water or electricity, the only furniture being a bed my aunt had had carried in and the carpet Zuma bought. We were to stay there for three days.

The village was made up of the gigantic and not so gigantic houses of our relatives but it was also surrounded by lush forest that used to be farmed for yams and other crops back in the day. This meant there were probably all sort of creatures living in that house.

In the evening, after pleading with us one more time, my aunt had a group of girls bring us a tray of red stew, rice, fried plantain, and two bottles of orange Fanta for dinner. We were so hungry and exhausted that it was the most delicious food we'd ever tasted. The girls also brought a barrel of well water for bathing. Even after washing in the dirty bathtub with cups of freezing water, it was still sweltering hot in the room we'd locked ourselves in.

"Geez!" I said, scratching at my itchy sweaty scalp. I planned to dunk my head in a bucket of water to wash my braids tomorrow. "How are we going to sleep in this heat?"

Zuma shrugged, sitting on the bed, looking miserably at the lit candles.

"I almost want to dump water on myself, soak my clothes and the bed!" I whined. I held my little battery-powered hand fan to my face. I sat beside her. We crossed our legs on the bed, afraid to touch the floor with our bare feet. "And we're probably gonna get bitten up by mosquitoes with that open window . . . "

"Will you just shut up?" Zuma snapped. "If you want to run to uncle and auntie's house, go! I'm staying here. What are we supposed to tell mom and dad when we get back? You think this is gonna make dad *feel* better? That a bunch of his relatives are greedy jerks even when he's sick? Who cares about mosquitoes, man. This is . . . "

Then we heard it and we both shut up.

Softly, *scrape, scrape.* Then *clunk,* like something falling. Then a more continuous *scraaaaape.*

It was coming from downstairs.

"What's that?" I whispered.

"Shhh!" she hissed.

Scrape, scrape. Quiet. Minutes passed. Then more *scrape, scrape.* It seemed to be moving away from us, toward the front of the house downstairs. We stayed frozen like that all night. Listening. Come morning, we were still in the same position. In the village, there were night-sounds that were normal, like the hoot of an owl, the clicks and chirps of insects, the screech of some animal we couldn't name. But what we'd heard was in the house and it only stopped at about the same time that the sun rose.

Someone knocking on the door forced us to leave our room.

"Hey," I said, smiling tiredly, as we slowly walked down the stairs. I pointed at one of the ceiling corners. "Looks like those nasty spiders are taking off because of us. The webs aren't just empty but it looks like the spiders actually cut them down."

"Cool," Zuma said. "I guess they aren't so stupid. I was gonna ask Tochi to come and crush them all today."

"Good morning," our aunt said when we opened the door. She carried a tray of breakfast: bottles of water, thick pieces of buttered bread, scrambled eggs, and a tin of sardines. She looked extremely relieved to see that we were okay.

"Good morning," we both said.

"How was your night?"

"Not so great, but we made it," I said.

"It was fine," Zuma said taking the tray. "Thanks for breakfast. It looks great."

We quickly ran back upstairs, anxious to eat. Zuma would be the only one eating the sardines, though. Those are nasty. As we walked past the Yoruba Room, I glanced in. Then I stopped.

"What the heck?" I shouted. "I knew something was missing downstairs!"

"What?" Zuma asked anxiously. She obviously wanted to eat before doing anything else.

I ran into the room without answering. "But how?" I said. "How did it get here?"

"No way," Zuma said, running up next to me, when she saw the carpet. "Did we lock all the doors?"

We spent the next several minutes relocking every door in the house and then locking all the rooms that had windows. "Someone snuck in here last night and is trying to mess with our heads by moving our carpet around," Zuma angrily said as she locked a door. "Not gonna happen again."

That night, night number two, we slept a little better. We were exhausted and went to bed at seven p.m. Plus, knowing that the noises were probably made by human beings related to us and that all the doors were locked set our minds at ease. At least until about four a.m. when we heard that scraping sound again. I was terrified, thinking maybe this time the noise was armed robbers or . . . zombies. My sister, she took it all a different way.

"Dammit," Zuma hissed angrily. "They're not gonna drive us out. This is *so* mean." She got off the bed, this time not caring that her feet were bare.

"What are you doing?" I whispered loudly.

"Gonna see who the hell that is!"

Next thing I knew, she was opening the door and going into the hallway with the flashlight.

"Wait!" I whispered, creeping behind her.

Quietly, we moved down the stairs, toward the scraping sound. My sister peeked around the corning, staying on the last stair. She flashed her flashlight. She gasped. "Shit!"

"What is it? What do you . . . "

She grabbed my hand and we ran up the stairs.

"What? What?" I shouted. "*What?*"

She pushed me into the room, slammed the door and locked it. Then she shut the window.

"Okay," Zuma said, calming down, sinking to the floor. "Okay, okay, okay, okay, okay. Oh my God, I wish we'd have . . . no, not really. Just . . . man. Alright."

"*What?*" I sobbed, sitting next to her with my heart pounding. She didn't answer. For minutes, we both just sat there, quiet and listening and sweating. The scraping had stopped.

"What was it?" I finally asked again.

My sister turned to look at me with red-rimmed eyes.

"A snake, a big black snake."

★

We spent most of the next day outside with our cousins. We didn't tell anyone about the snake. After sitting there feeling tired and scared and confused, we had both silently thought about dad and decided to spend the last night in the house. One more night. And then the wildlife in the house could do whatever it wanted . . . until people were hired to clean the place up.

Zuma said that the snake was over four feet in length and thick in body. That it was a dusty black and had yellow eyes. We assumed it was poisonous and that it had probably been prowling the house at night searching for rats or mice or whatever else lived in the house.

Our cousins took us for a walk down to a nearby lagoon and for hours after that we sat and played cards and forgot about our troubles. But eventually we had to return to the house. And that night was the most disturbing of them all. We'd locked the door as always and then we listened for the snake to start its foraging. Around three a.m., it started.

"Let's go see," I said. It was our last night in the house and, of course, I was scared, but something in me wanted to see that snake. If only to be able to talk about it when we got back to Chicago.

At first Zuma looked at me like I was crazy. It was a similar look to the one I had given the crazy Junk Man back in that Abuja market. Then she smiled. "Alright. Let's go."

We crept out the room with our flashlight and tiptoed to the staircase, but we didn't go down. We didn't get to see the snake either. Why? Because the carpet was on the stairs. No, it wasn't just on the stairs, it was creeping *up* the stairs. It moved like some giant stingray. We stumbled back as it glided by, hovering about an inch or two off the floor as it swam through the air. Zuma followed it with the flashlight.

Once it disappeared around the corner with a flick of a golden tassel, we both made a run for it to our room and shut the door. Then we just sat on the bed, speechless. I thought about the Junk Man. He would have laughed hard at the two of us trembling in our room like that. Shocked and shivering and mentally shifted. Shit.

"Did you see . . . "

"Shhh," my sister said as we sat there.

"It was a flying carpet!"

"Shhh," my sister snapped. "Don't talk or something. What if it hears us?"

"Well, we've been here how many days. I think it's probably safe to say . . . "

"Mukoso, shut up!" she said. "And it wasn't a flying carpet; it kinda just crept over the floor and stuff."

"Whatever, man. A carpet isn't supposed to move!"

"*No*, really?"

What we both agreed on was that neither of us was leaving the room again that night. Not with snakes and carpets and shit creeping and fluttering around the house. Danger abounded. So we stayed there and went to sleep. For the first time, we slept through what remained of the night. Be it from shock, mental fatigue, or just common sense, it didn't matter.

We woke up hours after sunrise, around eight in the morning. We dressed and washed in silence. And when our aunt came with breakfast, we didn't say a word. Instead we went and sat on the floor in the Yoruba Room and ate.

As we sat there with the empty plates, my sister nibbling on a sardine, I said, "Let's go find it."

"Why?"

"Why not?" I said. "We're leaving today . . . plus, it doesn't move during the day, at least thus far. I . . . don't . . . think, at least." I shook my head. "Come on, let's go *see* it."

"I . . . I dunno," she said. "Let's just get outta here and act like . . . "

"But it did!" I said with wide eyes. "We saw it, man."

We found it in the kitchen.

"Hello?" I said loudly.

Zuma frowned.

I shrugged. "Just making sure," I said.

Even as we looked at it, neither of us was dumb enough to start doubting what we'd seen last night. Sure, it was dark, yes, we were tired, and we were scared. But we'd seen what we saw; this periwinkle carpet with black thread designs and golden tassels was alive. And maybe now it was asleep. Who knew?

We stepped into the room, staying close together. Then slowly, we walked up to it. Still, it didn't move. It was spread out flat, taking up about a third of the kitchen's floor. There were a few lumps in it.

I squatted down and touched one of the rug's golden tassels. Then quickly before I changed my mind I lifted and threw the rug back over itself. We both jumped back. What we saw underneath still haunts me to this day. There was a big pile of those huge spiders, black, crushed, and dead. There were also several large dead rats and the brown black body of a smashed scorpion, too! To top it off, there was the black snake. I got to see it for myself after all. Coiled up, scaly black-skinned, and dead as all the other creatures under the carpet.

As we stood there, the carpet rippled and began to turn itself over and flatten itself out. Then it floated away from us a bit; later I would think it did this almost shyly. We didn't wait to see anymore. That was enough. We ran upstairs, packed our things, and dragged them down the stairs, trying not to look toward the kitchen. We spent the remaining hours in our aunt and uncle's house. I could almost hear the Junk Man laughing his giggly laugh.

★

As the airplane took off, flying us back to the United States, I couldn't help but think about the next time we'd visit. I had a feeling that the flying carpet that lived in our house was one piece of furniture our relatives would not steal.

"You think it'll be there when we go back?" I asked Zuma.

Zuma looked at me, then we both started laughing. We laughed and laughed until we looked out the window. Then I nearly screamed and Zuma just stared.

Do I need to say what we saw?

ICON

Journal Entry

This is going to be a good story. African rebels with the audacity and ability to cripple America's crude oil supply. Priceless. I am the smartest man alive. "Heart of Darkness," my ass. Feels so good to be back on the continent. The moment this plane touches the ground, the adventure begins. Watch me win a Pulitzer for this shit. Got to prepare notes and questions now. More journaling when I return from the swamp . . .

★

The mangrove trees looked like frozen many-legged beasts staring at something about to happen. The boatmen had the same looks of frightened anticipation as they rowed the small boat through the quiet waters. Thankfully the sun was on its way up.

Richard and Nancy wore jeans and long sleeve shirts despite the heat. They'd doused themselves with pungent-smelling insect repellent, too. The two boatmen, muscular men in their twenties, wore nothing but shorts. Nonetheless it was Richard and Nancy who were getting bitten up by mosquitoes and gnats. The swamp creatures obviously had a preference. Richard couldn't even feel the stealth insects bite. He tried to ignore his thoughts of malaria. Not a disease he wanted to catch again.

Even this early in the morning, the heat was thick and tangible. It settled on him like a heavy blanket and baked and stewed his skin. Even after a good shower, he still felt dirty. Couple all this with his super peppery, palm-oily breakfast of egg stew, fried plantain, and yam and it was no wonder he felt all around goddamn itchy and hot as hell.

"Fuck!" Nancy said, slapping the side of her face. Her hand left a red print.

"Almost there," one of the boatmen said. He pointed ahead. "See?"

Amongst the mangrove trees, dense bushes, and leafy palm trees, the village was a mere cluster of thatch roofed huts. Scrawny chickens strutted boldly about and a goat *baa*-ed from beside a hut. Richard could see people starting their day. Mainly women. They wore old rapas, t-shirts, and cheap plastic flip-flops. The air smelled of cooking fires and heated palm oil. The women swept floors, carried buckets of water on their heads, and chatted. Some stopped and shielded their eyes as they watched the approaching boat.

From somewhere, a boom box played Erykah Badu's "I Want You." Richard smiled to himself as he scratched a mosquito bite on his back. He loved that song. Nice to know it traveled far. They passed the village and moved slowly to a small bank a few yards beyond the last hut.

"Doesn't look so bad," Nancy said as Richard climbed out of the boat into the knee deep brackish water. He tried not to look down, afraid he might see a snake or some other biting venomous creature swimming around his boots. He'd already spotted a huge water bug. And something large and white rolled to the water's surface and disappeared a few feet away.

He focused on the village. Nancy was right. It didn't look like the hideout of rebels with nothing to lose. He frowned. For the first time since leaving New York, he felt a tiny pinch of doubt.

A month earlier, Richard had written a story for *Newsweek* about a "pirate" attack off the Nigerian coastline. They'd come in broad daylight firing AK-47s at a fishing trawler. They shot the ship's chef before the eyes of the crew. The poor man had bled out as the pirates stripped the ship of its valuables and causally ate the meal the chef had been preparing. Then they made their escape. But not before being spotted by three police patrol boats.

"I saw the whole chase," a fisherman told Richard. "The police were right behind them, three big speedboats! *Brrrt! Brrrt!* They blasted away at the tiny speedboat. How did they get away? Only the Blessed Father knows."

The story was significant because the culprits were from the NDPM, the Niger Delta People's Movement, a Nigerian terrorist organization bent on sabotaging and destroying any efforts Shell and other oil companies made to extract oil from this strip of the Niger Delta. Pirating was one of their ways to make money and gather supplies, the others being email fraud and kidnapping.

Richard spoke with three other witnesses and it was the same perplexed story. Somehow, though the police were in close pursuit and shooting like crazy, not one of the rebels was hit. Then the small boat entered the place where the police could not follow, the swamp's waterways. Only the locals could safely navigate them. It was excellent stuff. Richard wanted more. But when he tried to set up a meeting with these elusive rebels, he was coldly dismissed. Until now.

Mud squished under his boots as he made for the bank, a mosquito buzzed in his ear, something hissed and moved in the bushes to his left. He almost slipped and dropped his laptop bag in the water. "Shit," he hissed. When he looked up, he jumped back as fifteen AK-47-toting men came striding up the path. They wore dark green camouflage and black face masks with fresh green leaves stuck through the sides of the mouth and eye holes. They were all barefoot except for a few wearing flip flops and one who wore boots.

They had chains of bullets around their shoulders and necks. It was a grand show, Richard had to admit. One of the barefoot men also had a machete sheathed at each hip. From what Richard could see, they were all grown men, except two or three who were closer to ten years old.

He looked back. "N . . . Nancy, hurry up," he said.

She clambered out of the boat and fumbled with her bag as she tried to get one of her cameras out. "Come on," she muttered to herself.

"No pictures yet," one of the men demanded in a low imposing voice.

"Who are you?" the one with the machetes asked. He was not the tallest but he was tall and had a chest like defined steel, accentuated by the fact that he wore no shirt under his open, sleeveless fatigue vest. His chest was covered with symbols that looked drawn with a red marker. Richard could also glimpse a bit of a large elaborate red green dragon head tattooed on the left side of his chest. It probably extended over his shoulder down his back.

"We're the journalists who wish to interview members of the NDPM," Richard said, working to sound brave.

"Names?"

"Richard Banks."

"Nancy Armond."

The machete- and gun-toting man looked at Nancy, his head cocked. A cell phone rang from somewhere. The ring tone reminded Richard of the sound Tinker Bell made in the Disney Peter Pan movie. He bit his lip as the thought took him to the face of his five-year-old daughter. Another pinch of doubt.

The machete and gun-toting man reached into his pocket, brought out and answered his phone. "They're here," he said. He glanced at Richard and then Nancy. "A black American with short Bob Marley and a fat white woman named after almonds. She carries many camera, like flowers in a bouquet."

A few of the others snickered. He looked at Richard and Nancy as he listened. Though Richard couldn't see his face, he thought the man's eyes looked feral; this guy was definitely capable of doing some really crazy shit. The madman folded his phone and said, "Come with me." He turned to two of his men. "Obi, Effong, make sure their boat stays." He pointed at the two boatmen. "I know who all your wives are."

The boatmen looked terrified but nodded. "We stay here, sir," one of them meekly said. "No *wahala*, sir. No *wahala*."

"We have more things on the boat," Richard said.

"Nah, leave your shit here," the madman said. "For now."

Richard and Nancy nodded, exchanging a confident look. They were in. They followed the militants into the bush.

"You have your cell phone?" Richard asked Nancy in a low voice.

Nancy nodded. "But I don't know why I'm here if I can't use my cameras."

"We're just getting clearance," he said.

They walked along the dirt path for about twenty minutes. A strong morning sun lit the sky but little of its light made it through the dense foliage. Nor did much of a breeze. The heat and humidity pressed so heavily on Richard that his ears were ringing.

By the time they got to the first village hut, Richard and Nancy were prickly with fresh mosquito, fly, and gnat bites, and drenched with sweat, and their boots were heavy with mud. They'd taken the scenic route. *As if we couldn't see how close the damn village was from the boat,* he thought, annoyed. He could even see their boat sitting in the same place, yards away.

In the village, some old men sat at a small table staring at them as they passed. A woman was in front of her hut knitting a fishing net. A baby in yellow pants and a green shirt happily crawled around her. It was from inside this woman's hut that the Erykah Badu music blared. Now it was playing "On and On."

They stopped in front of four plastic white chairs.

"Sit," the madman instructed. Richard and Nancy quickly did so. He turned to one of the boy militants. "Saturday, go and get me something."

The boy named Saturday went into a nearby hut. A group of more militants, all masked and armed, sat inside another hut having a loud lively conversation in a language Richard could only identify as not being Igbo or Yoruba. One of these men came out to meet the madman. They greeted and spoke to each other in the same foreign language. The man might have been the tallest man Richard had ever seen.

"Damn, what a fucking giant," Nancy whispered.

"Gotta be what? Over seven feet tall?" Richard replied.

"How'd they find camouflage fatigues to fit *him*?" Nancy whispered after a moment.

"I was wondering the same thing," Richard said.

"They've got money."

"Yeah."

"This piss poor village is a cover."

"Yep," he said. "We're not in yet." His fingers ached to write this all down just as Nancy's probably ached to take pictures of these men.

A more ordinary looking militant joined the wild and tall one just as the boy named Saturday came out carrying a bottle of whiskey. The wild one grinned and took the bottle. He mumbled something and poured a bit to the side. Then he took a deep gulp. *Great*, Richard thought. *Alcohol is all this one needs.* He handed it to the tall one who did the same and then handed it to the ordinary-looking one who, without drinking any, came over and offered it to Nancy.

Nancy paused, and looked at it. She smirked. "Sure," she said, taking it and taking a swig. This was so like her.

The wild one laughed as did the others. "You're supposed to give it to the man first, almond woman," he said. He shook his head. "You American women are something else." He pulled up a plastic chair and sat across from them. The other two stood behind him.

Nancy handed the whiskey to Richard who took a swig and then handed it back to Nancy who took another. She handed it back to the wild one. For several minutes they passed the whiskey around and soon the bottle was empty. Richard found himself feeling nicely spirited. He'd just begun to relax when the wild one who seemed to be the leader suddenly jumped up, his cell phone ringing its twinkle tune.

"So what are those symbols?" Richard asked, slightly slurring his words. "What do they all mean?"

But the leader had brought out his cell phone and was looking at the screen. He seemed to be reading something. *A text message*, Richard thought. *Whoever it was doesn't want this guy speaking out loud.* He exchanged an uneasy look with Nancy.

"Icon," the tall one said. "The man wants to know about your symbols."

Even through the thin mist of whiskey, Richard heard, caught, and shelved the name in his mind. Icon. The wild one who was the leader was named Icon. Didn't sound Nigerian at all.

"Eh?" Icon asked, his attention still on the screen of his cell phone. "Okay," he muttered, putting his phone back in his pocket. He looked up. "Almond woman, do you want to know, too?"

Nancy shrugged and nodded. "What I want is to take your picture, but sure, I wouldn't mind knowing."

"Whipping boy!" Icon called. "Get your ass over here." An unmasked boy immediately came running. He couldn't have been more than nine. He wore a tattered black t-shirt and old looking jeans. He had three short black lines etched into each cheek. Richard wasn't sure if these tribal markings were Hausa or Yoruba; one of those, definitely.

Icon brought a small jar from his pocket and grabbed the boy by the shirt collar. The others in the hut came out to watch.

"Every soldier must do his time," Icon said, as he dipped his finger in the white paste that was in the jar. He was breathing heavily with excitement. Richard suddenly had a very bad feeling.

"Richard?" he heard Nancy moan beside him.

"Shh, quiet," Richard hissed. "Don't bring any attention to yourself." Still, he was curious to see what this man was about to do.

Icon smeared paste onto the boy's face. He drew a circle on the boy's forehead and what looked like a Star of David on the boy's bare arm. Then he stood back. "They call me Icon because I can draw 'icons,' loaded symbols that speak the unexpected," he said. "The fucking kill-and-go and all those *oyibo* white men who come here and hunt us like chicken . . . " He grinned and shook his head. "Give this boy a gun and it becomes a different game." He pointed his gun at the boy. All the men around him quickly moved away from him.

"Icon, dis no be necessary, o," the tall one said in his low voice. The ordinary one shook his head with obvious pity but did nothing to stop it.

"What the fuck?" Nancy shouted.

"Hey! No! Don't! Wait!" Richard screeched, holding up his hands. "We believe you! We . . . we've read the papers! We're journalists! You believe in Egbesu, right? The . . . the deity of warfare? That's what those symbols mean, right?"

"That is superstitious bullshit," Icon said, his gun still pointed at the boy. "I want you to report what you see here. This is the real thing, my man. Oh, wait." He brought down his weapon. Richard sighed with relief. Icon strode over to him. "Better yet, *you* shoot him," Icon said.

Richard backed away. "What?"

Several of the militants immediately pointed their weapons at both Richard and Nancy.

"What did you think when you came here?" Icon asked, cocking his head. "That you would shake my hand and call me brother without really getting your hands dirty? Just like a typical Black American." He paused, glaring at Richard. "It is time for you to go."

Richard whimpered, stealing a glance at Nancy. "Okay," he said. "Fine . . . *fine*! We'll go!"

"We had no intention of letting either of you in," Icon added. "Our great leader Biko Niko is a man of his word. He told you 'no' in his email, yet you think by throwing your money around you will still get in? You have no respect."

Several of the militants sucked their teeth loudly and grumbled agreement.

"I . . . I'm sorry." Richard said.

"We both are," Nancy added.

"Go," Icon said. As Richard made to move in the direction they'd come, Icon grabbed his arm and said, "But first, you get your hands dirty." He shoved the gun in Richard's hands and stood back. "Pull the trigger or my men shoot you."

Richard stood there with the AK-47 in his hands. He'd never held a gun. It was heavier than he'd imagined. Were these even NDPM militants? He was no longer sure. But one thing he knew was that he and Nancy were on their own. He twitched, the gun pointing at the cowering boy.

"I won't!" Richard cried, his body beginning to shake. "No way!" He glanced at the boy and quickly looked away. He couldn't stop the tears of terror from running down his or the boy's face.

"Look at this fucking white black man," one of the militants goaded. "Idiot *akata*. What's doing you? No *blokkus*."

Richard just stood there, sobbing. Some of the men began to laugh. Nancy tried to give him a reassuring look. It helped. He took a deep breath and started to calm down. A little humiliation was better than killing a little boy. He was looking down at the gun in his hands when Icon swiftly stepped up to him from behind, grasped his finger, and squeezed.

Blam!

The boy that they called Whipping Boy was blown right off his feet, his flip-flops flying in different directions. He hit the ground and was instantly silent.

★

Journal Entry

I've returned from the swamp covered with its slime.

Only in this journal will I say shit about what happened.

I'm still shaken. I'm still in shock. I hope this plane back to New York crashes. Why should I return home?

How can I have done what I did?

This is what I happened:

That crazy mutherfucker who calls himself Icon, the one who draws symbols, he put that poor boy there. No more than a few feet away. Imagine bullets smashing into your body from that close proximity! Now imagine that you are just a poor down-trodden boy who was trying to be a part of something you sensed was destined for greatness.

Now imagine that you are me, an African American searching for an African story within an African story, who's never touched a fucking gun in his fucking life, despite all the stereotypes about black men, who's never seen someone die or murdered, who grew up poor but not desperate on the south side of Chicago, whose parents were teachers who were part of the civil rights movement, you see this little boy's smooth dark brown skin, sweat on his smooth forehead, terror in his young face. He has sad dark eyes that haven't seen much because he has only been alive for about nine, ten years, nearly the same age as my own son.

Icon's gun was warm from his hands when he shoved it into my hands. Then he pressed my palm to it. That man was full of a kind of heat that could get near and tear out the throat of any president. I stood close to him. I felt that heat. I know. I know.

My hands shake as I write this. I'm a murderer. Africa made me a murderer.

The boy was shaking. The Whipping Boy.

Icon pressed my finger to the trigger and I twitched. It was my finger that caused the gun to shoot. My reflex. My nerves. It was my arrogant presence that brought me to that place to put me in that position to kill a little boy.

My God, I should have known better! Nigeria is a fucking jungle full of jungle people.

I blew the boy off his feet. His flip-flops flew off. Both of them.

The smell of hot steel, burned flesh, my hands slippery with black gun oil and the sound of Nancy hyperventilating as she fell to her knees and that fucking fucker Icon laughing and smacking me on the shoulder and saying, "Well done. Well done!"

And I sunk to the muddy ground, my quivering hand over my mouth, hollering, "What have I done? What have I done?" Some bird screeched from nearby. No wind blew. The morning sky above was clear, not a cloud, blue as can be. It should have been black. It should have split open to let hell swallow me up.

I had been so sure those men would kill me if I didn't shoot the boy. I didn't want to die. But I didn't want the boy to die either. He was my son's age. He was like my son.

Icon was still chuckling as he walked up to the boy's body and pulled him up and dusted the kid off.

"Well done, Victor," Icon told the boy.

Victor, that was the boy's real name. Not fucking Whipping Boy. Or maybe Victor was now his name and it was something else before I shot him. A name of rebirth because I swear that boy was dead!

Victor looked bewildered, there were tears on his face but . . . he was otherwise unscathed. Just fine. The boy looked at me and nodded. I stared. Stared at the symbols on his chest. He had been a few feet away. I did not miss. And I'd seen him blown back. Smoke wafting from his chest. He'd lost his flip-flops.

I saw a white flash. Nancy had pulled herself together enough to do what she came to do. Several men aimed their guns at her.

"No, no," Icon said, motioning for the men to stand down. "We have nothing to hide."

I don't know about that.

Neither of us spoke on the boat that took us from that village. They dropped us off on land near a busy road not far from our hotel with one final warning.

"When you write about us in newspaper," one young man said, "tell the world this: If you people don' listen, if your oil companies don' get out, we crumble your economy. And maybe we take down Nigeria economy, too. You go see dis country fall to small small pieces like Biafra War. We at war with everyone. And like you know, we hard to kill. No one go at peace till you people listen to us." Then they sped off in a hail of splashing water.

Nancy showed me the photo on her computer. She hadn't only taken one. Nancy has balls, no doubt. The first was a dark photo of the boy just after Icon drew the symbols of him. Nancy truly has courage. She'd turned off the flash and held the camera discreetly at her side when she took the photo.

Despite the shade from the trees, the six point star on the boy's arm and the circle on his forehead glowed a soft pink. And they looked crisp and clear and solid. I noted how perfect the star and circle looked. As if it had been made on a computer and not by Icon's hand, the thickness the same all the way around.

Speaking of hands, the second photo, which was of some of the militants standing nearby, caught a bit of Icon, mainly his hands, and a bit of his chest. I don't think any phenomena in the photos were glitches from the camera and neither does Nancy. There was a pink vapor emanating from his hands all the way up to his elbows. And more of it wafted from his chest.

The third photo was a full shot of Icon standing there looking powerful and smug, and there was the pink vapor again, coming from his chest and dripping from his hands like liquid heat. I didn't see this vapor when I was there.

That place is a cesspool. Oil companies should get out while they can. Who knows what all the pollution and exploitation has made those people into? And who the fuck cares? Leave it alone. Fuck Africa, fuck Nigeria. Fuck history. And fuck this story. Nobody is ever going to hear it.

THE POPULAR MECHANIC

Anya was high up in a palm tree when her mother called. She thrust her hand into her pocket, fumbling for her portable. "Shit," she hissed, as it screeched the Nigerian national anthem a second time. Finally, she grasped and held it before her face, shielding the tiny screen from the sun's glare. "Hello? Hello? Hi, mama."

She clutched the tree with her thighs and leaned back against her leather sling.

"Can you hear me, Anya?" her mother asked.

"Yes, mama," Anya said. She frowned. She could see the brown rosary in her mother's hands. Something was wrong.

"Are you in a tree?" her mother asked, looking past Anya.

"I just finished my first semester in *medical* school, mama," Anya said with a small smile. "No lectures about palm wine tapping only being for men. It relaxes me." She paused. "Mama, what's wrong?"

"I don't want to alarm you. Especially if you're in a tree."

"Mama, just tell me."

"Come home immediately . . . Your father . . . "

Anya's heart jumped in her chest. "Is he okay?"

"I don't know," her mother said, now looking openly distraught. When Anya had returned from school a week ago, she was surprised at how tired her mother looked. Even now Anya could see the bags under her mother's eyes.

"What do you mean?" she asked, grasping her sling.

"He isn't here! I don't know where he went! He's in one of his moods . . . he threw a wrench at me. He was yelling . . . in English."

"Shit," Anya hissed. It was always English when he was angry. She brought her phone closer to her face. She didn't see any bruises, at least not on her mother's face. "Mama . . . "

"I'm fine. Just come home."

"I'm on my way."

She folded her cell phone and put it in her pocket. With a shaky hand, she pulled the wooden straw from the large bunch of shiny red palm kernels just below the tree's crown and put it in her pocket. The round gourd she'd hung just below the straw was full of milky-white palm sap. She held the gourd to her nose and closed her eyes for a moment. It smelled so very sweet and flowery. Once fermented, it would make a good batch of palm wine. Her father would be delighted.

"If I can find him," she mumbled.

Though tapping palm wine was considered a man's job, it was Anya's favorite hobby. She'd always loved climbing trees but she'd started tapping palm wine when she was fifteen. It had brought a rare smile to her father's face that first time and she'd been doing it since. Nevertheless, despite her efforts, as time progressed, she saw her father smile less and less. These days, he was in "one of his moods" quite often. Volunteering his body to the American scientists had been the biggest mistake of his life.

If there was one thing Anya had learned in the past year it was that if something was not broken, *don't try to fix it.* She and her medical school friends debated about this quite often. Anya was always the one wildly against any surgery that made a good normal life even "better." To Anya, if a medical condition wasn't life threatening, or possibly a crippling deformity, then it should be left alone to do as nature wished it. Her father's life had not been in danger, nor was he deformed. He'd just had one arm.

Anya's mother was a schoolteacher and her father was a mechanic who owned a spare parts shop. Anya hadn't grown up rich but her parents were always able to give her what she needed. Ten years ago, when she was thirteen, her father made what would turn out to be the second biggest mistake of his life.

"Did you hear about it?" her father had said as he ran into the house that day, a big grin on his face. "One of the pipelines in the forest burst! Free fuel!"

Nigeria was one of the world's top oil producers. Yet and still, as the years progressed, the Nigerian government had grown fat with wealth harvested from oil sales to America. The government, to the great detriment of the country, ate most of the oil profits and could care less about what the process of extracting the oil did to the land and its people. On top of all this, ironically, Nigeria's people often suffered from shortages of fuel.

Anya's father's business thrived more from the sale of bicycle and *okada* parts and portables and computer repair than anything to do with cars and trucks. Fuel in Nigeria was liquid treasure. On the black market it was more valuable than clean water. Thus a burst pipeline attracted desperate pirates of all kinds.

Anya's father grabbed two buckets and was off. Anya had heard him describe what happened next many times over the years. It was usually after he'd had several cups of her palm wine. When his mouth grew loose and pensive. He usually told the story in Igbo.

★

I ran to the site with great speed. I was so excited, *o*! With those buckets of fuel do you know how many bicycle parts I could transport in that useless piece of shit truck we have?

Since I'm big and strong, I was easily able to get to the front. There was a big big pool of fuel and over a hundred people gathered around it. It was like a pink pond. The fuel was coming out of the pipe like a fountain! Men, women, children, Igbos, Ogonis, Efiks, Yorubas, Hausas, Ijaw. We all may fight a lot but we're all here together struggling, too. I even saw a white man there! We all needed fuel. Bowls, bottles, buckets, wheelbarrows, and jerricans; we used whatever we could to collect it.

The smell was overwhelming, *o*! Stung my nose and stuck to my clothes. We all withstood it with runny noses, turning our heads to the side and spitting, thinking we could just wash our clothes and bodies afterwards. Drink lots of water, beer, and palm wine to cleanse our systems. Fill our bellies with fu fu, soup, and plantain once our containers were full. It was madness. It's still madness. Look what that damn government has turned us into. Robot zombies scrambling for a sip of fuel!

I remember laughing as I ran home with those full buckets. On the way, I passed a market women carrying buckets of all shapes and sizes balanced on her head; she'd come to cash in on things, too. Smart smart woman. I put down my buckets and fished out some naira and bought two more from her. I balanced them on my head and went home.

You remember this part, right, Anya? When I came home with the fuel, put it down, and took the new buckets back for more? You kept asking what I was doing but I was too hurried to answer. One bucket was bright orange and one was blue. Oh, if it weren't for that lady being there to sell them to me. But how can I blame her? Eh? She was just being business savvy, no? I'd have done the same if that were my trade.

So I was on my way back. When I got there, I was about to step around a group of fat women and elbow my way in again. They were laughing and talking about selling the fuel they collected. We all were going to make a fortune. That's when it happened. I heard it first, a soft "phwwwooom!" Then all became heat and light. I don't remember a thing after that. Just waking up in that filthy sloppy slimy hospital.

★

Someone near the pool of gasoline had needed a cigarette and lit a match. Anya's father was burned on his face and his entire right arm was burned to the bone. He was *very* lucky. He'd not been that close to the gasoline pool and burst pipe and the bodies of the plump laughing women in front of him had shielded him from the giant fireball that rushed past them all like an unleashed demon. All of those women died. Anya's father was one of fifteen survivors. All together, ninety-nine people were killed in the explosion, including an infant who'd been strapped to her mother's back.

Anya's father ended up having his severely-burned arm amputated and undergoing several surgeries on his face. He'd returned to his spare parts shop months later, plagued by nightmares of pain, fire, gasoline, and burned flesh. Still, he was as strong and ambitious as ever. He worked hard to train his left arm to do the job of both his right and left arms. And he succeeded.

Life settled down for Anya and her family until a year ago, seven years after the explosion, when the Americans came offering several million naira to ten one-armed individuals willing to try a new cybernetic arm transplant. Anya's father was the first to sign up. The newspaper advertisement said that the new arms would be like having the arm of Superman.

"Imagine how fast I'll be able to repair things with it!" he'd told Anya's mother. "Especially now that my left arm is more trained than my right used to be! Ah, ah! I'll be beyond ambidextrous!"

Her mother only laughed. She thought he was joking.

Her father didn't tell her mother when he left. She received a call from the hospital that night and Anya had gotten a call the next morning at school.

"Why is this room full of wire cobwebs?" her father asked her mother the day he'd left the hospital and stepped into the house. The cybernetic arm transplant had gone perfectly. There was no sign of rejection and it responded to the lightning-fast commands of his brain as if it were his own flesh. It could bend in all directions and was strong enough to lift a car. The arm looked like a perfect replica of his original except that the skin was of shiny gold metal instead of dark brown human flesh. It was made of a special carbonano alloy, the lightest and strongest material ever made by man. It was like a strong plastic that was not plastic.

"Why are computer chips embedded in the walls?" he asked his wife the next morning, looking forlorn. "What are you trying to do to me? I only asked for a new arm!"

The Americans came by once in a while to see how he was doing and type his words into their portables. The side effects of the transplant were well noted. Periods of delusion, paranoia, and mild incontinence were all on the list. They couldn't explain any of them. Anya was sure that none of the results from her father's experience—from the delusions to the incontinence—would reach the American newspapers or scientific journals.

Anya also wasn't surprised to learn that this same company was now seeking out one-armed American volunteers for their new cybernetic arms. Anya guessed that the scientists had since worked out enough of the kinks to safely experiment on their own citizens. Regardless of what the Americans did with their information, time, and money, she still had to somehow help her mother take care of her changed father.

When she reached the ground, she dusted off her jeans and black tank top and tucked her gourd of sap into the basket on the back of her bicycle. As she rode past the open-air market, she noticed that it was busier than usual. But people seemed to be moving in the opposite direction, some of them leaving their booths. She didn't have time to wonder about this. Thankfully, it made the going easier for her. By the time she got to her street five minutes later, she didn't even have to dodge one *okada*.

Her mother was standing on the front steps of the house.

"Is he back?" Anya asked frantically as she pedaled onto the driveway.

Her mother's face was wet and puffy from stress and tears. Anya didn't need an answer.

"Okay," Anya said, taking the gourd from her bike. "Take this, put it in the refrigerator. I'm . . . I'm going to go look for him." She gasped as she realized something.

"What?"

"Momma, there's fuel shortage," Anya said.

"So?"

"I think . . . momma, wait for me here!" she said, hopping on her bike and riding off as fast as she could. She knew where everyone was going, where the exodus ended. "Papa, what have you done, *o*?"

All she had to do was follow the people, who she now noticed were all carrying buckets, cups, jerri-cans, large bowls, plastic containers. After a while, she could have also followed her nose, the smell was so strong. It stung and bit at her nostrils and eyes. As she came down the small hill, she saw the situation clearly.

The raised pipelines ran behind several homes, some large and modern, others tiny and basic, a patch of forest extending behind them all. Her father stood before the burst pipeline, beside the stream of fuel. It was fist sized in diameter and it must have been flowing for over an hour, for a large pool of fuel had formed. It was a dark pink, almost like watery blood. The area was crowded with what looked like over a hundred people, all jostling to get to the pool. Anya's father stood proud, a citizen before his people. Men, women, and a few children knelt on both sides of him, scooping fuel into containers.

"In an orderly fashion!" her father was saying in his gruff voice. He held his cybernetic arm to his mouth as he spoke and his voice carried farther than humanly possible. Anya frowned. When had he built a microphone into his arm? How'd he know how to do that?

"I repeat!" he said. "I broke open the pipeline, so we do this my way! I see you all glancing at my arm. It's right for you to fear it. You don't want it around your neck or crushing your ribs. So stay calm, cool, take your fill, and let your neighbor in."

"Papa!" Anya called as she worked her way down the hill to him. She was still too far for him to hear or see her.

"We are clever pirates! Use your brains! If anyone gets the urge for a cigarette, control yourself until you've returned home and bathed! Turn off your cell phones! Don't rub metal containers together! Be careful as you take, o!"

"Please let me pass," Anya said when she couldn't get past a group of men waiting for their turn. "That man's my father!"

One of the men turned and looked at her and then moved aside.

"Thank you," Anya said, relieved.

"You should take him home," the man said.

"Papa!" Anya said, standing before the pool of fuel. As she looked at her father standing on the other side of the pool, the fumes made her eyes water. When he noticed her, he grinned bigger than she had seen him grin in years.

"See the color?" he said. "Looks like thin weak blood! Ha! It is diesel fuel." His eyes were red . . . everyone's eyes were red. He raised his voice and addressed those scooping up the fuel. "So do not put this in your cars! Use it for heating!" He looked at Anya. "Unfortunately, because we Nigerians are so stupid, we must send this stuff overseas for proper refining. We have all the oil but we can't make proper car fuel! We need the white people for that. Ah, ah, it's embarrassing."

"Papa, you really did this?"

"Of course!" He flexed his shiny metal arm. "Tore the pipe open like paper. Anya, there are conspiracies, stinging wires, implanted computer chips everywhere. But we should still try and do what we can."

Anya coughed, her chest hurting as she inhaled the tainted air. "It's not safe here."

"I will close it up in a few minutes," her father said. "A little sip won't hurt anyone. Especially since we're all so thirsty."

Anya shook her head, trying to clear it. She was starting to feel dizzy. She had to get her father out of here. She started to push her way past people standing on the edge of the pool but this close to the liquid treasure meant more aggressive and stubborn people trying to get their fill. The pool was about two feet deep. Thinking only about the fact that something could ignite the fumes and gasoline at any second, she decided to slosh across.

"Anya! What are you doing?" her father exclaimed, stepping in to grab and pull her across the pool.

Anya's heart was beating fast. "I won't let anything happen to you this time, Papa," she exclaimed. The fuel soaking her jeans was cool against her skin. "Please! *Biko*! Let's go!"

He looked at Anya's soaked pants. "Why did you have to go and do that?" he asked, looking irritated. "It can burn you!"

"Papa, please."

"No." But he looked at her soaked pants again and frowned. "They owe me. They owe us all! I should be using this damn arm to make them pay!"

Anya could feel her skin beginning to itch. She blinked away tears from her stinging eyes. "You don't know my side of it, Papa," she said. "You don't ask. You think it only happened to you?"

"Yes," he said, a stubborn look on his face.

"Papa, come home." Any moment, anything could ignite the very air.

"I will come when I'm finished here. Go home and wash up. This shit will eat through your skin."

"I'm not leaving you." She looked up at the clear sky. At the shining sun. All it would take was the slightest spark. She leaned against her father, pressing the side of her face to his stubbly cheek. "Papa, we need you. Mama and me. You're still human, right? Nothing concerning *oyibo* can be more important than that," she said. "Nothing."

He didn't move, his gaze falling on the pool of pink volatile liquid that Anya knew had plagued his dreams for ten years.

"It begins to evaporate as soon as it hits the air," she whispered in his ear.

He looked at Anya's wet pants. "I'm going to close it now!" he said. He raised his arm and spoke through his microphone. "Enough is enough, people! I will close this stream now before anything happens."

Anya heard curses and protests from the back of the crowd.

"Wetin dey do you?"

"Na idiot like this that keep us rolling in poverty!"

"What's doing you, old man? Eh? Do you see any Olopa police?"

One voice really caught Anya's attention. It came from her left. The young man stood with three other men, all of whom were filling very large plastic containers. "You close that and I open your head," the young man had said. An AK-47 was slung over his shoulder. Anya gasped, stepping in front of her father. Her legs shook at her own audacity as she looked at the barrel of the gun.

"You want to come and stand up to me, you idiot?" Anya's father asked, gently pushing Anya aside.

The young man took his gun in his hands and pointed it at Anya's father. "My friends and I will finish getting our fill, then you can do whatever you want, sir."

"You have no respect for your elders," Anya's father said, putting his cybernetic arm on his hip. "And on top of that, you're very very ignorant. You fire that thing and we all go die."

The man glared at Anya's father, his large nostrils flaring. He slung his gun over his shoulder, returned to his container and started using the plastic cup to fill faster. Anya couldn't help but smile, though her legs still shook and her sinuses stung. What had gotten into her father? What had gotten into her? She suddenly felt like laughing.

Her father turned to the pink fountain.

"How do you plan to close it?" Anya asked.

"Very carefully," my father said, kneeling next to the stream of fuel. He spread the index finger and thumb of his cybernetic hand and then pinched the steel. The flow immediately stopped. Anya noted the acrid metallic smell even with the fumes. Her heart skipped as she understood what her father meant by "very carefully." Her father was a true mechanic.

He held his hand to his lips. "Go home now," my father announced. "Use and sell what you have taken for good things. Keep your mouths shut and only tell stories of the Igbo Robin Hood Pirate Cowboy Man who took what was owed to him and shared the wealth." Several more people shouted curses at him but that was all.

He brought his hand down and winked at Anya. He gazed at her with clear eyes that reminded her of when he had been a mechanic with two human arms. He held out his cybernetic arm and Anya took his hand. It was warm, the metal hard, his grasp gentle.

"Oh," he said, taking his hand from hers. He picked his own three large buckets of fuel with powerful arm. "Can't forget these."

As Anya led her father away from possible death by incineration, he said, "The cobwebs have become wires, Anya. Those white people owed me three buckets of fuel."

As they walked home, her father carrying his sacred buckets and Anya wheeling her bike, her father laughed. He spoke to her in Igbo.

"You and I," her father said. "We both like to work with our hands. That's why I'm a mechanic and you want to be a surgeon and when you are on break, you climb trees and tap palm wine." He paused. "When someone does something to you and you feel that hot fury, you will react with your hands, too. Those Americans were lucky that I chose to spill their pink blood instead of their red blood. Crush necks of steel instead of flesh. Those goddamn Americans. Like vampires, even in the Nigerian sun."

"You're lucky both of us aren't fried like plantain, Papa," Anya said. She had a terrible headache and the skin below her knees felt both hot and cold but oddly, she felt good, really good. As if a weight had been lifted from her chest. "Papa, you won't do this again, will you?"

"Why would I?" he said, looking perplexed.

They were silent for a while.

"I've got some palm wine at home," Anya said. "Want some?"

"Fresh?"

"Mhm."

"By your hands?"

"Yep."

He beamed and patted Anya on the shoulder with his only human hand. "It is a good day."

WINDSEEKERS

She didn't want to kill him the second time.

She crouched over him amongst the flowers, her skin blacker than her shadow, her seven thick locks dragging in the soil. And as she sliced his smooth neck with her sharp machete and inhaled his last breath, she gazed into his eyes. Her nose stung from the tinny smell of blood and lemons.

Her homeland, Calabar, was very far from here but that didn't change who he was and the direction in which his blood flowed. As it ran sticky, soaking her big hands with warmth, she frowned. It didn't matter that the first place she'd killed him was as an Aborigine man in Australia. Nor that this second time, he'd caught her eyes with his and forced her to watch until he was gone. Arro-yo looked over the trees. This was Ginen, where all things began and all things finished. And in Ginen, everything completed itself in threes.

★

Arro-yo blended in easily but her sandaled feet hurt. She wasn't used to so much walking and she was hot in her long blue summer dress. For a while, she watched people sell everything from bottles of sweet smelling oil, to foul smelling meats, to wood, flora powered generators, to budding potted plants, to milking goats, to everything else. Children ran about, some with purpose, others for play. People shouted, laughed, and the air smelled of perfume, water vapor, smoke, and sweat.

In so many ways, this place was like West Africa. But in many ways it was not. For one thing, the skyscrapers here were easily higher than any edifice found even in Asia or America. And they would grow higher, for they were actually large sophisticated plants. When she first came to this place, Arro-yo'd gone up to one of them and actually touched its walls. It was solid but still had the yielding roughness of plant flesh.

In all of Ginen, especially the city of Ile-Ife, the people had accomplished something more advanced than any society Arro-yo had seen in her many travels: A happy weaving, interlocking, meshing of technology and plants. A true symbiotic relationship between man and flora.

It was a strange man who had told her the path to Ginen.

"The people there is lost," he said, taking a puff from his cigar. His breath had been horrendous and Arro-yo thought he knew it. "Used to know how to communicate with all them plants, trees, bushes. They forgettin' things now. Black folks is the same wherever they go."

Arro-yo smiled to herself. She always felt this way when she was in the city of Ile-Ife. This was a city of legend. As the strange man had said, legend had it that the people of the land used to be able to talk to its creative plants. Arro-yo shook her head. Legend also had it that many people of Ginen used to be able to fly and they were called Windseekers. But Arro-yo knew, even in these civilized days, if someone were revealed to be a Windseeker, he or she would be plucked from the sky and tied to a tree until death came.

Before Arro-yo came here, she'd been in Louisiana. Very few people there had heard of Ginen. Those who had were either afraid to talk about it or spoke of it with a hushed reverence. Centuries ago, though the number of different languages amongst them was many, most of the Africans dragged to America knew the word Ginen. As they were forced to forget, it came to be known as the mythical Africa, their heavenly homeland from which they were taken and to which they'd return after death.

Some remembered it as the world of the dead under water. A Hades Atlantis. Still, some didn't view it as a physical place at all. Instead it was the realm of consciousness that the mind was taken to when he or she was being ridden by a deity. After several visits, Arro-yo knew that no one ever got it right; unless they were one of the very very few who had been there and back. Ginen was the mother of the motherland, where Africans migrated from, Africa's Africa.

She stood for a moment thinking about all the things she had in her blue satchel. She liked to collect small items whenever she visited. She was sure she could barter with something. Maybe one of her earrings that looked like raindrops from the ocean. They glinted in the sun in such a way that she suspected she could buy a lot with them. She sat down in a grassy area reserved for picnickers next to a woman talking loudly on her red palm-sized portable. That was when she felt the tug.

Like a fishhook embedded in her mind. When it had her, she couldn't turn away. The more she struggled, the deeper it dug. Her guard went up like a spiked gate around a house. The sun was high in the sky, roasting all the sellers, buyers, browsers, and observers but now the sun seemed too bright. It splashed everything and everyone with light. But to Arroyo, the feel of the crowd was good. Nothing worse could happen in this place other than someone getting overcharged. But still, she scowled. She scanned the milling crowd.

All these people. Do they come every day? There were entire smiling families walking about, moving tightly together, as if they were one creature. Small trees blooming with sugary smelling lavender flowers stood here and there in the market, like sentries posted to keep watch. The ground was carpeted with bright green grass that stayed healthy and fragrant even with all the trampling. It was a beautiful place. But something was suspect. Her mind was like radar.

Where is? . . . There.

When her eyes finally found him, the young man was staring at her and he was frowning, his nostrils flared as if he smelled something unpleasantly familiar. She was suddenly sure he'd been following her for a while. He'd spotted her the moment she landed in the forest. Just outside of the city. For several seconds, they just stared at each other.

Black . . . like me. But not African, she thought. *His clothing . . . he's from here. Same shade. He carries a rucksack. He wears green, dark green. All green. Hmmm.*

She stood up, keeping her eyes on him, and began to walk. He followed her, maintaining the same distance whichever way she moved. It was as if he could read her mind; he knew every direction she'd go. She dodged a man carrying a bunch of ripe bananas on his shoulder but she kept her eye on her follower. He in turn kept his eye on her as he maneuvered around a woman carrying a large plastic looking gourd of water on her head. He didn't take his eye off of her even as drops of cool water dripped onto his clothes. Arro-yo walked fast through the market, a bubble of tension expanding in her chest. She was moving so fast, her neck craned in one direction, that she got a cramp in her ribs. However, she kept moving.

She made it to the market outskirts onto the paved street. The farther she walked, the more the market and the city tapered. It happened fast, as if the city had run out of energy. The number of electric cars that passed by slowly dwindled to nothing. Arro-yo was glad because the flat vehicles sped horribly fast and had no regard for pedestrians. The bartering along the street was less passionate, the sellers looked less hopeful and the buyers looked less interested. The buildings got smaller, growing in less artistic shapes. They went from large expansive structures with thick foliage walls and fleshy radio antennas and leaf-like satellite dishes poking from to the roofs to less looming building, living quarters, apartments, houses, homes, broken down homes, empty lots next to homes, forest. By the time it was just the two of them, they were surrounded by palm trees, brambly leafy bushes, and only the sound of birds, insects and the occasional snort of what lurked behind the foliage.

The road had gone from perfect black paving to bumpy red orange dirt. Arro-yo glanced behind her. The Ooni palace and several of the tall buildings were easy to see, especially the top of the palace, which bloomed into a giant blue disk of a flower with purple petals. The city of Ile-Ife was a series of smaller buildings looming around the purple palace like an audience surrounding a performer.

He walked on the other side of the road, directly across from her now, only a few yards away. He was taller than Arro-yo, slightly, and even through his flowing attire, she could tell was capable of moving fast. He had long fingered hands, veins raised against the skin. He was strong. His sandals slapped the dirt as he was easily able to keep up with Arro-yo's fast long legged pace. His green pants that managed to span past his ankles were caked with red dirt from the road, as the hem of Arro-yo's long blue dress was. There was a small mirror about the size of a fist embroidered into the left hip of his pants and smaller coin-sized ones around the cuffs of his shirt.

If he doesn't explain himself soon, he's a dead man, she thought.

"Who are you?" he said from across the street with a nod of his head. "Why do you track me?"

Arro-yo frowned, keeping her eyes straight ahead. The young man's voice was low but it made the tips of Arro-yo's fingers tickle. It had an edge to it and she wondered where he hid his weapon because he surely had one.

"*I'm* not tracking *you*," she said. She stopped walking to face him. They stood quiet, glaring at each other. He was an invasion of her space. Arro-yo never traveled with a companion.

"Your actions tell me otherwise," he said.

Arro-yo shrugged. He wasn't making sense.

"I don't care. I go where I please," she said.

"As I do."

"Then please go."

"If you do not follow me."

Arro-yo paused. Her blood pressure was rising. *What an insult*, she thought. *What would I follow him for?*

"What is your name?" he spat.

"You best ask me that, more politely. I'm growing tired of you."

For the first time, his face softened. Just the tiniest bit. *There would be no slashing and killing tonight*, she thought. She relaxed. She didn't like killing.

"Tell me your name and I'll tell you mine," she said.

He took a step closer and she held her hand up.

"Stay there," she said.

He shrugged.

"Ruwan Sanyi," he said, puffing up his chest. "Originally of the Northern people."

"Originally?"

Ruwan looked away.

"I was not made to live my entire life in a place that is older than time but it is where I am originally from, yes."

He stepped back, crossed his feet and sat down in the middle of the road, looking up at Arro-yo. He held out his hand and nodded his head. She looked down at him for a moment, humphed and then sat down across from him cross-legged. When she met his eyes, only two feet away, she shivered, as if there were several fingers tapping her neck. His eyes were a dark brown, almost black. As far as she could tell, he had a lot of hair and it was held in a green net. His long legs butterflied out and Arro-yo wondered how he was able to sit so comfortably cross-legged. She would have to stand up in a few minutes.

"What is your name?" he asked again.

Arro-yo paused, gazing at him further.

"Arro-yo."

"That is not your real name."

"No," she said. "Few can pronounce my true name."

He nodded.

"You know in the north . . . " he cut himself off and shook his head smiling. "You dress like a northerner and northern women are beautiful like you but, no, you are not from there."

Arro-yo chuckled, shaking her head. *Women like me are never beautiful,* she thought. She knew when someone was trying to distract her.

If northern men are beautiful like him, I'll have to make a long stop there. But this man makes my locks want to stand straight up. All I need is an opening and I'm gone, out of here.

"Come with me," he said, standing up holding out a hand. "I want to show you something." He paused. "If you are not afraid."

Arro-yo got up quickly, her face scrunching.

"*Afraid?* Of you?"

"Obviously I am physically superior to you."

"Don't overrate yourself," she said. And she was telling the truth. She didn't have any fear of Ruwan, at least not physically. She nodded. "Okay, show me what you want to show me then we'll part ways."

They walked for an hour through the trees. By the time they got to the clearing, the moon had replaced the sun. Surrounded by high palm trees and bushes with heavy water-filled leaves, the clearing was carpeted by large red open-faced flowers with fuzzy orange centers. The smell was sweet and lemony. The moonlight gave the flowers a haunted look, lighting up the centers and darkening the petals.

"This," Ruwan said with a dramatic sweep of his hand, "is a place I like to come to often."

Often? All the way out here? I can barely see the palace. The north must be miles and miles. "It's nice?"

Arro-yo put her arms around her chest and took the place in, trying to hide her smile. She had a weakness for natural beauty and she was having trouble resisting the urge to run to the middle of the field and sit down. It would be like wadding into a sea of flowers with only her head above the surface. There was a slight breeze and it swirled the scent into her nostrils.

"Come, let us sit and talk."

She followed him to the center and they sat down. Arro-yo took a deep breath and looked across the field. It really was like swimming in a sea of flowers. They sat for a while both of them looking into the sky at the stars.

"In my village, when I was young, my great granduncle used to sit us all down and tell us stories," Ruwan said after a while, rubbing his lightly bearded chin.

"Yeah, we did the same thing in my village," Arro-yo said. Under the moon, their garments looked the similar color of turquoise.

"And what village are you from?"

"It's not important," Arro-yo said.

Ruwan cocked his head but didn't press the issue.

"Do you know of the tale of how the tortoise got its cracked shell?"

Arro-yo thought for a moment. She knew many stories that her grandfather used to tell the children of the village on full moon nights, when one didn't need a candle or a flashlight. Everyone would go to the courtyard. Once you sat in the group before grandfather and he began talking, the outside world fell away.

"Hmmm, maybe a version of it," she said. *Goodness knows that the stories and folktales of Ginen are almost interchangeable with those of West Africa,* she thought.

"The tortoise flies into the sky with some feathers he finds to join some birds having a party on a cloud," he said. Arro-yo nodded. "When he gets there," he continued, "he tells everyone that his name is Allofyou. The birds, not being too smart, welcome him and when the food comes and the cook says, 'This is for all of you,' the tortoise stands up and goes to eat. When he eats all the food, the birds get angry and throw him off the cloud."

"And that is how the tortoise got his cracked shell." It was the exact same story. Ruwan smiled, his eyes watching her. Arro-yo found it hard to smile back. As a matter of fact, the tight hitch of fear in her chest was back.

"Hmm," Arro-yo said. "So . . . one should not . . . fly if he's not meant to."

"Yes, to fly one must make himself as light as possible. Greed is heavier than lead." He paused, putting his arms around his chest. The mirrors sewn into the cuffs of his shirt clicked. "And so is a disregard of tradition."

When she jumped up, stepping back, Ruwan jumped up, too, his whole gentle demeanor changing to one prepared for battle.

"Why do you choose *this* story to tell?" Arro-yo asked in a flat voice.

"Do you know another version?" he spit. "There should only be one."

"What?"

Arro-yo froze. She was overcome by shock, anger, confusion and . . . fear. She felt ashamed of her fear. It had been a long time since she'd felt it. But she was a woman of honesty and so she still listened to her instinct. She turned and took to the air. She'd made it as high as the tallest palm tree, her dress grazing its rough leaves, when his hand clasped around her ankle. Then he pulled hard. She whipped her head around, snatching her machete into her grasp and pointing it at his neck. She went completely still when she saw the blade held to her midsection.

I know this man, she thought. *Oh, I know him well.*

He floated up so that he was pressed face to face with her, still holding

183

his knife in place. He pulled off the net that held his hair and it fell down his waist in chunky locks. She knew there were seven. They hovered in midair above the field of flowers in the moonlight, two Windseekers in a stalemate, a mix of blue and green garments blowing in the soft breeze. The palace was in full view but neither of them looked towards it.

It was in Australia and he was one of those who remembered, like me. And like me, he wanted to travel alone. So I had to kill him. Either that or he'd have followed me wherever I went. Yes, I remember. He had seven thick blond locks that ran down his back like tree roots that grew deep underground. And his skin was smooth and brown like the dark chocolate he sold. And he was stealthy as a cat. He owned a candy shop. That's how he got me, those chocolates filled with liquor and his familiar scent. Now he's come back, as this other.

"You think I didn't know that you keep a machete made of white silver with a blue handle strapped to the lock closest to your neck?"

Arro-yo paused, waiting for it to come back. She blinked when it did.

"You keep a two-sided blade with a green jade handle close to your hip," she said.

"You are claustrophobic," he said.

"You're afraid of tornados."

"You will have no children in this world or any other."

"Neither will you."

"If you let me love you, you would never leave me."

"You'll never leave me and that's why I have to kill you."

They paused glaring at each other. Their jaws clenching, their cheeks dimpling in the same places.

"Why do you pursue me?" he asked.

"I was going to ask you the same question."

He exhaled through his nostrils and increased the pressure of the knife on her belly. The sharp tip poked through her dress, drawing blood. She pushed her knife closer to his neck, slicing a thin red line. Ruwan brought his knee up and pressed it hard between her legs, his lips grazing hers.

Arro-yo could smell him above the lemony smell of the flowers below. She wondered if he'd brought her here so that the flowers would hide his scent. So she wouldn't remember him. Or maybe he really did come here often, he loved places of natural beauty just as she did. *How could I forget* him? she thought. Arro-yo rarely forgot anything. He had smelled strongly of mint. As they hovered above the ground, their lips met in a kiss. Ruwan's mouth tasted like cool green leaves.

Their knives held in place, they pulled at clothes with their free hands and pressed closer. Arro-yo balked at her loss of control and then gave into it. For the moment. For the moment she was lost. Lost in him, lost in herself. She sucked at his tongue and remembered a happiness she wanted to forget. Long ago, in a different time and place. With him. Her back arched, her legs wrapping tightly around him in midair, her silver ankle bracelet on her left ankle biting through his shirt into his back. They had yet to hit the ground.

Ruwan hugged her close and then grasped her locks, pulling them to his face and taking a deep, deep breath. She pressed her lips against his neck, where her knife had cut him and sucked his blood and she remembered that she knew moments in the sky when she traveled with him, side by side. She dropped her knife, as the tears ran from her eyes and he thrust into her. She was trembling, her eyes shut tight as more images came. There were times, a home, in the same place. In a remote place of flowers in Ginen, far from Ile-Ife. He'd killed whoever tried to kill them. He'd always worn green, she'd always worn blue. There were children. They floated to the ground, slowly, following a shower of clothes, intertwined, locked, inseparable, moving to the same rhythm. *I need him,* Arro-yo thought. But not bitterly.

"I need you," he said. His eyes were wet.

★

I was flying backwards, back through clouds and then leaves, till my feet hit the red dirt, my small feet from long ago. Back when my father would always look at me whenever he came into my room in the morning to check on my sisters and me. My feet were always caked with long dried mud. I'd say that I hadn't washed them the day before. That I'd been stomping on ants and traipsing around in the forest. But he was a smart man and he'd then ask me why the mud was so dry. And my mother would ask me why I was smiling so big as I spoke. They knew what I was doing, that I could do what I was doing.

Few people within my bloodline could fly. We forget more every generation. But I was born with a memory strong as the oldest trees. And the moment I became comfortable with it, I said goodbye to my parents and sisters and flew away to see the world. I pause. Or was it to look for him? My parents knew I'd eventually leave. I was born with dada hair. I emerged from my mother with seven long locks flopping on my head, each lock black as onyx. And I wailed when my mother tried to cut them. Somewhere else, he was wailing. When a Windseeker enters the world again, so does the twin of her soul, however many hundreds of miles away. And neither soul leaves until both have died. But I disregard tradition. I want to travel the skies alone. But he is like the rain to my body of cracked dry barren earth.

Arro-yo awoke with a start. Then a red dull ache. Her satchel and his rucksack were some feet away, as where their clothes. Ruwan was warm, curled close to her, his arm around her waist. His two-sided blade was held tightly in his hand. She stared at it for a moment, absolutely shocked. Even in his sleep she could see how he clutched the knife, with surety, finality. The blades shined, reflecting the skin of his arm. The same shade as her skin. She started to slowly get up and winced. When she looked at his hand, she saw blood dribbling underneath. Her abdomen ached but not unbearably. During their stalemate, his blade had jabbed her deeper than she realized.

The pain was a blessing. For she could easily have been the one who woke up with a knife to her throat. And he wouldn't have hesitated, as she didn't. Her machete was sharp and she sliced fast, her arm muscles working. Skin tearing. Veins and arteries severed open. The blood flowed fast and hard to the beat of his heart. If she had thought about it, she wouldn't have done it. And if she didn't do it, he would have killed her the minute he awoke, for he was like her. Halfway through slicing his throat, blood pooling in her lap, his eyes opened but his strength had followed the course of his blood and he was weak. His body shuddered three times, then he simply lay looking at Arro-yo, blood coating the very lips she had kissed not an hour ago. Her hands shook as she finished, a mixture of her own and Ruwan's blood on them.

Arro-yo knelt close to Ruwan's face, her locks dragging in the soil around him. His eyes held her until he was gone. *I've killed myself,* she thought. When her face started to crumple, her chest started to hitch and her eyes started to sting, she let his head drop to the ground. She stood up, swallowing the wail that wanted to erupt from her lips and shake the clouds in the sky. She looked down on him for a moment. She glanced at the blood on his hands, the same blood that coated her belly and her crotch. She shuddered. Then she mechanically gathered her clothes, slipping into her blue dress, not bothering to wipe off the blood. She quickly took to the air.

She'd return to Africa for a while, maybe Madagascar where she could rest in the trees and the people were open to someone like herself. Where she could possibly get back to who she was before, the fearless Arro-yo. But deep in the back of her mind, she knew this would be a waste of her time. This time he had changed her. Or maybe he had changed her back in Australia. Though she pushed it way back in her heart, the grief she felt threatened to consume her. And as she flew, her tears mixed with the condensation of the clouds. Never had she felt so alone. Grief.

When she got a chance, she'd wipe her tears. On a moonless night, she'd break a kola nut, dip it in peanut sauce and alligator pepper and set one half at the foot of a palm tree and eat the other half. Afterwards, she'd soothe her senses with freshly tapped palm wine and spend the rest of that night looking to the sky. Then she'd sit and sharpen her machete, for when she returned to Ginen. The third time was always the most charmed and she had to be ready.

BAKASI MAN

Hunchbacks are very expensive. But this was not why we killed Bakasi. And what happened to him after his death was part of some darker politics.

★

You must understand, hunchbacks are not normal people. Even when they die, security has to be stationed at the gravesite for at least the first year, to prevent robbers from digging them up. It's the hump that people want. A hunchback's hump is said to be the source of his or her great power.

So you see why the evil man we call Bakasi was so feared yet respected. Not only was he bent over, his twisted spine snaking up into a profound hump, but he had one green eye. Green as the treetops during rainy season. In a place where eyes are always brown, Bakasi's green eye was a thing of much talk.

Rumor has it that when he was young, he was always at the top of his class. Some say his powerful hump bestowed this great intelligence upon him. Others believed his teachers gave him the highest scores because they were terrified of him. Whatever the reason, Bakasi went on to study medicine, specializing in midwifery and endocrinology.

I cannot imagine such a man bringing babies into the world and curing skin ailments but apparently he was a different man back then. I have a few friends who were delivered by him, one of them who is even Agwe (the very tribe he'd come to despise so much). People say he was full of love and had excellent bedside manners.

Bakasi even came to be called the Man with the Magic Hands. I don't know what happened to him along the way but whatever it was made him more crooked than his spine. It must have been the fact that his truest passion was the most crooked business of all: politics.

He got his chance to pursue his dream when the elections for state secretary came around. He was also a great orator. Wherever he spoke a large crowd would gather. Some came to see his great hump, hoping to glimpse its magic. Many believed that if the sun shined directly on it, you could see green sparks softly popping from it. Others came to hear his deep resonating voice. It was so strong that even with the largest audience, he never needed a microphone.

Others came because he spoke of lifting up the community, bettering the schools and hospitals, instilling methods that would bring more business to the community. His goals sounded so logical and realistic that people would leave his speech glowing as they did after a spirit-filled Sunday mass. He wasn't scapegoating us Agwes in the beginning. He was elected and promptly began to work toward a better Ndi State.

His work as secretary must have shown him how powerful my people are. Well, not powerful but hardworking, resourceful, and organized. There are few of us but we are ambitious and industrious. There is nothing cruel, clannish, or greedy in our ways, not more than any other group of people's. If no one will stick up for us, I will.

When Bakasi decided to run for Ndi's Head of State, his speeches took on a different flavor, a flavor that reflected what many in the greater community of Ndi State were thinking. Suddenly the Agwe became his reason for all of Ndi State's problems. We were greedy, miserly, nepotists, the scourge of Ndi State. We were few, so our votes amounted to little. He won by a landslide and that was when the trouble really began.

★

Bakasi had come to hate us and began to openly say so. And his hate was contagious. To make a long story short, things became very bad for my people.

You will never understand what it's like to walk in my shoes. You will never *be* in my shoes.

My father and I often sat up late at night talking about him. Always, in the room at the center of our house is the most secure place, where no one can hear our hushed voices. For if any of the Bakasi Boys or their many spies heard how we spoke of Bakasi, they'd have burned down our house, murdered our loved ones, and slandered the names of our ancestors and future children in the newspapers and market.

Bakasi the Hunchback had become a murderer, a worker of black magic, a dictator.

★

Three days ago, he gave a speech.

We knew he would because there were riots three days prior at one of the state's biggest markets. It would have looked bad for him to stay quiet. What happened at those riots? Some Agwe were fed up and went crazy. Ten people were killed, even more injured.

It was time.

★

There were five of us.

Me, Rosemary, Effiong, Ralph, and Victor. There are more of us now but we were the soul of it. We were the ones who took it into our hands first. I don't know what we started but I believe my father when he said it was inevitable . . . though this fact does not absolve the guilt I feel.

I was there. I was a part of it. No one saw it coming, except us. But we couldn't have predicted how severely things would explode.

Bakasi gave his speech at the university auditorium. He should have known there would be trouble where adult students dwelled. Where people like Rosemary flourished hidden between books and exams. Rosemary was Agwe but she was tall, beautiful, and tactfully quiet. Bakasi's people were aware of her as they were aware of all Agwe students at the university but she was left untroubled because she didn't seem like a threat. It was Rosemary who scoped out the auditorium and planned what we did.

She, Victor, Effiong, and Ralph had snuck in two nights ago with sacks of food, among other items. We all had mobile phones to stay in contact. Thus they had everything inside before Bakasi's security came and started checking people for weapons at the door. The security people were not thorough, or they would have checked the entire auditorium before letting people in. Bakasi was arrogant.

I came a few hours before the speech and was stationed in the front. I melted into the huge crowd waiting outside to see him. If you saw how spectacular his entrance was, you'd understand why so many gathered here.

The street was cleared of all cars and hawkers and pedestrians were banned from touching the roads. It was believed that the roads were like Bakasi's fingers, that he could touch anyone who touched them. Bakasi, it was said, liked to clear his mind before a speech, so it wasn't a good idea to be on roads that he planned to travel. Those of us in the crowd stood in the grass.

I knew he was coming when the black shiny Mercedes started to pull up. One every minute for ten minutes. They'd park next to the auditorium until the entire place was surrounded by polished black chrome and metal. Then the green Hummer came up the road, driving slowly, like a gigantic careful chameleon. By this time my legs were aching and I was breathing heavily with anticipation. Finally I'd see what this man looked like up close. This man who had turned our state upside down.

"Here he comes," I said to Rosemary on my phone.

"Okay, Issa, time to stand true," she said. I could hear the smirk on her lips.

"I'm ready, are you?" I said.

"I've been ready since this man had my brother expelled, my mother's fruit stand burned, and my father beaten in the damn streets."

I nodded, though she couldn't see me.

"Once the door is open, Rosemary, we won't be able to close it." But I didn't say this with fear.

"Like my mother always says, 'He who digs a pit for others will inevitably fall into it.' "

Then she hung up and I was alone.

As Bakasi's vehicle approached, a woman next to me fainted, a man on the other side of me began to babble and snicker, several people looked at each other with wide eyes. There were hundreds of us all standing there feeling more emotional than we've ever felt, for different reasons. Most loved and revered Bakasi, a few certainly must have hated him. I wondered how many people were Agwes. At least two of us were, judging from the stern look on a woman's face a few feet away.

The closer Bakasi's truck got, the quieter everyone grew. Soon all you could hear was the soft purr of the truck's engine. It had green and white flags planted in the front and back of the vehicle, snapping softly as the breeze blew.

The vehicle pulled up to the front of the auditorium. It stopped and from nowhere, five men in military uniform and olive green berets ran up with a green carpet. They unrolled it before the car. By this time, it was completely silent. Even the people waiting inside the packed auditorium had quieted, somehow aware of Bakasi's presence. One of the military men opened the door.

A long large shapely leg extended out. It was like the leg of a giant, a female one. She wore gold stockings that disappeared as the rest of her stepped out of the Hummer covered by her long green and gold rapa. So so tall. And her gold head wrap made her two feet taller! Bakasi's wife was a giant and I wondered how she could even fit into that vehicle.

She was beautiful in her largeness, fat off of the suffering of others; her chubby dark brown face carrying the most striking eyes and her lips were like upside down hearts. She stood next to the vehicle with a slight smirk on her face, her bejeweled hands clasped at her ample belly. Then a black shiny shoe peeked out of the vehicle. It was slightly turned inward. Bakasi was pigeon-toed. Bakasi's hump was so big that he did not step out of the vehicle as his wife did. He rolled out!

It happened so fast and with such agility that the entire crowd gasped. Then he stood up as straight as he could, which wasn't straight at all. He wore an all green caftan and pants, hemmed with gold. Specially made to suit his magically evil hump. There were gold hoops in his ears and his black shoes were also tipped with gold.

Then there he stood, pushed forward by his glorious hump that controlled all he did, including his body. I didn't see any green sparks flying from his hump but I knew this man had power. His face was smooth skinned and he was oddly pretty. His eyes washed over all of us. I especially noticed his one green eye and it felt as if he was looking at me in particular. That eye was so so knowing. As if it could look into a forest and see the past, present, and future. As if it could see where we all came from and where we all would end up. I shivered, positive he would look right at me and know what the five of us planned. We would be thrown in jail and quietly executed, our bodies covered with lime and thrown in shallow graves. But no such thing happened. Somehow he did not see what lay shortly ahead.

He grinned arrogantly, tenderly taking his wife's hand. They walked into the auditorium through the back entrance. He was surrounded by twelve of his uniformed guards. Bakasi Boys. As they entered, those of us still outside heard the people inside burst into applause. I, along with everyone else, ran inside through the main entrance.

As I entered the auditorium my heart leapt. But Rosemary was right, the guards were so focused on Bakasi inside now that they had stopped checking people for weapons at the door. It was hot and stuffy and the air was heavy with the smell of people's armpits and oily brows. Minutes passed before Bakasi stepped up onstage to speak after. There was a long introduction from the chancellor of the university, so I had enough time to push and shove my way near the front. I wasn't as close as Effiong, Rosemary, Victor, or Ralph but I was close enough.

"People of Ndi State, welcome," he said. His voice vibrated through the entire building. As always, he needed no microphone. "Fellow people, we give praise and honor to God Almighty for this day specially appointed by God Himself. Everything created by God has its destiny and it is the destiny of all of us to see this day. You the good people of Ndi State elected me, a man who had walked through the valley of the shadow of death, as your Head of State, to head this administration. I believe that this is what God Almighty has ordained for me and for my beloved Ndi State."

I bit my lip with irritation. My hands were sweating. I knew where each of them were. I could see them. I waited.

"I have found it necessary to address you once again in the course of our nation's history. In view of the unfortunate development three days ago, I'm in touch with our armed forces and they have all pledged their unflinching support and loyalty to the state government.

"Three days ago there was sporadic looting and rioting by a few disloyal and misguided and sad Agwes in some isolated parts of three Ndi State markets, followed by an embarrassing radio broadcast stating that my soldiers opened fired on innocent civilians."

My hand twitched near my pocket. *Wait,* I told myself. Not long now.

"Fellow people, you will all agree with me that the reasons given for this grave misconduct of these few civilians are significantly motivated by greed and self-interest. The Agwes involved decided to make themselves into a state security nuisance for no other cause than base avarice. I promise . . . "

I saw her stand up and heard her at the same time. Her voice was loud and clear, like Bakasi's.

"No more promises! We all know that your promises are death to our community in disguise!" Rosemary shouted from Bakasi's right. She didn't wait and neither did the rest of us.

Click click, bam bam bam!

I was rushing forward as I aimed and shot at Bakasi on stage. My aim was certainly not perfect but it was good, Effiong had taught me well. Before me, Bakasi looked as if he had small roses blooming on his chest and legs. He was still standing, although around him everyone moved away. Even his magnificent wife. In the end of life, you're always alone.

Nevertheless, any moment, his guards would throw their bodies over him, several of them were already crouching and shooting into the crowd in the direction of Rosemary's voice.

Then I threw my gun and was running with the rest of the people. Images of Bakasi on stage jumped in my head. We had to have hit him with over thirty bullets. He was dead on his feet before his men were able to throw their bodies over him. As I fled, I didn't feel as I thought I would. Guilt, disgust with myself . . . I felt those but only a little. What I felt most strongly, however, was that we had opened the door . . . or was it that we had dug a pit?

Women were screaming, men were shouting, children were gasping, and I kept running. After that, I'm not sure exactly how it happened. People just went mad. Outside, violent fights broke out between groups of men and women and people began looting nearby shops and setting buildings on fire. The black Mercedes that weren't driven off were kicked at and jumped on, their windows smashed and their insides set afire. There was a tint in the air, I recall. Something sour had spilled out from the auditorium to the streets. Bakasi was a Pandora's Box, his hump housing all the vilest spirits and poison, and the bullets had opened him up.

We met in the place we said we would, in an old shack a half-mile from the auditorium. We had to get down low, for outside there was chaos. Agwes fighting Kodobas, Agwes fighting Agwes, Kodobas fighting Kodobas. It seemed few could tell who was who and simply took out their anger on whoever was close by. Children killed mothers. Mothers killed fathers, men beat women. Yes, we stayed down low.

"Where's Rosemary?" I shouted. Someone's body hit the window above us and it cracked.

Ralph, who had blood dribbling down his face, looked at me.

"You couldn't see?" he said.

"I could," Victor said. He wiped sweat from his brow.

"Oh Christ, oh Jesus, what have we done!" Effiong moaned, slapping at his forehead.

Outside someone screamed.

"You hear that?" I spat. "Do you think the mere killing of a man did this?"

"But we *started* it," Effiong sobbed. "If we didn't . . . "

"We did *not* start this!" I shouted. "*We* did not start this! Bakasi did! It was there all this time. We've all known it! We had to cut off the head before it . . . " I had to take a breath. "What . . . where is Rosemary?"

But I knew the answer. She was back at the auditorium. And she, like Bakasi, was riddled with bullets. Rosemary was dead.

At that moment something flaming flew through the window and we got to our feet and started running.

★

Killing and chaos in the streets for three days.

I fear for the life of my father and sister and myself, though no one has come for me or the others over our assassination of Bakasi. They couldn't even find his body when all the smoke cleared. Many suspected that his hump had taken him back to the spirit world. But that day, forty-eight people were killed in the melee outside the auditorium, the newspapers reported. There was no mention of Rosemary. I guess they didn't want to further humiliate Bakasi by saying his main killer was a woman. More have been killed since. The president will be sending troops today and Ndi State has been declared a state of emergency.

Yesterday, Bakasi's body was left outside of the administration building. It reeked of decay and his hump had been cut off! This additional murder of Bakasi had nothing to do with us. I won't be surprised if whoever did it turned it to ashes and is selling the ashes on the black market for millions and millions of naira. These are dark times . . . no matter what you do.

Report that in your American newspaper and tell me if your readers won't shake their heads and think, "Even with all that sunshine, the place is still the Dark Continent." As if that is the soul of my story.

THE BABOON WAR

My father and I thought my little sister was crazy.

We were at the kitchen table sipping hot tea and eating leftover jaloff rice when she came home. We were home because of the strange heavy rains. All the fishermen were. Fifteen minutes ago, a storm had rushed in out of nowhere. Thankfully, we hadn't thrown our nets out yet. A weird morning, indeed. It was about to get weirder.

My little sister walked into the house. She looked like hell, soaked from head to toe. She was supposed to be at school. My first thought was that the odd storm had torn the roof off the school. But the entire school, roof and all, was made of concrete. She'd have been safer there than in the house.

Then my heart leapt as I noticed the bleeding cuts and scratches on her cheeks and arms. There was a deep gash in her left leg, the blood running down, staining her white wet socks red. Her uniform was torn in the front, back, and sides. She was spattered and smeared with mud. Her schoolbooks were so wet they were practically mush. But . . . she was smiling, smiling triumphantly. I wondered if she'd taken a blow to the head.

My father and I rushed to her.

"Emem, oh my God, what happened?" my father exclaimed. He took her face into his hands and touched a cut on her brow. I knelt down for a closer look at the gash on her leg. I shuddered. It looked more like a series of small puncture wounds. *What the hell did that?* I wondered.

"Come sit down," my father said. He didn't wait for an answer, pulling her to the dinner table and sitting her in one of the chairs. My sister giggled as she sat and my father and I gave each other a worried look. I quickly prepared a cup of tea for her.

"Put in two tea bags," she insisted in her high voice.

I frowned. She liked her tea bitter, but too much caffeine stunts your growth. Granted, Emem was already tall for a ten-year-old but we certainly didn't want to stop the process. A tall woman in our clan fetches a high bride price. And with such height, not even her husband will mind if she went to school past her teens. Emem was definitely made for school. Not only was she at the top of her class but she loved both reading books *and* the work and craft of fishing. I looked at my father. He nodded. "Just for today," he said.

I set the dark tea in front of her. She didn't move to take it immediately as she normally did. She loved tea. She always snatched at her cup of it, afraid that my father or I would change our minds and take it away.

Instead, she played with the bracelet around her wrist as she gazed at her tea. She'd made it months ago from three tiny bronze bells she found on the beach a few weeks ago, after a torrential storm. The night before, some fishermen said that they'd seen something like a falling star streak across the sky and land in the forest that borders the water. I didn't think anything of it at the time. People are always seeing strange things in the forest. I myself have seen several tungwa floating amongst the trees as I've canoed my way home at night. I flashed my torch on one once. Tungwas really do look like floating skin balls. This had dark brown skin.

The little bells my sister had found looked harmless and common. Like something that might have fallen from a girl's fancy dress or a child's toy. Emem had strung them on some old rope and made a bracelet out of it.

Emem softly placed an object on the table. It pulsated and hummed every time those bells on her wrist tinkled.

"What is that?" my father asked, sitting across from and gazing at it. I preferred to stay a few steps away. Whenever I looked straight at it, my eyes dried out and my heart beat irregularly. I felt a squeezing in the back of my throat and tasted a metallic tang on my tongue. And in the back of my mind, I swear I saw clouds burst and waters rise. My little sister looked at me with the eyes of a girl who had conquered great things.

Then she started telling us a very bizarre tale.

As she spoke, my father and I realized we hadn't been paying enough attention to Emem, so wrapped up we were in pulling fish from the waters. They'd been so plentiful, of late. How could you really blame us? As mama told me the day before she passed, "A family must survive." I guess.

I sat down beside Emem. Despite the object on the table. I sat protectively beside her and listened to every word she said.

★

The war started ten days ago.

Emem and her two closest friends, Nka and Asan, had been walking to school together since they were five years old. They considered each other sisters. Because they lived near the ocean, their walk was longer than most of the other girls'—about twenty-five minutes. They usually got to school with little time to spare.

Emem never complained. She'd always been one to analyze a situation and, if there was no way to improve it, accept and work with it. Of course, if there was a way to make it better, she'd move heaven and earth to do so.

Ten days ago, an opportunity to reach school earlier presented itself. Emem and her friends usually took the main road. But this day, as they walked, Nka noticed a bush beside the road. It was heavy with *mbe mbe* berries. Ripe ones, most of which were a sweet black or deep red. Nka had sharp and observant eyes when she was undistracted by conversation. Emem and Asan relied on Nka to spot groups of annoying boys from school, fast cars, and *okada* motor bikes careening up the road.

Nka giggled and ran to the berries, Emem and Asan following close behind. They'd eaten several handfuls when Nka noticed the break in the trees to her left. A narrow dirt path. Its entrance was marked by three wooden planks pressing down the foliage. The wood was warped and white with salt, as if it had been at the bottom of the ocean.

It was Asan's idea to check out the path. She was the most curious, always wanting to know what was going on. Plus, because of their berry-eating, they were going to be late and this path looked as if it went straight to their school.

"Come on," Asan said.

Asan and Nka looked at Emem. She was best able to swiftly consider all angles of a situation. She cocked her head. Then she grinned and nodded. "We better hurry!"

When they crossed the wooden plank, Eme noticed that their sandals made an odd wet trippity-trop-slap, trippity-trop-slap that seemed louder than normal. They walked for about ten minutes in apprehensive quiet, only Emem's jingling bracelet breaking the silence. The path was squishy with mud and the air smelled swampy. Yet Emem saw no standing water or pond anywhere.

"Ssp!" something hissed softly from nearby.

"Hhaah," something else whispered. Emem assumed the noise came from birds or some other small beast. The clicking sounds were probably insects. Emem heard bushes and grasses being brushed aside. Three times, large seeds fell from the trees, almost hitting Emem.

"Maybe it wasn't such a good idea to try the path," Emem mumbled. A moment later, it started raining. All three of them cursed. It hadn't looked like rain at all when they'd left home.

"Shh!" Asan suddenly said, whirling around.

"What?" Emem shouted over the sound of rain hitting leaves. "I didn't . . . "

"Quiet!" Asan snapped, wiping her wet face.

"Something's watching us," Nka whispered into Emem's ear, squinting into the trees. "Some *things*. I can see . . . their eyes." She gasped, huddling up to Emem. The rain stopped.

"Wait!" Emem whispered, trying not to push her off. "I can't . . . "

Asan huddled in, too.

"What do you see, Nka?" Emem moaned.

But Nka was too busy looking around to answer. Asan started whimpering, pressing closer. The trees and the humidly pressed close, too. Emem could feel her own sweat mixing with the rain, water further soaking her school uniform. She grasped her backpack of soggy books more tightly. The bells on her bracelet softly jingled. Immediately, the tree branches above and the bushes before them shook. Then, hollering a war cry, about ten baboons burst through the foliage, a whirlwind of fangs, claws and brown grey fur.

Emem, Asan and Nka, screamed but didn't run. Instead they pressed into each other, a mass of brown bodies in navy blue and white uniforms. They burrowed their heads into each other's shoulders, Nka into Emem's, Emem into Asan's, Asan into Nka's. Emem felt one of the baboons yank hard at her bracelet. When the bracelet didn't snap, the baboon gave up.

Baboons were crafty, violent, and meat-eating when the urge took them. Children were taught early in life never to play with, feed, or run from baboons. They moved in well-organized packs and had sharp fangs inches long. To flee invited attack. But the baboons lived deep in the forests, so there wasn't much to worry about . . . unless you were young people in a forest and outnumbered.

None of the girls saw the baboons pull at their clothes or slap at their legs. Nor did they see the beasts finally open the girls' backpacks and take their lunches of chin chin, fried plantain, and sandwiches. Emem and her friends realized this after the baboons ran off, shrieking in victory.

Emem, Asan, and Nka stood there, listening and looking at each other. They started walking. Emem felt like laughing, the result of a mixture of intense terror and realizing she was unhurt. They emerged on the far side of the school, stepping off the path into bright cloudless sunshine. Immediately, their clothes started drying.

The path *was* indeed a short cut. Emem smiled to herself. *Completely worth it*, she thought.

Even if it was a short cut, they should have been about fifteen minutes late. Instead, they were fifteen minutes *early*. How this was possible, none of the girls could guess. None of them cared. Emem looked at her friends and they grinned and slapped hands.

"Nothing good comes easy," Emem said.

"That was crazy, though," Nka said.

"*Ah-ah*, I thought we were going to be eaten alive, *o*," Asan said.

They laughed. Emem plucked at her clothes. *Nice*, she thought, sarcastically. Still, she couldn't help but wonder what it was all about. Baboons may be crazy, but there was usually a reason behind their madness. But then again, the baboons *had* stolen their lunches. *But what of the rain*? she thought. She shrugged. Near the ocean weather always did whatever it wanted and no one questioned it.

The next day they took the path again. They hadn't planned to, but in a way they had. After finishing her homework, Emem had packed her lunch early, taking extra care to wrap her orange and biscuits with paper and a tight rubber band and placing it deep in her backpack. Her friends later told her that they, too, had secured their lunches.

However, none of this made a difference when they got halfway down the path. Again, the baboons attacked, scratching and slapping. One of the baboons ran at Emem, shrieked, bared its sharp fangs and turned up its upper lip. Emem almost wet herself as she stumbled back, raising her hands to shield herself against the insane creature. The jingle of her bracelet seemed to infuriate it even more but she didn't know what to do. Again it started raining and again their lunches were stolen. Despite it all, once again, the girls made it to school impossibly early, with nothing more than a few scratches from running through bushes and shoving branches aside.

They did this nine days in a row.

Each time, the baboons attacked. But the attacks grew progressively worse, too. They'd snap at Emem and her friends. Lash out with their claws, inches from skin. Emem knew that sooner or later one of them would get seriously hurt.

Emem and Nka would buy little snacks like boiled eggs, cashews and peanuts to eat during lunchtime. They would share with Asan, who never had enough money to buy lunch. They told no one about their ongoing war with the baboons. It was an unspoken pact between them. But they were not going to let the baboons drive them off their chosen path. Not for anything. It just didn't seem right. And none of them was raised to give up, especially to stupid baboons.

On the ninth day, Emem realized she was angry. They'd been attacked as usual, but this time, the baboons didn't even care about their lunches. One of them jumped on Emem's back and ricocheted off, pushing her up the path. Another ran up Nka's back and tore at her short hair. Asan threw her lunch at one of the baboons. They merely stepped aside, hissing their warnings as the three girls ran up the path to school.

"Who do they think they are?" Emem suddenly shouted during lunch as their stomachs grumbled. This day she didn't have any money for snacks and neither did Nka. They'd spent the rest of their allowances on lunch the day before.

"Stronger than we are," Asan said.

"I don't care!" Emem said. "Every day, they attack us . . . ooh, sometimes I just want to tear their furry hides off!"

Nka rubbed her eyes. "They can bite . . . "

"So can we!" Emem snapped, flinging her hands in the air. Her bracelet's bells jingled angrily. "I'm sick of it! This can't go on! And I'm *not* going to stop using the path. I'm not going to be driven off by some . . . some idiotic monkeys!"

Nka nodded rigorously. "That would mean they'd win. We shouldn't let them win," she said.

"Why don't we just hide most of our food in our clothes?" Asan said. "And let them steal the stuff we keep outside our person?"

"That's stupid," Nka said, sucking her teeth. "You think the baboons won't smell the food on us? How would you like a baboon tearing at your clothes to get to some chin chin?"

"They don't care about the food!" Emem said. "And they were tearing at us today."

"Maybe we should try paying them," Nka said.

So the next day, when the baboons came running, the three of them held out packages full of orange, mangos, and udara fruit.

"This is our payment," Emem shouted. But the beasts kept coming, howling their war cry. The three of them dropped their food and ran down the path to school.

"Shit!" Emem shouted, when they emerged at the school, impossibly early as usual. "Now what?"

At lunch, they sat nibbling from small bags of cashews, plotting. Within minutes they had a new plan. It didn't involve running away or taking the long way to school. No, those days were over. Their plan wasn't complicated, either.

★

The next day, as they walked down they path, Emem could feel her heart beating in her mouth. Her palms were sweaty. She opened her mouth to breath. The forest felt especially close today. Above, clouds gathered quickly. She held her bracelet silent.

Ten days of being robbed and harassed will do strange things to a person. Some people will retreat and withstand whatever hardship they must in order to avoid being robbed again. Some will just stand there, indecisive. Others will go get more people and hope for the protection of numbers. But some . . . some will stand and fight no matter how unlikely the odds of victory.

Emem's father was fond of saying that some people carry the spirit of warriors. That this spirit doesn't change just because one is reborn into the body of a tiger, rat, butterfly, tree frog, or even a little girl. That this spirit will always be looking out from within whatever vessel the Unknown has placed it within. That it will look upon the world as a place where it will *never* be dominated. Emem could relate to this, as she knew her friends could, too. Maybe that was what attracted them to the path in the first place.

Emem felt a surge of excitement and anticipation. She was eager.

She led the way, then Nka and then Asan. They carried books in their back packs. They carried no lunches. They were silent as they walked down the path, backs straight and necks rigid. They listened, watching the trees and bushes.

They walked for five minutes. This was the farthest they had ever gotten without being attacked. Emem laughed and said, "I guess they only come when there's food." But then . . . they came. They came faster and harder than ever. There were over fifteen of them this time.

Emem, Nka, and Asan formed a circle, their backs to each other. As they rushed, Emem felt as if her heart would leap from her chest. Her legs felt like warm rubber. She could hear Asan grumbling something beside her, maybe a prayer. Nka was breathing heavily.

Emem's perception narrowed. She no longer saw her friends. All she saw were the baboons that came at her, long fangs bared, claws out. They looked twice their size, with their brown gold fur aggressively puffed up, their orange eyes wide.

Emem's foot connected with the face of one baboon. It grunted, knocked back. Her fist connected with another's chest. She felt a satisfying crunch. At the same time, she punched another in the head, her bracelet jingling loudly.

It started raining. Heavily.

Even as it fell to the side, the baboon she punched managed to snap its mouth dangerously close to her arm. Another sunk its teeth into her left leg. She felt a searing pain in her back as another slashed at her flesh with its claws.

She didn't make a sound, her eyes, nostrils, and mouth wide, taking in air, smell, and sight. She kicked and punched and scratched and bit. Her mouth filled with fur and baboon skin. She spat it out, saliva and blood dribbling down her mouth. Her short nails dug past fur to skin to fat to muscle. She screamed a warrior's cry as she stomped hard on the head of the baboon she knocked from her leg. Its head caved in, white-grey brain squishing out. Some got on her sandal, its jelly-like warmth wetting the skin on her foot. She smelled salt, copper, and soil. Every sound was razor sharp. She slapped a baboon away.

Instinct told her to run for her life.

All she heard was her breathing.

Her mouth tasted tangy and bitter.

All she saw was the dirt path. Bushes and trees to her right and left.

Her feet splashed through wet slippery mud.

She fell.

She got up.

She ran.

She slapped at branches, stems and leaves.

She felt no pain.

Not yet.

★

All three of them emerged from the path onto the school grounds with soiled clothes and ripped school bags. The ground here was firm and dry. The sun was out.

They'd been beaten terribly.

Asan had a scratch on her forehead that bled heavily into her left eye. Nka's clothes were the filthiest, for she'd rolled on the ground in battle, kicking and grabbing at fur. She still grasped a fistful of bloody flesh and fur in a shaky fist.

Emem was still angry, but she didn't know why. She was just angry. She took a tissue from her school bag, spit on it, and wiped Asan's face. They were still inspecting themselves when one of the larger baboons emerged from the path. Emem stiffened, readying herself. Nka and Asan gathered behind her.

"You want more?" Emem said, holding her fists up. Her muddy bracelet jingled, strong and true. Emem froze and then looked at Asan and Nka with wide eyes.

"Did you feel that?" she asked.

Nka was looking at the dirty soles of her sandals, rubbing her forehead. Asan met Emem's eyes but said nothing.

The baboon stopped and sat on its haunches looking at her. Emem was sure the others were lurking behind it somewhere. She could hear her classmates talking and laughing in the schoolyard not a half mile away. If the three of them made a break for it, they might be able to outrun the baboons. Would the beasts pursue them so close to so many other human beings? It didn't matter. She wasn't going to run.

Emem frowned. The baboon's fur wasn't puffed out. It looked so small. And, as it sat there looking at them with its golden eyes, it seemed almost pensive and human. Emem could see a patch of blood on its flank. She hoped she'd been the one to do that.

Slowly, other baboons emerged from the path. Some of them limped, dragged an arm, bled freely. Two of them had to be helped along. The one who sat in the middle of the path continued staring at Emem. It was holding something in its hands. Emem squinted. It was black. Very very black and about the size of a golf ball. The baboon's hands shook as it held it up.

"I think it wants to give that to you," Nka said.

Asan laughed. Emem felt the urge to laugh, too. As if she would step up to that huge group of baboons. She wiped her forehead. At the sound of the jingle of her bracelet, the thing in the baboon's hands pulsated. Just as it had done moments ago. Then *doom*! This time she was sure the ground shook. The deep sound made her teeth vibrate, her skin prickle, and the inside of her nails itch. Behind her, in the school yard, she heard people exclaim with surprise. Suddenly, the day grew cloudy. There was a rumble of thunder in the distance.

"What *is* that?" Emem whispered.

"Go get it," Nka said, pushing her forward. "I think we won it."

"What?" Emem asked looking back at her.

Nka was awed and despite the blood dribbling from a cut on her chin, she was smiling. "We won," she said. "I . . . I think they were guarding something. They didn't want to take our food after all, not really. They thought we were trying to take that thing. And we *won*!"

Emem looked at the waiting baboons. The thing in the baboon's hands throbbed again, but this time the shockwave it sent was much smaller. Maybe this explained the weird forest and how fast they kept making it to the school.

"Why me?" she whispered.

"I don't know," Nka said.

"I think she's right," Asan said.

"Then *you* go," Emem said.

Asan shook her head and stepped back.

Emem turned to the baboons. Adrenaline still ran through her veins, as did her warrior's blood. She took a step forward. The next step was easier. Soon she was standing amidst twenty baboons. They smelled of sweat and rain. The baboon holding the object stood up tall on its legs. Emem held out her hands. Her bracelet jingled and the object softly pulsated again, this time more gently. The baboon placed it in her cupped hands. It was warm and hummed softly, like something charged. It was light as a feather and gave off the slight scent she'd have associated with alligator pepper. Without further adieu, the baboons left one by one.

Emem, Asan, and Nka stared at the object. It was like holding a piece of midnight. Emem could see twinkling stars and the vast darkness of space inside it. Nka and Asan refused to touch it.

"We ran back up the path when the rain started," she said. "It only made sense to come right home. We didn't know it was going to be a full storm, though."

"Well, thank God you're alright," father said.

"You could have been blown away," I said.

The three of us stared at the object on the table. It was making the whole kitchen smell like alligator pepper and the windows were fogging up from the moisture it exuded.

"I guess this thing is mine," my sister said, playing with her bracelet and yawning. She picked up her tea and sipped it. "Whatever it is."

My little sister looked so exhausted. I wanted to yank off that bracelet and throw it into the ocean. But somehow I knew the rope wouldn't break.

ASUNDER

Nothing is new.

Everything has happened before and will happen again. You will be another person in another time in another place like this with this same choice to make. Let me tell you about yourself many lives ago, when you had this choice to make, the same odd and unlikely lesson to learn. This time your name was Nourbese and your dilemma was with your husband, Osaze.

Love was easy for you to give, especially to Osaze, who was the one you were meant to be with. Everyone in your village knew this, so when you two decided to get married at the age of fifteen, no one objected. Both of you were an oddity in your village but not because you were anything so amazing, genius, or unique. Actually both of you were fairly normal children . . . well, except for the exceptional love that existed between you two from the day you met.

You and Osaze met five years before. During the festival of the sun, the day when it rose the highest and hung the longest. It was a wonderful day because there wasn't a cloud in the sky. The air smelled sweet with the scent of budding lilac flowers. The land you lived in does not matter. It was a place very far from here with dry sandy grounds and gnarled wide-growing ancient trees. The people there wore long flowing garments that kept the body cool. And their lives revolved around both the sun and the large variety of flowers that grew year-round in the dry heat.

The day you met Osaze was a day of leisure for the community, and everyone gathered in the village's common area that sat in the center of the expansive croplands. The food people feasted on would be foreign to you now. Flowers of all shapes and sizes and textures. But not the flowers you know. These flowers were like meat to a leopard, like the hearty soups, sandwiches, stews, and roasts you like to eat. These flowers were their sustenance.

There was singing and dancing. There were friends and family who were finally able to talk leisurely and catch up on things. You had come with your parents and siblings, two younger brothers and an older sister. Your parents had brought a large mat and you and your sister were sent to buy some food that you would eat before the sun reached its highest point and the dancing began.

Somehow, in the crowds, you were separated from your sister. At the age of ten, you had a bad sense of direction. You tended to get carried away with your surroundings, your attention taken by the sweet, sour, and salty smell of roasting, boiling, and frying flower petals. All the sweeping colors of people's clothes, the blue sky, the soft sting of the sandy breeze. The sound of people talking, bees working, the click of grasshoppers, the zip of humming birds. You were so overwhelmed by it all, that you lost sight of your sister, who always walked with purpose and speed.

You were looking up at a large blue wildflower that was being visited by several ruby-red hummingbirds. Behind you, the festival crowds were coming and going. That was when you realized that you'd forgotten to keep an eye on your sister. You gasped, realizing that you were lost. You looked around frantically, nibbling at your nails. But all you saw were unfamiliar people. You stepped away from the large blue flower, unsure of which way to go.

Someone tapped you on your shoulder and when you turned, you met smooth brown eyes. His skin was the color of honey dripping down the brown stem of a wall flower. He was of a lighter shade than you were, yet he must have spent much time in the sun because something about him glowed. He held an oily-looking bulbous yellow flower out to you, its stem was long and green and slightly transparent, as if it were full of water. It gave off a sweet tart scent that made you think of lemons and sweet cane candy. He had what looked like a hundred of these same flowers balanced on his head.

"I don't have any money," you said, but you couldn't stop looking at his eyes and the way his hand did not shake as he held the flower out to you.

"But your mother will," he said. "Where is she?"

"I . . ."

"You're lost."

You frowned and looked away.

"I'm just . . . looking around," you said.

"No, you're lost," he said, shaking his head. "I know lost when I see it."

"You don't know anything," you said. "All you know is what I tell you."

"My father says there is plenty one can know about someone without them even speaking," he said. He was still holding the flower out to you. And without a word, though you didn't know why and you had no money, you took it. You took it and held it to your nose and smiled at him and he smiled back at you. And you two stood there shoulder to shoulder watching the crowds for several wordless minutes in front of that tall blue flower crowded with hummingbirds.

Can ten-year-olds fall into a love deeper than that of a man and a woman of a hundred years? A love deep like a forever blooming flower? Impossible, you say? You say impossible because you don't know any better, haven't had the chance to learn. You will.

Back when you were Nourbese and Osaze was in your life, you knew nothing *but* love. You two spent much time together from that day on. Osaze lived only minutes away from you and every morning, before school, before it was time to garden, before you did your other chores, you'd find each other and sit ear to ear and close your eyes.

It was something no one else of either of your clans was capable of. You two were the first and the last. You swam in each other's minds, thought out the problems of the world together, built empires in your heads, grew acres of fruit and vegetables in your souls.

The place where you two tended to spend the most time became a garden in itself. All types of flowers grew around the spot next to the garden of white cupped flowers behind Osaze's house, where you two would sit and travel within your minds. The spot where you both sat became cushioned with green soft moss.

Yours and his parents were bothered and in awe of the love you two had for each other. Thus they left you two alone to do as fate had obviously decided. The day you two were married at the age of fifteen was a quiet day. Few people attended. To most, you and Osaze were married the day you met. The actual traditional ceremony was an afterthought. Your mother didn't even know why it was necessary.

After that day, however, you two never left each other's sides. So this day *was* necessary. It marked the next phase for you and Osaze. You worked in the fields together, went to school together, studied together, lived together, spending half the time with your family and the other half with Osaze's.

When you were both nineteen, you finally decided that it was time to consummate your marriage. You had not waited on purpose. It was more that you were so intimate, that it never occurred to you. When it did it was like the sky opened up and swallowed you and when it set you back down in the sand, you'd looked at each other and imagined the sky full of fluffy clouds. From that day on, you were never seen farther than two feet from each other. It was around this time that people began to refer to you and Osaze as Osanour and you were fine with this, for you two had begun to feel like you were one.

You thought as one mind, part male, part female, all compatible. Because plants grew well around you, people often sought and paid for your blessing of their crops, for the community was one supported by the land. And your blessings always yielded results.

A house was built for you in the center of the community croplands. Here you resided enjoying the hot sun, dry but fertile land, and each other's love. You grew so close that even your hair began to knit together. Your closeness attracted your hair like roots to water, especially during the night. And soon, you literally couldn't move more than two feet from each other, for you were connected by a thick thick rope of coarse hair. Your hair was a dark dark brown, his was a sandy brown. And so the rope was like honey and root tea.

When you were thirty years old, you didn't know what to do when you became pregnant. You had forgotten that you were capable of producing something that was not part of you. You had forgotten that no matter how much you loved Osaze and no matter how much you were called Osanour, that you were still also Nourbese. He had forgotten that, though he wasn't capable of producing children, you were.

When your body began to change, and you both became aware that you were no longer just you, Osanour, there was unease. Your belly grew so huge that it became difficult for you to press your body against Osaze when you slept, as you had done since you'd got married.

Your space felt invaded by a foreign presence that wasn't that foreign. It was other. When you pressed your ears together, you still swam within each other's minds, experiencing thoughts and emotions, but there was now something else. Another voice, one that giggled and clung. One that was full of images neither of you could interpret.

You began to feel you needed space from Osaze. Just a little. A few more feet. Your body grew so hot in the sun, as it expanded. Osaze's hands grew more eager as your breasts began to swell and your scent changed to something irresistible to him. It badgered him at night and he covered your face with kisses as you slept, his hand on your belly, making you feel too warm.

You began to feel bothered when people called you Osanour. You wanted your name back because you were you, no matter how much you loved Osaze. You were you. *You* were the one with child. You insisted this but no one listened, so used they were to seeing you and Osaze as one. It seemed that to the community, the child inside you just became a part of Osanour, too. And you didn't like this either.

You started to cry often for no reason and Osaze could not console you. Osaze understood fully that things were changing and he began to brood. He couldn't bear that you were unhappy. And his neck constantly hurt because you were always pulling your head away from his as you tried to get more space.

You both knew when the baby was due to come and you knew what you would name her. You'd name her Ikuku, the term for the sacred winds which were believed to hold everything together. By then, you had made your decision.

"Today," you told him, one night. "Because the baby will come tonight."

Neither of you wanted to do it, really. But it was the only way to put things back in balance. No longer would your hair hold you together.

Ikuku would. You walked to your parent's home where you knew you would find your mother and father working in their garden.

"Papa," you said, your voice slightly shaking, your hands pressed into the small of your back. "Osaze and I need you."

"You and Osaze?" her mother said, releasing the rope of vine she was pruning. She looked at your father and you noticed that there was a slight smile on her face. You see, you were her child and when you met Osaze, she knew she had lost you to him for good. Or so she thought. She always dreamed that one day, you'd at last come back to her as Nourbese, her daughter. Today was that day.

"Yes, mama," you said. "Your granddaughter arrives tonight." You paused, knowing that once the words were spoken then they would come true. You felt Osaze's arm come around your waist and rest on your belly.

"We need you . . . to separate us," he said, looking her father in the eyes. Then he looked at the machete her father had in his hand.

Osaze's parents were also called to bear witness to the event and by the time they arrived an hour later, a crowd of siblings, cousins, uncles, aunts, and villagers had gathered.

"Please, papa," you desperately said. "Do this quickly before more people come."

By this time, your eyes were like a rare rain cloud and Osaze clung to you as if to let go would cause him to fall. Osaze's parents huddled with your mother as your father sharpened his machete with a stone. You were very aware of the whispers. Several people had even come up and pleaded with you and Osaze not to separate.

"Please," one man said, placing his hand on Osaze's shoulder. "Our crops will fail, *o*."

"Why are you doing this?" a woman said, taking your hand and squeezing. "Why not wait until after the baby?"

"You have made this place flourish," an old man said, his wrinkled light brown hands clasped tightly together. "Now you want to make it die?"

"You will die if you do this," an old woman said with tears in her eyes. "And then your baby will."

At this, Osaze had looked at you and you looked away. And again, you had mumbled the response that you had mumbled to the others, "It must be done." It was a sacrifice that needed to be made. But this time, you shivered. You weren't sure if the process would kill you. You weren't sure if the hair had become more than what it was. When cut, would it bleed? What a tragedy it would all be if all three of you died.

And if we don't die, well, what if it hurts? you thought. If the pain was too great, the child would suffer trauma, too. But if *you* died . . . your father would cut the baby out of you. Your mother had told you about such a thing that had been done when a pregnant woman's heart had stopped. The child that had been cut from the woman's body was one of the children you'd grown up and played with before you met Osaze.

Doubts filled your head and maybe they made your head too heavy, for you still laid yourself on the sandy ground when the time came. You and Osaze had purposely lain three feet apart to give enough space to cleanly expose the thick cord of golden-brown twisted hair. You were face to face but when you looked at Osaze he would not meet your eyes.

You wanted to reach for Osaze's hand as you lay there but you didn't. Osaze didn't try to reach your mind, either. You patted your belly as the child gave a soft kick.

"I will do it now!" your father loudly announced. He was sweating freely, large drops tumbling down his forehead and from his thick white black afro. But his hands held the machete tightly, firmly.

You glanced at the rising machete, which glinted in the desert sunshine. And then you shut your eyes just as the machete came down. But Osaze kept his open, so you were able to see it happen anyway. You'd never forget how the first chop left a deep gash in the hair. It made a meaty sound and reminded you of the first gash made in the neck of a bull when it was slaughtered. A perfect deep, mortal slice. You were certain that you smelled the copper smell of blood.

Now it would have to be finished. You saw stars before your eyes and you felt Osaze's closeness retreat. It was like letting out your breath after you'd been holding it for nine months. It felt . . . good.

Your father chopped and chopped. And you could hear the gasps of the crowd with each chop. You could feel your head able to move back a bit more with each chop. Until the last chunk of hair gave and you both came loose. Osaze slowly sat up, his rope of hair flopping on his shoulder, but he was looking at you. You were farther away from him than you'd been in a decade.

"Osaze," you whispered as your mother helped you up. Osaze's mother came and helped, too, for you were quite heavy with your pregnancy. Your father just stood there staring. He'd later bury the machete he'd used in the sand.

The rope of hair on your head felt heavy and light at the same time. You leaned on your mother and straightened out your long green dress to hide the anxiety you felt from being so far from your true love. You took a step toward him but before you could get closer something in your belly gave, and liquid splashed down your legs into the sand.

"Osaze!" you screamed. He was running to you before you even spoke and had you in his arms before you could take another breath. You were not too heavy for him to hold up. "Take me home," you said. You looked behind you. "Mama!"

"I'm coming," your mother said. And so did your father, Osaze's parents, your aunt, and the rest of those standing around.

Osaze didn't leave your side the entire time. He placed his warm hands on your cheeks and absorbed as much of your pain as he could. Afterwards, he'd have burst blood vessels dotting the whites of his eyes and speckling his neck. As dawn approached and the birds of the desert began to sing, the voice of your first child sang to the air. She was a fine and healthy girl.

After that day you and your husband were called by your respective names and, as two individuals with a profound connection, you raised your baby. Your daughter took much pleasure in running from you to Osaze and back to you, her strong legs relishing in the exercise. And when she was two, she learned to climb the tough stems of the flowers in the flourishing croplands.

So you see, once again, you learned that sometimes love is best when two are separate.

TUMAKI

Dikéogu Audio File Series
begun April 8, 2074
Current Location: Unknown Region, Niger
Weather: 36° C (98° F), N.I.U.F.
(Not Including Unpredictable Factors)

*This audio file has been automatically
translated from the Igbo language . . .*

Tumaki

I found the electronics shop two blocks from my hotel. All I needed to do was go in the opposite direction of the market.

The small store was packed with all sorts of appliances and devices. A few were from Ginen, like the solar powered e-legba that was part machine and part plant and the very small unhealthy-looking glow lily. Most everything else was very much from earth. Thin laptops, standard e-legbas, all kinds of coin drives, batteries, and hardware like bundles of wiring, piles of microprocessors, digicards, and every kind of tool imaginable. It was a tinker's dream. It was my nightmare. Way too cramped. I planned to be quick.

To make things worse, the place was air-conditioned. The minute I walked in, my skin instantly started to protest. I wrapped my hands around my arms as I stepped up to the counter. A woman stood behind it. At least I thought it was a woman. I'll never get used to burkas. Maybe it's the southeastern Nigerian in me but those things are creepy.

About fifty percent of the women in Niger wore them. Most are made out of stiff cotton and a cotton screen covers the women's faces. You can barely see their eyes. These women, especially when you see them walking down the street at dusk or dawn, scare the hell out of me. They look like ghosts, all silent and mysterious. No, I've never liked burkas.

"Yes?" she asked. Ok, so I had been standing there staring. I never knew whether I was supposed to speak to these women or not. And since I couldn't see their faces, I was even less sure.

"I . . ."

She sighed loudly, rolled her eyes, and held out a hand. It was a careful hand. My mother would have described it as the hand of a surgeon. Her nails were cut very short, the palm of her hand slightly calloused. Her fingers were long and they moved with a precise care that reminded me of a snail's antenna.

"Hand it here," she said.

I gave her my broken e-legba.

She turned it over, tapping the "on" button. The damn thing only whimpered. Never have I been so embarrassed. All e-legbas do that when they're broken. There are different whimpers, weeps, moans, or groans depending on the type of breakage. What kind of obnoxious engineer programmed them to do that? It's bad enough that the thing is broken. Why should a machine act like a whiny child?

"What'd you do to it?" she asked. As if my e-legba was some living creature.

"It's a long story," I said.

She turned it over some more between her antenna-like fingers and laughed. "This is practically a toy," she said. "This is your only personal device?"

"It's a prime e-legba," I insisted, indignant. "An electrical god of the best kind."

She laughed her condescending laugh again. "A lesser god, if a god at all. With a weak solar sucker, sand grains in the fingerboard, a faulty *and* cracked screen and probably a smashed-up microprocessor."

It gave a sad pained groan as if to stress her points. I wanted to grab and hurl it across the room. *What do I need it for anyway?* I thought. But in the back of my head, I knew I wanted to watch my mother's news program. And I had a copy of *My Cyborg Manifesto* on it, a much needed Hausa/Arabic dictionary, and it picked up a fairly decent hip-hop station whose signal seemed to remain strong wherever I went.

"I can fix it, though," she said after a while.

"You?"

She looked up, her dark brown eyes full of pure irritation.

I stepped back, holding my hands up. "I'm sorry," I said. "I . . . my mouth is what it is."

"It's not your mouth that bothers me," she said. "It's your brain. My *mother* owns this shop. Not my father. Does that surprise you, too?"

I didn't respond. It did surprise me.

She nodded. "At least you're honest." She paused, cocking her head as she looked at me. Then she brought my e-legba to her face for a closer look. As she inspected it, she talked to me. "My mother's an electrician. She taught me everything I know. My father's an imam. He tries to teach me all he knows, but there are some things that I cannot digest." She laughed to herself and looked up at me. "You're not Muslim, are you?"

"No."

She grunted something that sounded like, "Good."

"But you are, right?" I asked.

"Sort of," she said. "But not really."

"Then why do you wear that damn sheet?" I asked.

"Why shouldn't I?"

"Because you don't want to," I said.

"You don't even know me."

"Do I need to? A sheet is a sheet." I saw her eyes flash with anger. I kept talking anyway. "Doesn't matter if you look like a giant toad with sores oozing puss. You shouldn't . . . "

She pointed a long finger in my face like a knife. "You have got to be . . . " She stopped. I saw where her eyes flicked to. The black tattoos on the bridge of my nose from my time as a slave on the coca farms. I could tell she got it. She understood my obsession with free will.

"My mother and I are electricians and this town is dominated by patriarchal New Tuareg ways and even stronger patriarchal Hausa, Old Tuareg, and Fulani ways. People here still . . . expect things. My mother and I play along. My father, well, he prefers us to play along, too. Everyone's happy."

"Except you have to live under a sheet."

"Business is business," she said with a shrug. "It's not so bad. I get to be an electrician who is female." She looked me in the eye. "Plus, sometimes I don't want people looking at me."

That was the excuse my close friend Ejii often gave whenever she wore her burka. I didn't buy it from Ejii and I didn't buy it from this girl.

"Well, other people's problems should be their business, not yours."

"In an ideal world, certainly," she said. "So, can you pay?"

"Yes."

"In full?"

"Yes."

She paused, obviously deciding whether she could trust me. She brought out a black case and opened it. Her tools were shiny like they were made for surgery on humans not machines. She started to repair my e-legba right there. It was a simple gesture, but it meant a lot to me. She'd noticed my tattoos, considered them, yet she trusted me. She *trusted* me.

Minutes later, a woman came in, also draped in a black burka. Her mother. I was about two feet away from her daughter. It was too late to step back from the counter.

"*As-salaamu Alaikum*," the woman said to me, after a moment's pause.

"*Wa 'Alaykum As-Salām*," I responded, surprised. She glanced at my tattoos but that was all.

People came in and out of the store. Her mother helped customers, sold items, chatted with them. But I was focused on the electrician fixing my e-legba. I ignored my claustrophobia and the freeze of the air-conditioning. I didn't want to leave. I didn't want to move.

She had my e-legba in pieces within three minutes. She tinkered, fiddled, replaced, and tinkered some more. After about a half hour, she looked up at me and said, "Give me a day with this. I need to buy two new parts."

"Okay," I said. "I'll see you tomorrow then."

From that day on, that store became my second home. Her name was Tumaki.

★

Poetry

My e-legba was nothing to Tumaki. She could take apart and rebuild the engine of a truck, a capture station, a computer! She could even fix some of the Ginen technology. You should have seen what she did to that pathetic glow lily that I saw the first day I was in the shop. She got that plant to do the opposite of die. Once, she tried to explain to me her theory of why nuclear weapons and bullets no longer worked on earth. She started talking physics and chemistry. I remember nothing but the intense look on her face.

She was a year older than me and planned to eventually attend university. I wasn't sure if she liked or just tolerated me. When I was around her, I couldn't stop talking.

"We just use pumpkin seeds," she told me one day while she worked on an e-legba. We were talking about how to make egusi soup.

"See. That's where you people go wrong when you make the soup," I said.

"Us people?" she said, as she unscrewed some tiny screw.

"You people. Yeah. You know, those of you who live here in Timia," I said. I shrugged. "Anyway, Nigerians call it egusi soup for a *reason*. Because we use egusi seeds. Goat meat, chicken, stock fish, fresh greens, peppers, spices, and ground *egusi* seeds. What they serve in the restaurants here is a disgrace."

"Fine, we'll call it pumpkin soup, then," she mumbled, as she placed another screw. "Makes no difference to me."

"Ah ah, I miss the real thing, *o*," I said, thinking of home. "With pounded yam and a nice glass of Sprite. Goddamn. You people don't know what you're missing." I wished I could shut up. I didn't want her asking me any new questions about home. All I'd told her was that I was from Nigeria.

She only glared at me and loudly sucked her teeth. I grinned sheepishly. I was just talking, totally drunk on her presence. No matter how much rubbish I talked, though, she never got distracted enough to lose track of what she was doing. She could listen to me and work on a computer like she had two brains. Tumaki was genius smart. But she was also very lonely, I think. I figured this might have been why she didn't tell me to get lost. Maybe it was also why only two weeks after I met her, she did something very unlike her.

★

I was half asleep when I heard the banging at my hotel room door. It was around two a.m. I don't know how I heard it, as I was outside in deep REM sleep on the balcony. It was rare for me to sleep this well.

When the banging on the door didn't stop, I got up, stumbled across the room, no shirt on, mouth all gummy, crust in my eyes, smelling of outside and my own night sweat, barely coherent. I opened the door and came face to face with a black ghost. Death had come to finally take me. That thing from the fields outside the cocoa farms I'd escaped was back.

My eyes widened, my heart slammed in my chest. If my mind hadn't finally kicked in and my eyes hadn't adjusted, I'd have brought an entire storm into the hotel room to fight for my life. Then Tumaki would have learned the secret I'd kept from her just before that secret killed her.

"Tumaki?" I whispered, stepping back. I ran my hand over my dreadlocks. They were probably smashed to the side. I must have looked like a madman.

She laughed. "How'd you guess?"

A thousand emotions went through me. Delight, pleasure, excitement, horror, fear, confusion, worry, irritation, fatigue. I slammed the door in her face.

"Shit!" I hissed, staring at the closed door, instantly knowing it was the wrong reaction.

She banged on the door. She was going to wake my neighbors. I quickly opened it. "What the hell are you doing?" she snapped.

"Trying to save my neck," I said.

She sucked her teeth loudly. "Let me in," she demanded.

Oh my God, I have no shirt on, I realized. My heart pounded faster. I looked down both ends of the hallway. I saw no one. But who knew who might have been listening or peeking out? I grabbed her arm and pulled her in. "You could get me killed by coming here," I whispered. I didn't know what to do with myself. Tumaki's family was highly respected. She was the imam's daughter! No girl went to a guy's hotel room in the middle of the night! Period. Especially not to meet a guy like me. Especially if anyone suspected that I was a meta-human.

"Nah," she said. "They'll just chop off one of your hands."

"Not funny," I said, as I looked for a shirt. My room was tidy as I barely had use for it. I don't like messes, either. My clothes were neatly folded on one of the beds. Four shirts, one caftan, three pants. I grabbed a semi-clean cotton shirt. "What are you doing here?"

She shrugged and walked past me to my balcony. The scent of the incense she liked to burn in the shop touched my nose. Nag champa. I loved that scent, though when I bought some and burned it in my room, it didn't smell as good. She stepped over the mat I'd been sleeping on and took in the view. She inhaled and exhaled. "Nice," she said.

"Tumaki . . . "

"You sleep out here?"

I sighed loudly. "Yes."

"Why?"

"I like to," I said.

"You don't like the indoors."

"No."

She looked back out. "Makes sense."

There was a cool breeze. This was probably what allowed me to sleep so well. Despite her presence, my head still felt a little fuzzy. It had been while since I'd slept that deeply and to be ripped from that kind of sleep was jarring. "Tumaki, your parents are going to . . . "

She laughed and whirled around, her eyes grabbing mine. "Let's go to the desert!"

"Eh?"

"Just out of town," she said. "For a little while. I never get to do anything."

I opened my mouth to protest.

"I'm often in my library late into the night. Sometimes I sleep there," she said. "They assume that's where I am if I'm not in my bed. They can't imagine me being *anywhere* else but alone in my library. Trust me."

★

We could have taken her scooter but we walked. I didn't know how to drive one and, even at this time of night, too many people would remember a woman driving a man on a scooter. It was *always* the other way around

For once, I was glad she was wearing her black burka. In the night, you could barely see her. But I didn't have to see her to be aware of her close proximity. It was the first time we were completely alone together—no mother in the back room or customers looming. But it wasn't the first time I felt this strong attraction to her. It didn't make sense. I didn't even know what she looked like! But the sound of her voice, the scent of her nag champa, the dance of her graceful hands, just being close to her, I've never felt anything so real.

Each time I stepped into that shop, my heart started hammering. I'd get all sweaty. My mouth dried up. When talking to her and she had to leave for one second, I'd feel so impatient. She was my last thought before I went to sleep and my first thought when I woke up. Tumaki, Tumaki, Tumaki. I hated feeling like this. No, I didn't trust it.

I was sixteen with no experience with women. Well, there was Ejii. I definitely liked Ejii, who'd been a shadow speaker. But that had really never taken off. Two meta-humans? That probably would have been a little much. But this thing with Tumaki came out of nowhere. I didn't like things that just came out of nowhere. I didn't like surprises.

"I wanted to go see that spontaneous forest so badly," she said as we walked in the moonlight.

I laughed and shook my head.

"I did," she insisted. "But I didn't have anyone to go with."

Tumaki had told me that all of her friends had been married off. Now she barely ever heard from them except for baby announcements. It was as if they entered a different world. They had, in a way. The Married Woman World. In Timia, that world had no place for friends.

"Spontaneous forests can be dangerous as hell," I said. "Especially when you don't know what you're doing."

"Not all the time."

"You want to take that risk?"

"Yep."

I almost laughed. She sounded kind of like me. I was glad that damn forest was long gone. I think she'd have gone in there and I'd have had to go after her. As we passed the last building, a man on the camel slowly passed us on his way into town.

"*As-salaamu Alaikum*," he said to me.

"*Wa 'Alaykum As-Salām*," I responded, trying not to meet his eyes. Tumaki stayed quiet. Every part of my body was a sharp edge. How must we have looked heading into the desert with nothing but ourselves? *Oh Allah, they are going to lynch me, o*, I thought.

"Relax," Tumaki said when the man was gone. "He didn't know it was me."

"You knew that guy?"

"He was my uncle."

Before I could start cursing and going ballistic, she grabbed my hand. It was warm but not soft. I stared down at her hand in mine. I had no clue what to say or do. I considered snatching it away. She was the kind of girl who would slap the hell out of you if you did something to her that she didn't like. Don't let the burka fool you. I'd heard her tell off a man who'd tried to cheat her on the cost of an e-legba repair. She'd handed the man his masculinity on a silver platter.

"Dikéogu," she said. The sound of my name on her lips . . . *Let them cut off both my hands*, I thought. I wasn't letting go of her hand for anything. "Come on," she said pulling me along. "No time for you to start losing it."

★

We didn't go out far. About a mile. Timia was still within shouting distance. Between the luminance of the half moon and the dim light from Timia, it wasn't very dark here. By this time, the thought of having a foot or hand chopped off or being publicly whipped for fornication, attempted rape, or some other fabricated camelshit had faded completely. Tumaki filled my mind like a rainstorm.

And I knew she liked me, too.

The cool breeze was still blowing and she opened her arms as if to hug it. Her burka fluttered. She looked like a giant bat. I laughed at the thought.

"I *love* the wind," she said, her eyes closed, at least I thought they were.

I suddenly had an idea. I focused on the breeze and the rhythm of my breathing. The breeze picked up. Tumaki laughed with glee, her burka flapping hard now.

"When I was a little girl, before I had to start wearing this thing, I used to run outside on windy days," she said. "There was this one day in the school yard where suddenly this giant dust devil whipped up! Everyone went running away from it. I went running *to* it."

She laughed and whooped, whirling around. I increased the breeze to a wind.

"I managed to get in the middle of it," she said, raising her voice over the wind. "It twirled me around and around and around. I felt as if it would suck me into the sky! My skirt lifted way up and everything." She turned to me, her burka billowing around her. "My father beat the hell out of me that day. For shaming Allah. I have a scar on my face from it."

A ripple of anger swept through me at the thought of this. And I lost control of the wind. *Whooosh*! It swept from the desert floor to her ankles and blasted upwards, taking her burka with it.

We both stood there watching it flutter back down many yards away. Then slowly our eyes fell on each other.

Almond shaped eyes. Skin dark like the night. Lips like two orange segments. The African nose of a warrior queen. She was taller than me and lanky in her red t-shirt with a yellow flower in the center and an orange patterned skirt that went past her knees. She wore her thick hair in two long cornrowed braids, the moon made it black but I suspected it was closer to brownish red. She had a long scar on her left cheek. Her hand went right to it.

Now she knew what I was and I knew what she looked like.

There was a flash of lightning from above. I could feel it in every part of my body and soul. It started to rain. We were soaked. But we didn't care. We ran around in the sandy mud and lightning and rain. We threw mud at the sky. We laughed and screamed and it rained and rained. Was it because or me of the will of the skies? Both, I'd say.

I grabbed her wet hand and pulled her to me. The first time I ever kissed a girl was accompanied by a chorus of simultaneous lightning, thunder, and a torrential rain and tasted like the wind and aquatic roses.

The moment was poetry.

Glow Lily

Tumaki wore her brown-red hair cornrowed at the shop or at school. Basically whenever it was under a burka. When she was at home or with me, she let it out into the big bushy tangled afro that it wanted to be. I liked it best when it was out. So did she.

Her parents knew little about us. They only saw me in their shop, when I'd come around. I wasn't stupid. Her parents were progressive but they were still Muslim. I was lucky that they allowed me in the store at all.

Her parents named her well. "Tumaki" meant "books" in Hausa, which her father was extremely fond of. During those wonderful six months, I spent most of my time in two places, in Tumaki's arms and in her library, which I learned was an underground room behind their house. It was a place that she had made hers. Her space. That was the only reason I could stand being in a small underground room. The room was like Tumaki's soul.

She'd even reinforced the walls with concrete all by herself three years ago. She'd also installed a winding metal staircase. She said she hired some guys to help with it, so I guess the library wasn't *completely* secret. "About four years ago, this room just appeared," she told me. "My mother believes it was made by one of those giant underground worms. It might have dug the hole for eggs and then decided that it didn't like the land or being too close to humans."

"I believe it," I said. Ejii had once told me about "reading" the mind of one of those weird giant worms. She said it was obsessed with the number eight or something. The creatures definitely had strong opinions about stuff.

Tumaki had tons of books stacked down there. Books on physics, geometry, geology, biomimicry, African history, nuclear weapons, novels, biographies, how-to books, old magazines. She didn't discriminate. She loved information. She had an old beat-up couch and two tables and gold satiny pillows with tassels. Glow lilies that she'd cultivated lit the room. The place was always cool even during the day. It smelled like the nag champa she loved to burn and the curry she liked to eat. And there was always soft Arabic music playing.

We didn't go back out to the desert but we did explore the more progressive parts of Timia. We went to late night tea shops where people spoke freely, tea cups in hand, about whatever was on their minds. Once in a while people talked about meta-humans, mostly as if they were the scourge of the earth.

Usually when there was meta-human bashing, we'd stay for a long while. I really wanted to understand the root of their hatred of people like myself. Fear, arrogance, ignorance, you take your pick, those people suffered from all those. But eventually, I'd start getting really steamed. The way those guys would talk (always guys, women never spoke in the tea shop discussions), it was like they weren't on earth during the Great Change. Like they were untouched by it. They thought they were so "pure." It was ridiculous. More than once, Tumaki had to drag me out before I threw hot tea in someone's face. The last thing I needed was for people to know I was a meta-human.

Tumaki and I were quiet as I walked her home on these nights. After that night in the desert, we didn't speak of my abilities. She didn't ask about them and I didn't really want to talk about them. She knew I was a rainmaker, what more did we need to discuss?

We went to secret poetry slams held by students, usually in empty or abandoned buildings. Here I heard some of the worst poetry ever. But Tumaki seemed to enjoy it and none of these people bashed meta-humans. So, though I made it a point to tell her the poets stunk, we kept going to them. She knew most of the students here and again her burka protected her, as it did the identity of most of the women there. If word ever got back to her father about her being out at night *and* with me, she'd have more than just a scar to show for it.

"But my father isn't the monster you're imagining," she insisted during one of our conversations about her scar.

"Any father who puts a mark on his child is a monster," I said. "I don't care if he's an imam."

I'd never spoken to her father. Tumaki had tried to introduce me once but I wasn't up for it. He was one of those "big chief" men in Timia. The kind that struts around followed by guys who will admire even the toilet paper he wipes his ass with. His expensive embroidered thick cotton robes were always a heavenly white—how do you keep your clothes that white in a place where there is so much dust, eh? His long beard was bushy and dark black, his hair cut short, not one grey hair on his head. You could tell he was a proud proud man. I didn't like him.

"You don't know him," Tumaki said.

"I beg to differ," I mumbled. I'd known many like him, including Chief Ette, including *my* father.

That afternoon, she asked her mother if she could take the day off from the shop. Then she took me to the market square to see her father speak. We stood out of his sight, beside the booth of a man selling dried grasshoppers. The seller absentmindedly munched at a grasshopper leg as he listened to Tumaki's father speak.

Her father sat on a table before about a hundred young men who sat on the ground. He had their full attention. Every single one. I wished I could command that kind of attention . . . in a positive way.

Around them, the market went about its business, but people were

TUMAKI

obviously preoccupied, listening to Tumaki's father. I spotted her mother on the other side of the square. She was trying to be inconspicuous as she stood, fully veiled, in the shade of a cloth shop. Even the shadows couldn't hide the pride in her stance.

"And then *whoooosh*! the sweetest smelling wind ever imaginable," her father said. "Everyone agrees the smell of the Great Change was like billions of blooming roses. It made your skin feel new, soft like a baby's backside. Allah is great, *quo*. If you were not there to witness the Great Change you will never be able to fully imagine it. The Great Change was Allah's return. All its results are Allah's will."

He paused dramatically, then his eyes widened and he pointed his index finger up beside his head. "Now you have these *foreigners* who know nothing about us. Who do not respect local traditions. They slaughter cows indiscriminately. They consume goat milk." He spat to the side; several men in the audience did the same. "And have you ever shared tea with these people? They take one cup and then get up and leave when there is a whole pot left! What kind of nonsense is that?" Several people in the audience sucked their teeth and grumbled. I noticed more, however, were starting to look around, uncomfortable.

"They openly disrespect Islamic tradition. Look at all the addicts addicted to that . . . that drug, that mystic moss they brought with them. How many die from eating other people's personal peppers? A whole family died from them a month ago when a woman mistook one for a normal pepper and used it to make stew."

"And the worst thing," he stressed, his voice rising. "The worst thing is that they come here from their world and think they can tell us that we have gone wrong. They say the Great Change has made the earth and its people unnatural. They doubt the will of Allah. They take their own lives for granted." He narrowed his eyes and looked at his audience and then around the market. "You know who you are. You know who you are."

My mouth practically hung open. Beside me, Tumaki gave me a small smile and nodded. Tumaki had insisted that her scar had been an accident. A stupid mistake of an overprotective father. I'd scoffed. "Why do you protect him?" I'd asked. I was sure he'd done it on purpose,

231

because he didn't want her to be too beautiful. I assumed he was the usual non-progressive ego-driven type of guy that I was used to seeing. Okay, so I had to revise how I felt about Tumaki's father.

He was a traditional imam, certainly, but this man was open-minded. And the man had balls. The "foreigners" he was griping about were Ginenians, people from the world of Ginen. No one did that! The people of Timia practically worshipped Ginenians. And though he didn't openly say it, the meaning was clear: he was *defending* meta-humans. Can you imagine? In a town where meta-humans where treated like, well, cockroaches, here he was saying that meta-humans were the "will of Allah." Maybe Tumaki's scar *was* an accident caused by the hand of a scared father. Maybe. Even people who do good things can still do terrible things once in a while. He should have never scarred his daughter's face. I don't care what was going through his damn head.

More people gathered. Women, veiled, unveiled, gathered at the periphery of the all male audience. There was a young girl standing not far from me whom I think was a metal worker, as Tumaki's necklace was softly pulled in the girl's direction.

There was some booing. A few Ginenians had come to listen, too, and some local people simply didn't like what they were hearing. But mostly there was silence and attention and a deep sense of fear. His words were obviously inflammatory but many agreed with him. He was tapping into Timia's quietly festering disease. That thing that was on everyone's mind that no one dared to speak of.

He spoke with a casual eloquence that made you listen, consider, and fear for his life and your own for being there. You could see where Tumaki got her humanity. I felt my heart in my throat when I glanced at her as she looked at her father. I knew I had to deal with my parents eventually, my parents who had sold me into slavery because I was a meta-human. *Not yet*, I thought. I couldn't imagine leaving Tumaki. *Will she come with me?* I couldn't imagine that, either.

When her father finished speaking, I still refused to meet him. No one wants to meet that kind of man while knowing you've more than kissed his daughter. No way.

★

Not long after that, invigorated by his speech, Tumaki and I went into the part of Timia where drugs deals, prostitution, and other illegal transactions took place. It was her idea. I'd seen such places plenty of times since escaping the cocoa farms. I knew damn well that they existed and thrived. But I guess Tumaki was pretty sheltered.

"I need to see it," she told me.

So we went. One thing I noticed about Timia's ghettos is that you didn't see one Ginenian. You saw them at the poetry slams and always in the tea shops but never ever in ghettos. I guess that was sinking too low for them.

Sometimes Tumaki and I just walked the streets at night. Because we could. And I knew Tumaki liked the risk of it, though deep down she knew that I'd never let anything happen to her.

Nonetheless, we spent the most time down in her library. We didn't have to wait until night to go here. I'd meet her here after she finished school, when she didn't have to work, or on her days off on the weekends. We'd simply read and enjoy each other's company. It was the first time I'd really had a chance to sit down and educate myself since my abilities had begun to manifest. Back home, school was not a good place for me. I was "The Boy That God Was Angry With," "The Kid Who Kept Getting Struck By Lightning," the butt of everyone's jokes.

"This book was amazing," Tumaki would say, shoving a thick book in my hand. Or she'd say, "You've got to read this! It'll change your life!" I couldn't not listen to her. I was in love with her, I guess . . . if I want to use that cliché overused damn-near-meaningless word.

Anyway, I must have read hundreds of books in those months. Reading kept thoughts of my parents at bay. And it helped me make sense of the strong anti-meta-human discrimination I saw in Timia. I was slowly running out of money but I'd cross that bridge when I got to it. I wasn't thinking about my future at all.

I read about witch hunts, persecution, racism, tribalism, infanticide. I read about the genocides that had taken place in the world so many decades ago. In Germany, Rwanda, Bosnia, Sudan, Kosovo. I memorized the eight stages; classification, symbolization, dehumanization, organization, polarization, preparation, extermination, and denial. I, of course, read extensively about slavery and those who fought for freedom. I read about the pollution and eventual nuclear destruction of the environment.

I read about camels. I read *The Autobiography of Malcolm X*. (I usually don't care for super old books like that when it's not history but I liked this book very very much). Tumaki made me read some of those novels about Muslim women . . . not bad, except for the ones that were mostly about perfumed and oiled girls dodging eager men and landing a rich princely husband.

My brain must have doubled in size.

Rainmaker

Tumaki didn't wear make-up. Even without the burka she had no need for it. She only lied when she had to. Like when her mother asked about me. She told her that I was just a friend and that I was harmless. Her mother would have had me beheaded if she knew that I knew every part of Tumaki. Every part.

Tumaki wasn't deceptive and because she grew up around trust, it was easy to learn to trust me. She quietly worked hard to earn mine. At first, I couldn't see past her looks. Then, as time passed, yes, I began to trust her, too. Bit by bit.

You think of the times in your life where you actually accomplish something useful and good. Where you create love and beauty. Then when you reach the bad ugly place, where everything is a rainy prison, you understand that life is meant to be lived. We are meant to go on.

That's what I tell myself here. Each day we get closer and each day those good days with Tumaki get farther and farther away. Soon it will be as if they never happened at all. It will be as if none of this happened. It will only be the wind, the rain, the lightning, this great storm.

★

Paradise Lost

Now, listen.

I'm not telling the story of my relationship with Tumaki. That was gloriously normal. Textbook stuff. She and I were good together, when you didn't count all the outside stuff—like her being from a Muslim, fairly well-off family, and me being a meta-human ex-slave who'd been rejected from his basically Catholic stinking-rich family. I told Tumaki a little about my past. And she didn't ask much more. She knew the basics. My secrets were not her preoccupation.

The story I'm trying to tell started when Tumaki's father disappeared.

Recall the incident I saw with the little boy shadow speaker. I saw so much of that in Timia. Meta-humans treated like radioactive cancer-causing evil infidel waste. Meta-humans were threats to small children and wholesome family values. They caused women to become sterile. They were the cause of all that had gone wrong. It was the Ginen folk spreading these stupid rumors.

But local people took to it like fish to water. They loved the Ginen folk like people love superstars and the wealthy. You could see it in their eyes. Women would swoon over the young Ginen men. Men would chase after Ginen women like they'd lost their damn minds. I have to hand it to the Ginenians, they had style. Their clothes were always the most fashionable. They had a way of speaking that sounded like music to your ears—I think some of this had to do with the magic involved in their language. And they always had money from selling their rare items.

It was the people, the natives of Niger, who took to calling meta-humans (and anyone who sympathized with or gave birth to them) "cockroaches."

It was a slow disease in Timia. I might have left that city if it weren't for Tumaki. Hiding away in her library, I didn't realize how bad it was getting. Not until the day she came running down the winding staircase, shaking, eyes wide and wet. I'd been waiting down there for an hour.

I jumped up and ran to her. "Tumaki! What . . . "

She snatched her hand from mine as she threw off her dark blue burka and let loose a string of obscenities that even impressed me.

235

"What?" I asked again. "What happened?"

"My papa!" she shouted. Her left eye was twitching as she sat down on the couch. She stood up and started pacing. Then she made to go up the staircase. "I have to make sure . . . "

I grabbed her hand. "Will you tell me . . . "

She whirled around. The look on her face made me back away. I thought she was about to punch me. Her panicked rage practically burst from her skin. "They took him!"

"Who?"

"Some men." She shook her head. "And one woman. All of them strong like oxen. People were cheering! How can that be? People of his own home!"

"But why?"

"People are suddenly disappearing all over Timia," she snapped. "Haven't you noticed?

I shook my head.

"Oh Allah! They took my papa, *o*!" she wailed. She screamed and moaned. I didn't dare touch her. Eventually, minutes later, she knelt down and was silent. She shut her eyes. When she opened them, she was calm. She stood and grabbed my hand. "Come, Dikéogu," she said, her voice steady, her eyes blank. "I don't care what my mother says."

We went up the stairs, across the yard, into her house.

Her mother didn't care, either. She didn't ask why I was with her daughter alone or why I was in her house. It was the house of wealthy folks. It reminded me of my home in Arondizuogu, but not as obnoxious. The floors were wooden, not marble. The furniture was plush, sturdy, and well-made but probably not black leather imported from Italy.

There was a large picture with a white silk veil over it. I assumed this was a portrait of Tumaki's father. The house reeked of burned rice and Tumaki had to run to the kitchen to turn the heat off the pot. Her mother just sat there on the couch. She wore no burka and she stared blankly ahead. It was my first time seeing her face. Tumaki was the spitting image of her mother.

"It was only a matter of time," her mother whispered. "Of course they'll take the imams first. Right there in the mosque. They have no respect."

Tumaki brought her a glass of water. Her mother took it absentmindedly. Tumaki looked at me and then back at her mother. "He should have kept quiet," her mother said. She whimpered. "He used to watch windseekers fly about at night when the bats were out, when they thought no one would see them." She set the water on the rug beneath her feet.

That day, I moved my things from the hotel into Tumaki's home.

★

I walked the streets, letting people assume I was a slave. The slave of Tumaki and her mother. I went shopping for them. I helped Tumaki in their electronics shop. I went to tea shops to listen to gossip. The government was finally doing what "needed to be done," some drunken blockhead said. Everyone, including me, mumbled assent.

"Soon this city will be free of meta-humans and troublemakers." More mumbled agreement, this time a bit livelier.

"Good riddance," a woman muttered.

It was all happening so fast.

★

Within one week, I stopped seeing meta-humans with obvious characteristics in Timia. No windseekers; they brought wind wherever they went. No metal workers; they attracted things like earrings, necklaces, and keys just by standing near people. No shadow speakers with their weird eyes. Professors started disappearing, too. And certain students, many of whom we'd seen at the poetry slams, disappeared, too.

Two weeks later, Tumaki's mother's shop was ransacked, then burned down. Two days after that, her mother disappeared from her own bedroom.

The streets were busy and, dare I say, jubilant. Something was very wrong with these people. It was as if they'd been programmed and then the program had been turned on.

Tumaki and I dragged as much food and water as we could into the library and hid there. We read books and enjoyed each other but avoided talking about anything serious. Especially about the fact that I was a rainmaker and she was a female electrician and student.

We were down there for three days.

By the third, we were smelly, hungry, and angry. And that was when we heard people rushing down the stairs.

Now, when you've been cooped up for that long in a small room, you become concentrated. You know every sound. You know every angle. And you're a bundle of nerves. We'd been waiting for three days for something to happen.

Tumaki had her mother's best hammer. I had myself. But nothing could have prepared us for what came down those stairs. There were four of them. Tall, dark-skinned, bald, even the woman. They wore white long kaftans, the woman a white flowing dress made of the same flawless material. They moved swiftly down the winding stairs and they made not a sound. I mean, *not . . . a . . . sound.* Silent as ghosts. Once in the room, they zoomed right at Tumaki and me.

I shoved Tumaki behind me. She tried to shove me behind her. It didn't matter. With my peripheral vision I saw one of them zip right at Tumaki, grabbing her in his clutches. It all seemed to happen in slow motion. I turned, my mouth open. He slammed Tumaki against a bookcase. She winced, mournfully glancing at me. He had teeth like a snake, fangs. *Vampire?*

"Let her g . . . " I was grabbed from behind.

But I saw it sink its teeth into Tumaki's neck as she raked her nails across its face. Its skin tore away but there was no blood. It didn't let go. Tumaki's eyes went blank.

I was grappling with the woman, trying to get back to Tumaki. She said into my ear, "Where do you think you're going, cockroach?" Two more of them grabbed me.

I didn't hear a sound from Tumaki. But I heard the sound of her hammer dropping to the floor. In all that scuffling, I heard that.

I'd had enough. I stopped fighting. I focused. I let burst the most powerful surge of electricity I could produce. It made a low deep deep *thud*!

Screeches like you would not believe.

Like rabid rats trapped in a tiny tiny cage.

Spitting and hissing and high-pitched screeching.

They fled up the stairs. I don't know if they flew or ran or oozed or what. All I knew was that they took Tumaki. She was gone. They must have picked her up like a sack of dried dates. They'd sucked the life from her and then they took her.

"Oh Allah, what is this, *o*?" I screamed. Then I just screamed and screamed until a darkness fell over my mind.

★

The only gift my father really ever gave me was a thick book about an Igbo poet named Christopher Okigbo.

A line from his poetry: "For the far removed, there is wailing."

★

It was several things about Tumaki.

It was her books. It was the fact that she *hid* her books. Maybe one of the men who'd helped her install the staircase that led down to her library had told on her. It was her tinkering. It was how she knew to wear her burka despite all this. It was her pride. It was her wanting to attend university. And it was probably her parents.

I have no doubts about why they killed her.

★

I went mad.

Darkness crowded in on me. Down there in her library, all alone. I barely noticed. Tumaki was gone. I'd seen one of those creatures bite her. Her eyes had gone out. Like a light. I loved her. I was consumed by terror, shock, rage, shame. I tore at the neck of my caftan. I had no one left. A breeze lifted up around me.

It oozed up though the library floor like some ancient crude oil. It pooled around me, whispering and sighing. It was nothing but a breeze. It was opportunistic, searching for a way into me. I could feel something else bubbling up in me, just as I could feel the darkness oozing around my feet: The Destruction. I wanted to destroy all things. Murder, mayhem, havoc. Crush, kill, destroy. "Yessssss," the darkness whispered to me, like the sound of whirling sand. "Sssssssssss."

Only my utter grief made me flee deep into myself instead of taking it out on what was outside myself, and maybe a tiny shred of humanity, too. I was lucky . . . in a way. In another way, I wonder if I'd have been better off succumbing to the thing from outside the cocoa farm that seemed to have followed me into Tumaki's library, like some lethal black smoky snake that had waited for the right moment to strike.

A large chunk of my life remains mostly a blank and the few short moments that I remember was just more badness. I do not recall leaving the library, or the city of Timia. I briefly recall, some idiot of a man grabbed me and told me I was going with his family to Agadez. He needed someone to help him with his camels. He read my tattoos as the mark of a slave, though they were of a slave and rainmaker. I let him. In Agadez, I slipped away in the dead of night two days later. My memory is blank for weeks after this. In the following months, I'd mentally surface for an hour or two, finding myself in this town or that town. So much blank memory. I'll not talk about the worst of it.

My mind was unhinged. I forgot Tumaki. I forgot myself.

Somehow I ended up in the desert squinting up at that curious tall man whose face was covered by an indigo veil. He stood feet away from me, unmoving like some djinni. I think it was being nearly dead that finally woke me up. The closeness of death has a way of awakening even the most damaged senses.

BIAFRA

When we talk about this woman, we always start off by saying: *What a time Arro-yo stepped into!* 1967. Our land has been named Nigeria and the Biafran War was upon us. Heavy and dirty. Anyone would have felt sorry for Arro-yo. This was not the place she remembered, but home was still home.

"Selfish," she hissed to herself as she headed there, blinking away tears. "I've been so damn selfish!" She'd been away a long time, seeing the world. Now, she had to get *home*. She had learned much while she was away. She knew about courage and fear, she knew about gain and loss. She certainly knew about love and anguish and murder of love. But now she was going to learn about mass death.

She'd read about it at the restaurant as she sat in the sun drinking a cup of milky tea. Someone had left the *Time Magazine* on the table after he had finished his meal. The headline read: "Biafra's Agony." She'd almost dropped her warm cup. Then, like so many of our people who were abroad, she'd felt the words deep in her bones.

Come home!

The rest she would learn along the way. You see, our lands had finally gained what the British called "independence." But when a place is made up of false boundaries strategically sketched and strictly enforced by foreigners, there will eventually be trouble. Many of the new rulers were chosen by the British, and these chosen men were magicians and sorcerers gone wrong. They used juju charms like magical walking sticks to repel bullets and secret elixirs to prevent poisoning. They wore sunglasses to hide their dry red eyes, eyes that always looked worried because they could see their victories, but also their deaths.

These leaders had intercourse with woman after woman, sapping their feminine lifeforce and then throwing away their shriveled, sad bodies. But those broken bodies still birthed children, giving these men thousands of sons to ensure that no power would be lost if they were assassinated. This of course, didn't matter, for inheritance is ignored in any *coup d'état*.

As the chieftaincy of our country was snatched by party after party, frustration eventually turned to violence. On May 30, 1967, our tribe's leader proclaimed the land of the Eastern Region of Nigeria as the Republic of Biafra. A grand name for a grand place. Oh, how it made us think of the great Biafran Empire so so long ago. "We will have it again!" we cried. Soon afterwards, Nigeria declared war on us. We, the men, women and children of the Igbo tribe, became Biafran soldiers.

We asked, "Igbo *Kwenu*?"

We responded, "Yah!"

Even as Arro-yo made her way home, she too asked and responded to these words. Igbo *Kwenu*? Yah!

When she got to Nigeria, as she flew home, there was combat in the forests and gutted villages. Bodies were scarred and killed by machetes, nailed to their huts, raped, torn by bullets and bombs. In Biafra, we invented the *Ogbunigwe* bomb and self-guided surface-to-air missiles to help us. Women became spies and soldiers. Children did their part, too. Scientists on both sides spoke of developing nuclear and biological weapons. But our weapons could not match the Nigerians', whose were supplied by foreigners. And then the enemy was able to cut off our food supplies and we began to starve, we began to lose faster.

After years of being away, this was the warring land that our Arro-yo flew into. There was no place for guilt here, but she bore it and it consumed her.

Her first day back in Nigeria, still hundreds of miles from her village, she came across an exodus. Now she saw it with her own eyes. Thousands of people were going southeast. They were Igbos fleeing from the north, back to Igboland, what was now called Biafra. They were tired, scared, and hungry. For a while, she just stood there staring.

She wanted to continue her journey home, but these people were desperate and she had skills that could help.

"I am finished being selfish," she said to herself.

She approached people and said that she was a nurse. She found what she needed in the nearby forests. Herbs, bark, flowers, leaves. She brought down fevers, eased pain, stitched up machete gashes with palm tree raffia, fished out bullets, helped people fight their infections, and she watched some die. It wasn't quick for these people. It took nights and days of pain, crying, and sometimes a resigned motionlessness.

Once Arro-yo sat with a girl of about ten. Her name was Onwuma and her family had been killed by soldiers who'd raided her village in the north. The girl had no one to look out for her but herself. She was too young and soon she began to suffer from kwashiorkor. The girl had been eating only handfuls of uncooked rice for weeks and her belly was swollen as if she carried a baby herself. Our Arro-yo knew it was too late to try and help her. The girl had lain still that night, her eyes open, looking through the trees at the night sky. All around them, people slept.

"I'll go soon," Onwuma said softly. "They're waiting."

Arro-yo wiped the girl's forehead with a wet cloth. She was hot. Arro-yo wasn't surprised at the way the girl spoke. The girl's name meant, "Death knows." It was an ogbanje name. This girl had probably been hearing the calls from her friends in the spirit world all her life. Now that the girl's family was dead, she had no one to keep her alive. An ogbanje child was always torn between family and his or her friends in the spirit world.

"Can you see them?" Arro-yo asked the girl.

"Yes," she said. "They're above us. In the trees."

"What do they look like, Onwuma?"

"Like . . . " she giggled softly. "Like large pretty green lizards with long long rough tails."

"What do they say?" Arro-yo asked.

"They say . . . " she trailed off in a sigh. Her breathing slowed. Arro-yo gently shook her.

"What is it?" the girl asked.

"I was asking you what your friends were saying," Arro-yo said, fighting to keep her voice still. The girl was so young. *She hasn't even seen much of the world, at least not in this life,* Arro-yo thought. *And the last part of her life has been riddled with things no child should ever see.*

"Who?"

"Your spirit friends."

"Oh," Onwuma said after a long pause. "There's one with its claw on your shoulder. It says thank you; that it's okay to let me go now."

Then she shut her eyes and never opened them again.

Soon after Arro-yo left this group of people, she tried to continue going home but before she could even get close to her village, she came across the real violence. The fighting. Men slashed and shot each other in the forests and in ruined towns and villages. Arro-yo saw many die every day. She flew into the sky to get away from gunless, machete-bearing, desperate men gone mad who tried to attack her. She was shot at several times, but somehow she was able to escape unhurt. Behind her, as she flew into the sky, she heard cries of shock and fear. Some ran away, others simply stared up. Still others threw themselves on the ground and shouted to her for forgiveness.

"No!" she'd shout back, tearfully. "*You* forgive me!"

The violence spiraled into a tornado, and our vulnerable, guilt-riddled Arro-yo was easily pulled in. She didn't know how many people she saved. There were children with bloated bellies that she dragged from fires. Men she slashed to ribbons with her blade for their attempted rape of women. She no longer heard the different languages people spoke. She didn't see the tribal markings on their cheeks or the styles of their uniforms. The people fighting all looked the same to her. She made her decisions according to who was hurt and who was doing the hurting.

The first time she saw the giant birds, she thought she had somehow stepped into another world. For where else would such monsters exist? But then she realized that they were made of metal. She remembered that these were airplanes.

She'd been in the forest, helping several sick men and women. There were also children in the group and a pregnant woman. She'd been tending to the pregnant woman when, suddenly, there was the sound of flapping wings. No chirps, squawks, or whistles. The birds were soundless except for their wings frantically trying to launch them into the air as quickly as possible. She didn't have to look up to know these were vultures. Only vultures behaved like that.

The woman Arro-yo was helping gasped loudly and jumped up. So did everyone else.

"What is it?" she asked, as she held the pregnant woman's arm, so the woman wouldn't fall. Before the woman could answer, Arro-yo heard the war cry of an enormous beast.

Whirrrrrrrrrrrrrrrrrrrrrrrrrrrrrrrr!

Then everything exploded. Arro-yo was thrown against a tree. The moment her mind regrouped, she flew up as fast as she could. Her clothes were covered with blood and chunks of moist flesh. She coughed, her nostrils filled with smoke and blood. But she flew and flew, higher and higher, her heart beating as if it would burst from her chest. She breathed with her mouth open. Once she was high enough to no longer smell smoke, she looked back.

They zoomed back and forth over the forest, destroying everything alive. Trees, bushes, grasshoppers, vines, human beings, plants, owls. For several moments, her mind could not comprehend what she was seeing. She had seen so many amazing things in her travels but this . . . man-made disaster . . . she couldn't understand it.

When the metal birds flew away, she flew down. Everyone was dead. She flew on. She didn't want to be around when the vultures returned as she knew they would. And somewhere else, there were people who were still alive and needed her. She'd forgotten that she needed to go home. To her, everywhere had become home, everyone was a relative she'd abandoned to go see other places.

She saw the metal birds of destruction many more times after that. She knew she couldn't stop them. They were too big. Too fast. Too murderous. She began to patrol the skies. Wherever the metal birds went there would be people in need, if anyone lived.

Those were days of blood. She did what she could, but she always eventually flew away. Like a lost bird searching for her home. But there was one man she could not bring herself to leave. She'd seen him running, looking back into the sky as the metal birds approached.

There were many others running. But this man caught her eye as she flew by.

His face was not familiar to her. He was just a man. His skin was dark, his eyes were wide, and he was shouting as he ran. Then the bombs exploded and she could no longer see him. She had to wait as the metal birds dropped the rest of their excrements of death. Then they turned and flew away. On the horizon, she saw another one coming but she didn't care. She flew down anyway.

She found him and he was almost gone. He was covered in his own blood, his clothes burned, his body quivering. His abdomen had been blown open and half of his face was gone. He called to a Creator in a language Arro-yo didn't understand. Where he found the breath to speak, she'd never know. His voice shook and his lips were coated with blood. Arro-yo stood over him, her mouth open. No words.

She clutched her chest. Her blue dress was stained with dried blood from others and her own sweat. She'd flown so many miles. She didn't remember the last time she'd slept. She could barely remember her own name. But here was another man dying, alone, at her feet. Still.

She fell to her knees and took the man's head in her arms. The man's one open eye looked at her and he stopped calling to his Creator. Arro-yo sat with the man's head in her lap until the man's body stopped shaking.

When this man died, it was as if she woke up. She remembered that she was Arro-yo from the Calabar region. But awakening to one's self can be painful. She leaned forward over the dead man, feeling her blue dress stretch and tear. The fabric was now old.

She wished the airplane she'd seen on the horizon would hurry and come with its exploding excrement. Then it would be finished. *Let it be done,* she thought. *I've had enough. I've had enough. I've had enough. Let me be reborn as something other than myself.* But she continued to live and breathe. And even with the man's body turning cold in her lap, she could feel the pull of the sky.

Minutes later, with care, with kindness, she lay the man down. Then she stood up straight, finally free of what had taken hold of her since she'd come back to the warring country of her birth. Snapped from her guilt. Then she flew home.

Those she saved who were Christian called her an angel. They said that she was sent from the heavens to help those who needed help. Those who were Muslim were sure that she was a servant of Allah. Others called her Yemeja, Mami Wata, and many other things. People now might compare her to a superhero of some sort.

But she was just a woman. Our woman, our Arro-yo.

And even after all this, our Arro-yo stayed. She remained. She did not fly away; for what good does it do anyone to run away from home? Even when home is in turmoil? When this woman who could fly found her home, she found round-bellied children, some who were her nephews and nieces. She found her mother carrying a gun and a wild look in her eye. She found her father's body in the ground, full of bullets. And Arro-yo never flew again.

Or that is what some say. We all tell stories about her. She is a legend. Still we don't all believe such a woman could ever be grounded; but worse things have happened.

MOOM!

She sliced through the water imagining herself a deadly beam of black light. The current parted against her sleek smooth skin. If any fish got in her way, she would spear it and keep right on going. She was on a mission. She was angry. She would succeed and then they would leave for good. They brought the stench of dryness, then they brought the noise and made the world bleed black ooze that left poison rainbows on the water's surface. She'd often see these rainbows whenever she leapt over the water to touch the sun.

The ones who brought the rainbows were burrowing and building creatures from the land and no one could do anything about them. Except her. She'd done it before and they'd stopped for many moons. They'd gone away. She could do it again.

She increased her speed.

She was the largest swordfish in these waters. *Her* waters. Even when she migrated, this particular place remained hers. Everyone knew it. She had not been born here but in all her migrations, she was happiest here. She suspected that this was the birthplace of one of those who created her.

She swam even faster.

She was blue grey and it was night. Though she could see, she didn't need to. She knew where she was going from memory. She was aiming for the thing that looked like a giant dead snake. She remembered snakes; she'd seen plenty in her past life. In the sun, this dead snake was the color of decaying seaweed with skin rough like coral.

Any moment now.

She was nearly there.

She was closing in fast.

She stabbed into it.

From the tip of her spear, down her spine, to the ends of all her fins, she experienced red-orange bursts of pain. The impact was so jarring that she couldn't move. But there was victory; she felt the giant dead snake deflate. It was bleeding its black blood. Her perfect body went numb and she wondered if she had died. Then she wondered what new body she would find herself inhabiting. She remembered her last form, a yellow monkey; even while in that body, she'd loved to swim. The water had always called to her.

She awoke. Gently but quickly, she pulled her spear out. The black blood spewed in her face from the hole she'd made. She quickly turned away from the bittersweet tasting poison. *Now* they would leave soon. As she happily swam away in triumph, the loudest noise she'd ever heard vibrated through the water.

MOOM!

★

The noise rippled through the ocean with such intensity that she went tumbling with it, sure that it would tear her apart. All around her, it did just that to many of the smaller weaker fish and sea creatures.

The water calmed. Deeply shaken, she slowly swam to the surface. Head above the water, she moved through the bodies that glistened in the moonlight. Several smaller fish, jellyfish, even crabs floated, belly up or dismembered. Many of the smaller creatures were probably simply obliterated. But she had survived.

She swam back to the depths. She'd only gone down a few feet when she smelled it. Clean, sweet, sweet, *sweet*! Her senses were flooded with sweetness, the sweetest water she'd ever breathed. She took a breath of water deep into her gills as she swam toward it. In the darkness, she felt others around her. Other fish. Large, like herself, and small . . . so some small ones *had* survived.

Now, she saw everyone. There were even several sharp-toothed ones and mass killers. She could see this well now because something large and glowing was down ahead. A great shifting bar of glowing sand. This was what was giving off the water that was so clean it was sweet. She hoped the sweetness would drown out the foul blackness of the dead snake she'd pierced. She had a feeling it would. She had a very good feeling.

★

The sun was up now, sending its warm rays into the water. She could see everyone swimming, floating, wiggling right into it. There were sharks, sea cows, shrimps, octopus, tilapia, codfish, mackerel, flying fish, even seaweed. Creatures from the shallows, creatures from the shore, creatures from the deep, all here. A unique gathering. What was happening here?

But she remained where she was. Waiting. Hesitating. Watching. It was not deep but it was wide. About two hundred feet below the surface. Right before her eyes, it shifted. From blue to green to clear to purple-pink to glowing gold. But it was the size, profile, and shape of it that drew her. Once in her travels, she'd come across a giant world of food, beauty, and activity. The coral reef had been blue, pink, yellow, and green, inhabited by sea creatures of every shape and size. The water was sweet and there was not a dry creature in sight. She had lived in that place for many moons before finally returning to her favorite waters.

When she'd travelled again, she'd never been able to find the paradise she'd left. Now here in her home was something even wilder and more alive than her lost paradise. And like there, the water here was sweet. Clean and clear. She couldn't see the end of it. However, there was one thing she was certain of: What she was seeing wasn't from the sea's greatest depths or the dry places. This was from far far away.

More and more creatures swam down to it. As they drew closer, she saw the colors pulsate and embrace them. She noticed an octopus with one missing tentacle descending toward it. Suddenly, it grew brilliant pink-purple and straightened all its tentacles. Then right before her eyes, it grew its missing tentacle back and what looked like boney spokes erupted from its soft head. It spun and flipped and then shot off, down into one of the circular bone-like caves of the undulating coral-like thing below.

When a golden blob ascended to meet her, she still didn't move. But she didn't flee either. The sweetness she smelled and its gentle movements were soothing and non-threatening. When it communicated with her, asking question after question, she hesitated. Then she told it exactly what she wanted.

★

Everything was changing.

She'd always loved her smooth skin but now it became impenetrable, its color now golden like the light the New People gave off. The color that reminded her of another life where she could both enjoy the water and endure the sun and the air.

Her sword-like spear grew longer and so sharp at the tip that it sang. They made her eyes like the blackest stone and she could see deep into the ocean and high into the sky. And when she wanted to, she could make spikes of cartilage jut out along her spine as if she were some ancestral creature from the deepest ocean caves of old. The last thing she requested was to be three times her size and twice her weight.

They made it so.

Now she was no longer a great swordfish. She was a monster.

★

Despite the FPSO Mystras' loading hose leaking crude oil, the ocean water just outside of Lagos, Nigeria was now so clean that a cup of its salty sweet goodness would heal the worst human illnesses and cause a hundred more illnesses yet known to humankind. It was more alive than it had been in centuries and it was teeming with aliens and monsters.

THE PALM TREE BANDIT

Shhh, shhh, concentrate on my voice, not the comb in your hair, okay? Goodness, your hair is so thick, though, child. Now I know you like to hear about your great-grandmother Yaya, and if you stop moving around, I'll tell you. I knew her myself, you know. Yes, I was very young, of course, about seven or eight. She was a crazy woman, bursting with life. I always wanted to be like her so badly. She had puff puff hair like a huge cotton ball and she'd comb it out till it was like a big black halo. And it was so thick that even in the wind it wouldn't move.

Most women back then wore their hair plaited or in thread wraps. You know what those are, right? Wrap bunches of hair in thread and they all stick out like a pincushion. They still wear them like that today, in all these intricate styles. You'll get to see when you visit Nigeria this Christmas. Hmm, I see you've stopped squirming. Good, now listen and listen close. Yaya sometimes wore a cloak and she'd move quieter than smoke.

In Nigeria, in Iboland, the people there lived off of yam, and in good times they drank palm tree wine. Women were not allowed to climb palm trees for any reason—not to cut down leaves or to tap the sweet milky wine. You see, palm wine carried power to the first person to touch and drink it. Supposedly women would evaporate into thin air because they weren't capable of withstanding such power. Women were weak creatures and they should not be exposed to such harm. Shh, stop fidgeting. I'm not braiding your hair that tight. I thought you liked to hear a good story. Well then, behave.

Not all of the women evaporated when they climbed a palm tree, but the parents of the offender were cautioned and cleansing rituals were performed to appease the gods for her misdeed. A she-goat and a hen had to be sacrificed, and kola nut, yams, and alligator pepper were placed on shrines. The people of this village did not eat meat, and to sacrifice an animal, one had to find a goat willing to offer itself for sacrifice. You can imagine how hard that must be.

Well, there was a young woman named Yaya, your great-grandmother. Most people dismissed her as an eccentric. She was married to a young conservative man whose job was to talk sense into families who were having internal disputes. He had a respectable reputation. Everyone loved him, since he had saved marriages, friendships, and family relationships. But his woman, well, she was a different story. She wrote for the town newspaper but that wasn't the problem. Her problem was her mouth.

She'd argue with anyone who was game. And as she was smart, and she was beautiful, so all the men in the village liked to engage her in discussion. The problem was she'd mastered the art of arguing and the men would either grow infuriated or stalk away exasperated. Rumor had it that the only argument she lost was with the man she married.

Yaya was a free spirit and when she wasn't arguing, she was laughing loudly and joking with her husband. But one day, Yaya was arguing with Old Man Rum Cake, the village chief elder. Cake was over a hundred years old and he liked to watch Yaya flit about the village. She both annoyed and intrigued him.

This was the reason for his comment about the glass of palm wine she was sipping: "You know women aren't even supposed to climb palm trees, let alone drink it when it is sweet," he said.

At the time, Yaya only humphed at his comment, and went on with their argument about whether garri was better than Farina with stew. Nevertheless, Yaya's mind filed the comment away, to chew on later. It didn't take much to get Yaya's gears going.

That very evening, she ravished her husband into exhaustion, and while he slept his deepest sleep, she dressed and snuck out of the house. Under the mask of night, she crept toward the three palm trees that grew in the center of town, wrapped a rope around her waist and shimmied up the trunk of one of the trees. She took her knife out of her pocket and carved a circle about a foot in diameter, her people's sign for female: a moon. Then she cut three huge leaves and brought them down with her, setting them at the trunk of the tree.

The next morning was chaos. Men looked confused. Some women

wailed. What was to become of their desecrated village? The chief called a town meeting—the culprit had to be located and punished. But who would do such a thing? What woman could survive such an encounter? Yaya almost died with laughter, pinching her nose and feigning several sneezes and coughs. Cake proposed that the woman who did it had most likely evaporated. "And good riddance to bad rubbish," he said.

The next week she struck again, this time tapping palm wine from one of the trees and leaving the jug at the trunk of the tree. Next to the moon she carved a heart, the sign for Erzulie, the village's Mother symbol. This time, it was mostly the men who were in an uproar. The women were quiet, some of them even smiling to themselves. A month later, Yaya struck a third time. However this time, she almost got caught. Three men had been assigned to walk the village streets at night. For the entire month Yaya had watched them, pretending to enjoy sitting near the window reading. She thought she had adequately memorized their night watch patterns. Still, there she was in the palm tree just as one of the men came strolling up. Yaya froze, her cloak fluttering in the breeze, her hands dripping with tapped wine. Her heart was doing acrobatics. The young man looked up directly at Yaya. Then he looked away and turned around, heading back up the street, reaching into his pocket for a piece of gum. Yaya just sat there, leaning against her rope. He hadn't seen her. He'd looked right through her. She glanced at the heart she had carved in the tree next to the moon. She gasped and then giggled, a mixture of relief and awe. The carving pulsed and Yaya knew if she touched it, it would be pleasantly warm.

When she got home, there was a green jug in front of her bed. She glanced at her snoozing husband and quietly picked it up and brought it to her lips. It was the sweetest palm wine she'd ever tasted, as if only a split second ago it had dripped from the tree. She plopped into bed next to her husband, more inebriated than she'd ever been in her life.

In the morning, her husband smelled the sweetness on her and was reluctant to go to work. Later on people smelled her in the newsroom, too. Many of her coworkers bought chocolates and cakes that day to soothe a mysterious craving. They began calling the mysterious woman who could survived climbing palm trees the Palm Tree Bandit and eventually, as it always happened in villages, a story began to gel around her.

The Palm Tree Bandit was not human. She was a polluting spirit whose only reason for existing was to cause trouble. If there was a night without moon—such nights were thought to be the time of evil— she would strike. The chief, who was also the village priest, burned sacrificial leaves, hoping to appease whatever god was punishing the village with such an evil presence.

However, the women developed another story amongst themselves. The Palm Tree Bandit was a nameless wandering woman with no man or children. And she had powers. And if a woman prayed hard enough to her, she'd answer their call because she understood their problems. Legend had it that she had legs roped with muscle that could walk up a palm tree without using her hands, and her hair grew in the shape of palm leaves. Her skin was shiny from the palm oil she rubbed into it and her clothes were made of palm fibers.

Soon, Yaya realized she didn't have to keep shimmying up palm trees. One moonless night she had contemplated going out to cause some mischief but decided to snuggle against her husband instead. Nevertheless, when she woke up, she found another jug of palm wine wrapped in green fresh palm tree leaves inside her basket full of underwear. There were oily red footprints leading from the basket to the window next to it. Yaya grinned as she quickly ran to get a soapy washcloth to scrub the oil from the floor before her husband saw it. That day, the village was alive with chatter again. And the Palm Tree Bandit's mischievousness spread to other villages, kingdoms away. Instead of an uproar, it became a typical occurrence. And the palm wine tapped was as sweet as ever and the leaves grew wide and tough. Only the chief and his ensemble were upset by it any more. Otherwise, it was just something more to argue and giggle about.

Eventually, women were allowed to climb palm trees for whatever reason. But they had to offer sacrifices to the Palm Tree Bandit first. Shrines were built honoring her and women often left her bottles of sweet fresh palm wine and coconut meat. No matter where the shrine was, when morning came, these items were always gone. So your great-grandmother was a powerful woman, yes, she was. Just as squirmy as you, girl.

My story is done, and so is your hair. Here you are, Yaya Number Four. Of this story, there's no more. Run along now.

AUTHOR'S NOTES

The Magical Negro
"The Magical Negro" was inspired by an incident that happened while I was at the Clarion East Writer's Workshop at Michigan State University. One of the writers wrote a story with a magical Negro in it. That week, the instructor just happened to be African-American bestselling speculative fiction writer Steve Barnes. He did a lecture about Magical Negroes. Still, I was pretty pissed off so to illustrate my annoyance, I fired back by submitting this story to the workshop. It went on to be published in *Dark Matter: Reading of the Bones* and was named a finalist for the Theodore Sturgeon Memorial Award.

Kabu Kabu
This is one of those stories where I have no memory of the story's origin. All I know is that I wrote it and then gave it to Alan and he worked it over and we went back and forth like that until it was done. I can say that I have always been fascinated by kabu kabus (illegal/independent cabs), danfos (commercial buses in Lagos), and okadas (motorbikes) in Nigeria. Also, well, my middle sister is named Ngozi, she's a lawyer who lives in a townhouse in Chicago and Vee-Vee's, the African restaurant on the north side of Chicago, is very good.

The House of Deformities
This is the first short story that I ever wrote, so please be kind with it. The year was 1993 and I was in my very first creative writing class. I was sporting a medium length afro, liked to wear knee-high black Doc Martins and my experience with being paralyzed due to spinal surgery complications was very very fresh. I was still using a cane to walk. I wrote this on a word processor and I haven't stopped writing since. Oh, and this is based on a true story and my sisters and I really do call it "The House of Deformities."

The Black Stain

My novel *Who Fears Death* is a post-apocalyptic novel set in a future Sudan. The main character is the product of weaponized rape: rape used as a weapon during war and genocide against women and their cultures and families. A year after its publication, it was optioned by Completion Films with Kenyan director Wanuri Kahiu attached to the project. Immediately Wanuri began asking me for more details about *Who Fears Death*. In particular, she asked me about the origin of the Ewu Mythology. (In the novel, the children of wepaonized rape are called *Ewu*, a derogatory term). Wanuri's question inspired this story.

How Inyang Got Her Wings

Arro-yo is a character who has haunted me for many years now. She is the first windseeker to tell me her story, flying around me long before Zahrah came along. Over a decade ago, I wrote a novel called *The Legend of Arro-yo*. It was never published but one of the stories won an award for best magical realism, two stories from the book earned me finalist accolades, and three Arro-yo stories went on to be published. On top of this, just about every book I went on to write blossomed from writing and exploring of this unpublished novel. This is Arro-yo's origin story.

On the Road

This is the first and only horror story I have ever written (so far). Writing it left me afraid of roads at night for weeks. It was inspired by a story the dean of my university told me about a friend of hers who'd visited Nigeria. Yeah, so, that creepy little boy, he's real and he's out there.

Spider the Artist

This is the first science fiction story that I wrote that I can clearly call science fiction. It first appeared in the *Seeds of Change* anthology and I thank editor John Joseph Adams for challenging me to write a science fiction narrative. After creating this story, the type of stories I wrote changed.

The Ghastly Bird
This story was the result of my disgust and sadness upon learning the true nature of the dodo bird's fate.

The Winds of Harmattan
Originally titled "Asuquo," "The Winds of Harmattan" is another story that I mined from one of the earliest versions of my unpublished novel, *The Legend of Arro-yo*. The Winds of Harmattan was about Arro-yo's aunt and meant to be a cautionary tale for Arro-yo. Of course, Arro-yo didn't listen and still managed to get herself kicked out of her village, as demonstrated in the story (also mined from *The Legend of Arro-yo*) "How Inyang Got Her Wings."

Long Juju Man
I eventually expanded this into a children's book that went on to win the Macmillan Writer's Prize for Africa. The short story and subsequent book were named after the infamous Long Juju Shrine of pre-colonial Arochukwu, Nigeria. This shrine was said to have divine knowledge, when in reality it was merely a tool used to trick and sell people into slavery. The name "long juju" was said to come from the idea that the shrine's *juju* went a *long* way . . . at least that's what my uncle said. This short story has nothing to do with slavery and plenty to do with trickery. I credit my Uncle Moses Okorafor for telling me all about the Long Juju Shrine one day when I visited him in Maryland (the American state, not the Maryland in Lagos).

The Carpet
When my oldest sister and I were in our early 20s, our parents sent us to Nigeria to visit my father's village. They wanted us to check on the house they'd had built in my father's village. When building a house in the village, you never truly knew the progress until you saw it with your own eyes. We were to stay in the freshly built fully furnished humongous beautiful white house with the red roof. Before we left, my sister bought a welcome mat that was shaped like a very happy cartoon

frog. When we arrived, we learned that indeed the house was gorgeous and finished. However, there was no running water, no electricity, and every piece of furniture had been stripped from its interior . . . by relatives. My sister and I were angry as hell and determined to stay in the house, regardless, to show respect to our parents. We managed to stay for three days. We slept on a bare bed. Those nights were full of mosquitoes and heat and there was a turkey right outside our window who would screech and cluck until the sun came up because it was being attacked by rats. And we were terrified because every night, something downstairs slithered around. Maybe it was a snake, maybe it was something else.

Icon
This is a story that is an even mix of the fictional and the real. Some of the words in this story come from individuals in Nigeria's conflicted Niger Delta whom I had no business speaking to.

The Popular Mechanic
The origins of this story is complicated and very personal. I wrote it when my father was very very sick. He suffered from Parkinson's Disease and Diabetes. Several moments in this story draw from some of the darkest times of his illness. At the same time, the conflict in the Niger Delta was raging and I was fascinated by the many instances of oil bunking.

Windseekers
This was the first Arro-yo story to be published. It was a finalist in the Writers of the Future Contest and published and illustrated in the resulting anthology. It's a story mined from one of the earliest versions of my unpublished novel, *The Legend of Arro-yo*. I must admit, looking back, I don't like this story very much. The ending really bothered me and I eventually changed it in the novel.

Bakasi Man

How do I explain this one? Well, it all started when my sister's superstitious ex-husband (who happened to be Igbo) said, "Hunchbacks are very expensive." It was all downhill from there.

Baboon Wars

I hate to totally validate a cliché about black people but . . . when my mother was a kid, she used to fight baboons. She was born and raised in Jos, Nigeria, a city in the predominantly Islamic and arid North. She talked about the soothing call to prayer of the muezzin from the minaret and the dust devils she'd play in. One day, she told me about how she and her friends used to have to fight baboons on their way to school. The baboons wanted their lunches. I imagined the rest.

Asunder

I can't believe I wrote a love story (I don't like love stories that are love stories only for love's sake), but that's exactly what this story is. This story was part of the only novel I've ever begun and not finished. The novel was called *Nsibidi's Script*. I stopped writing it in order to write my second novel *The Shadow Speaker*. This story is told to Nsibidi (who was also a character in my first novel *Zahrah the Windseeker*) in sign language by an idiot baboon. She's being told about her past life and why it's important that she leave home.

Tumaki

The short story "Tumaki" is mined from my novel *Stormbringer*, a sequel to *The Shadow Speaker*. I like for readers to read it without context. But if you must have some, all you really need to know are the following: The narrator is sixteen-year-old Dikéogu. He is Nigerian and a fledging rainmaker (one who can control the weather; this includes producing lighting from within and calling up the wind) who is avoiding his destiny. The story is set in a Post-Apocalyptic near-future Niger (the country directly north of Nigeria which is dominated by the Sahara Desert) where many of the laws of physics no longer apply, the barriers between worlds have disintegrated, and children (called meta-humans) are born with strange abilities. Dikéogu's e-legba (a sort of blackberry-ipod-laptop-esque portable device) is broken and he needs to fix it.

Biafra
This short story went on to win The Margin: Exploring Modern Magical Realism Short Story Contest. It is yet another story from my unpublished novel, *The Legend of Arro-yo*. The detail about the vultures came from an actually account from one of my father's best friends who also happened to be a Biafran War veteran. The ghost of the Biafran War (also known as the Nigerian Civil War) haunts every Nigerian family, no matter what side they were on or what tribe they belong to.

Moom!
"Moom!" is the first prologue (there are three for each "act") in my novel *Lagoon*. I'd read a news story about a swordfish in Angola that "attacked" an oil pipeline. Talk about a story that landed right in my lap. Another point of realism in the story was that the *FPSO Mystras* is a real ship.

The Palm Tree Bandit
"The Palm Tree Bandit" was the third story I had published. It was the second speculative fiction story I had published. I've always had very strong arms and for this reason, I've always been good at climbing trees. While in Nigeria, one of my granduncles saw me admiring a palm wine tapper collecting his bucket of sap at the top of a palm tree. He smiled and told me that women weren't allowed to climb palm trees. I think the reasoning behind this was that men could see a woman's underwear when she climbed the tree (as if a man can't just avert his eyes. Why must a woman always change her behavior in such situations?). This irritated me, of course. So I did something about it. I wrote a story in which the culture was changed and a super heroine who did the unthinkable was created.

PUBLICATION HISTORY

"The Magical Negro" first appeared in *Dark Matter II: Reading the Bones,* 2004.

"Kabu Kabu" (with Alan Dean Foster) is original to this collection.

"The House of Deformities" is original to this collection.

"The Black Stain" is original to this collection.

"How Inyang Got Her Wings" is original to this collection.

"On the Road" first appeared in *Eclipse 3,* 2009.

"Spider the Artist" first appeared in *Seeds of Change,* 2008.

"The Ghastly Bird" is original to this collection.

"Asuquo" first appeared in *Mojo: Conjure Stories,* 2003, reprinted as "The Winds of Harmattan" in *Black Arts Quarterly,* 2005

"Long Juju Man" first appeared in *Alchemy 1,* 2003.

"The Carpet" jointly first appeared in this collection and *The Dark,* 2013.

"Icon" first appeared in *Looking Glass Magazine,* 2010.

"The Popular Mechanic" first appeared in *InterNova,* 2007.

"Windseekers" first appeared in *L. Ron Hubbard Presents Writers of the Future,* 2002.

"Bakasi Man" is original to this collection.

"The Baboon War" first appeared in *Jungle Jim 7,* 2012.

"Asunder" first appeared in *African Writing Online,* 2007.

"Tumaki" first appeared in *Without a Map,* 2010.

"Biafra" first appeared in *Margin: Exploring Modern Magical Realism,* 2005.

"Moom!" first appeared in *AfriSF,* 2012.

"The Palm Tree Bandit" first appeared in *Strange Horizons,* 2001.

ABOUT THE AUTHOR

Nnedi Okorafor is a novelist of African-based science fiction, fantasy, and magical realism. Her novels include *Who Fears Death* (winner of the World Fantasy Award), *Akata Witch* (an Amazon Best Book of the Year), *Zahrah the Windseeker* (winner of the Wole Soyinka Prize for African Literature), and *The Shadow Speaker* (winner of the Parallax Award). Her children's book *Long Juju Man* is the winner of the Macmillan Writer's Prize for Africa. Her science-fiction novel *Lagoon* and young adult novel *Akata Witch 2: Breaking Kola* are scheduled for release in 2014. Holding two master's degrees and a PhD in Literature, Okorafor is a professor of creative writing at Chicago State University. Find her on Facebook, Twitter and at nnedi.com.